A small town in the Deep South isn't where most gay men would choose to go looking for love. But open hearts will find a way . . .

Growing up in the Bible Belt, Paul Dunham learned from a young age to hide his sexuality. Now he's teaching psychology at a conservative college in Georgia—and still hiding who he really is. If Paul hopes to get tenure, he needs to keep his desires on the down-low. But when an old college crush shows up on campus—looking more gorgeous than ever—Paul's long-suppressed urges are just too big for one little closet to hold . . .

Brandon Mercer has come a long way since his freshman year fumblings with Paul. Now he's confident, accomplished, proudly out—and the sexiest IT consultant Paul's ever seen. When Brandon asks Paul to grab some coffee and catch up, it leads to a steamy reunion that puts their first night of passion to shame. But when Paul's longtime crush turns into a full-time romance, he receives an anonymous email threatening to expose their secret to the world. If Paul stays with Brandon, his teaching career is over. Yet if he caves under pressure, he risks losing the one true love he's been waiting for. . .

Visit us at www.kensingtonbooks.com

Books by Wendy Qualls

Worth Waiting For

Published by Kensington Publishing Corporation

WORTH WAITING FOR

Wendy Qualls

LYRICAL SHINE
Kensington Publishing Corp.
www.kensingtonbooks.com

For Annabeth, who sprinted alongside me so we could both get All The Words Written,
and for Moe, who helped me make them the right ones.

Chapter 1

The chair of the psychology department was a mean, small man with a bad toupee and a permanent air of smugness pervading his office. His summons always evoked a feeling of impending trouble, but Paul stepped inside and closed the door anyway.

Doctor Kirsner looked up briefly, then went back to his typing. Paul waited in awkward silence for a full minute before his department head finally sat back in his chair and nodded for Paul to take the seat opposite.

"There have been some complaints about you," Dr. Kirsner announced.

"Sorry?"

He slid a stapled sheaf of papers across his desk toward Paul. "Employee code of conduct—you may remember signing it when you were first hired. I gather it's been giving you trouble recently."

Paul took the papers and flipped through, his mind whirring. Saint Benedict's wasn't officially a Christian college any longer, but it did hold its staff to a fairly archaic standard of behavior. Still, he'd done everything expected—*more* than anyone could reasonably expect—to ensure he never put a toe out of line. Tenure was so close he could taste it, and a major violation of the code of conduct would have been the easiest way for this new department head to knock him out of the running.

"I don't know what I could have done wrong," he said aloud.

Dr. Kirsner seemed to expect the denial, and leaned in for the kill. "Kissing," he hissed. "In front of students, no less."

"I'm sure that's not against the rules, and I wouldn't be dumb enough to do it in front of students if it were." *Plus I haven't kissed anyone in ages.*

"Ah. So your girlfriend didn't kiss you good-bye this morning in the parking lot, right outside my window?" Dr. Kirsner gestured to the quad outside. "You arrived at campus together well before classes started. She had an overnight bag. It doesn't take a lot of imagination to figure out what the two of you had been doing without the benefit of marriage." He tapped the code of conduct. "Which *I'm* sure *is* against the rules."

Oh. Paul heaved an internal sigh of relief that it was something he could explain. "She's not my girlfriend, and it wasn't really a kiss."

"Girlfriend, one-night stand, lady of the evening, it doesn't matter. The 'no immoral sexual conduct' clause covers having a partner stay at your place of residence overnight."

For all you know, we could have been having a tea party and playing videogames. Paul took a deep breath and counted to three before releasing it. "What you—and any student up that early—saw was *my sister* giving me two friendly kisses on the cheek as I said good-bye. She's been in France for the last two years and the kiss on both cheeks is a French thing she's picked up—there's nothing sexual about it. And surely whoever's complaining also noticed that she and I have the same color hair, same eyes, nearly the same facial structure, and a similar build. *Not* a girlfriend."

Dr. Kirsner's self-satisfied smirk froze on his face for a long moment, then slowly dissolved into a poor attempt at neutrality. "Sister?"

"*Twin* sister." Paul shrugged and tried not to grin too blatantly at seeing his overbearing department head at a loss for words. "We're not identical, obviously, but when we're together most people pick up on the family resemblance. I don't get to see her much anymore, so she stopped by after her flight got in—it's a long drive to my parents' house from Atlanta and I'm on the way. We took my car last night so I gave her a ride back to campus this morning to pick up her rental from the visitors' lot."

Paul was treated to the delightful sight of Dr. Kirsner trying very hard to fake a relieved smile and failing miserably. It was no secret the man wasn't fond of him. Paul refused to allow his private life to become cannon fodder in the departmental pissing match for dominance the way everyone else did and Dr. Kirsner could never quite wrap his head around why. The truth—Paul was clinging to the lingering security of being firmly in the closet—would have been the *coup de gras* for what would have been a short but promising academic career at St. Ben's. Much better to keep his mouth shut and let everyone think he was shy.

"Was that all, Dr. Kirsner?" Paul returned the department chair's fake smile with a much more genuine one of his own. "Because if so, I should really go prepare for class."

* * * *

The air still had a bit of a bite to it, but the sunshine felt wonderful and it was a beautiful Georgia spring day. Paul was more than ready to escape Dr. Kirsner's office and get outside for a while. The "prepare for class" line had been a bit of an exaggeration—his first lecture on Thursdays wasn't until eleven, which meant he technically didn't have to be on campus yet—but Danielle had been in a hurry to get home so Paul had planned to spend the morning in his office. Not that he'd accumulated all that much paperwork to do, with spring break so recently out of the way and no major assignments currently looming on the horizon, but sometimes it was nice to at least *feel* professional.

The quad was starting to awaken, too, some students stumbling blearily into the campus coffee shop and others wandering between early classes. Someone was bravely attempting a game of Frisbee shirtless, despite the temperature. Paul tried not to look, but it was hard not to notice that whoever-it-was had a lot to show off. He settled himself onto the low stone wall outside the psychology building and pulled out his phone, angling the screen to compensate for the bright glare.

"Paul Dunham?"

Paul looked up. A striking dark-haired man in khakis and a smart jacket stood before him. "Hi?"

The man grinned and held out his hand. "Been a while, so you may not remember me, but I sure as hell remember you. Brandon Mercer—we were hallmates freshman year."

Paul shook the offered hand on autopilot. It couldn't be, after all this time. *Brandon Mercer. Holy crap!* "Of course I remember," he said, his voice breaking a bit. "You were pretty memorable."

"So were you." Brandon took a seat on the wall next to him and cocked his head. "You teach here now?"

Paul smiled and shrugged, careful to seem casual. "Psychology. Finally got on the tenure track last year, so hopefully I'll be sticking around for a while. What have you been up to?"

"IT consultant," Brandon said. "Mostly security issues and such."

"I should have guessed from the beard." Paul nodded toward Brandon's neatly-groomed chin. "Your look screams 'computers.'"

Brandon laughed; the humor lighting up his eyes. "I'd say you were exaggerating, but you're right—in this field, it's practically a uniform."

It looked good on him. *Very* good. Brandon had been handsome enough ten years ago, when they were both eighteen-year-olds on the tail end of puberty, but the beard sculpted his face a bit and brought out the angle of his jaw. Which in turn matched the very nice angles making up the rest of him. *Handsome* was now a grossly inadequate word.

"What brings you back here, then?" Paul asked, managing to keep his thoughts from coming through in his voice. "I assumed you were off to make your mark on the bigger world."

"I'm based out of Atlanta now, but St. Ben's wanted someone on-site to take a look at something and I thought it would be interesting to see what's changed around here." Brandon raised his head and looked out over the quad, a small smile on his face. He was much less subtle about ogling the shirtless Frisbee player. "Not a lot, I'm guessing."

That was truer than Paul wanted to admit. "I like it better from this side of the desk, at least."

"Oh, I bet." Brandon fixed him with a knowing smirk and one delicately raised eyebrow. "Should I even ask?"

"Um." Paul could feel his face heat from the insinuation behind the otherwise innocent question. *Not really the time or place to talk about my personal life, especially after Dr. Kirsner's attempt to ream me out this morning—*

And Brandon seemed to get it. "Coffee," he announced. "You and me. Not here. Well, if you've got time, that is? I'm parked just around the corner. It'd be nice to catch up."

Paul swallowed and nodded. "That…sounds good. Thanks."

* * * *

The coffee shop was an independent little hole-in-the-wall, one Paul had heard of but never been inside. Its primary benefit seemed to be its distance from campus; the coffee certainly wasn't anything to write home about. Paul and Brandon got a corner table in the nearly-empty dining area and sat in silence for a little while. It felt oddly normal. And didn't at all explain the butterflies in Paul's stomach.

"So," Brandon started. "You finished up your degree at St. Ben's, then stuck with psychology?"

"Yeah." It had been the only field that interested him, even back then. "It's a pretty campus and it has a good cognitive program. Once I finished undergrad I went ahead and applied for the graduate program—it's close enough to my hometown to see my parents sometimes, and I didn't really want to go farther away."

Brandon nodded. "And St. Ben's doesn't have a problem with you being gay?"

Paul couldn't suppress his flinch, even though he knew nobody was listening. "I, um…"

Brandon's eyes widened. "You're still in the closet? *Seriously?"*

Like I have a choice. "Coming out isn't really something I can do right now," he admitted.

Brandon took a long sip of his coffee and didn't say anything, but the silence was just as eloquent as words. Finally he put his cup down and sighed. "I don't regret leaving, you know."

"I know."

"I didn't… I mean, I assumed my parents would freak out. When I came home that summer and told them I was gay. But they were fine with it. My mom gave me a hug and my dad and my brothers clapped me on the back and the next morning there were brochures for Emory and Georgia Tech sitting outside my room. Mom even called to get all my transcripts and paperwork from St. Ben's, so I'd have everything ready to transfer whenever I wanted to. And I lucked out. Georgia Tech doesn't usually take transfer students that late, but my dad's got a friend who works in admissions there and somehow they managed to pull some strings." Brandon flashed Paul a crooked smile. "It was the best thing to ever happen to me."

And it left me behind. Paul tried to smile back, but it probably came out more as a grimace. One year, then *nothing.* One year of longing looks and the uncomfortable awareness that this attraction wouldn't go away. One fabulous night when fate happened to put them both in the right place at the right time to admit to each other it was mutual. Paul had been forced to confront the fact that yes, he really *was* gay. And then finals were over and they both went home, and Brandon had never come back.

"How did you …" Brandon seemed to be picking his words carefully. "How was it for you? Staying?"

"It wasn't anything, really." *Confusing and frustrating, but that was nothing new.* "I just went back to not doing that. Nobody thought anything of it. Plenty of students here don't really date."

"So did you ever…" He trailed off and waved vaguely.

Paul stared down at the polished wood of the table with more focus than was probably warranted. There was a slight wave to the grain under the varnish. "Once," he admitted quietly. "Sort of. When I was in grad school there was a guy, and we kind of clicked. We got an apartment together eventually, to save on rent. It went from there."

"You said 'sort of,'" Brandon pointed out. Paul didn't look up, but he could *hear* his amusement. "How's that work?"

God, this is awkward. How can I possibly describe Christopher? "He was—*is*—kind of a lot to take in," Paul finally explained. "Friendly guy, but abrasive too. We never made it official or anything, but I never said no either. He made it clear he was interested in me after we had been living together for a while. We tried that for a bit, but I just couldn't. At least, not with him. It ended badly."

"You dumped him?"

"I guess so." Paul let out a long breath. "I didn't want to…to do everything he wanted to. We got in an argument and he wouldn't let it go. I finally moved out about a year and a half ago, when I realized nothing was going to change. Got my own place. He stayed at St. Ben's until this past September—not my department, but I still had to see him sometimes and it was always awkward. Honestly I was kind of relieved when he quit; the new IT lady is much easier to work with."

"And all this time, you stayed in the closet."

I did, and it sucks. "Pretty much." The words came out more evenly than he expected. "I had to, though—I can't leave St. Ben's. I have another year or two until my tenure review. And even though they don't require a statement of faith from their faculty anymore, having an openly gay professor isn't something the administration could easily overlook."

"I see." Brandon leaned back in his chair and studied Paul for a long moment, his face inscrutable. "So you're not claiming you're straight now? Dating women?"

Not really. He wasn't in denial, didn't argue with the label, just—being gay was inconvenient. Paul made a vaguely negative noise.

"You're missing out, you know."

He winced. Yes, he knew. The whole darn world seemed to be conspiring to tell him exactly how much he was missing out on. That kind of life wasn't compatible with working at St. Ben's, though. Speaking of which… Paul checked his watch and stood. "Look, I hate to cut this short—"

"Don't suppose you'd want to do dinner sometime?"

Paul snapped out of his self-pity party and only barely prevented himself from gaping at Brandon. "Like, dinner-dinner? Or date-dinner?"

"Either." Brandon smirked. "Don't you feel like we got separated too soon, back then? I agonized for ages over whether to call you once we went home for the summer, and even now I'm not sure why I didn't." He leaned forward in his chair, his long fingers practically caressing his little paper cup of coffee, as if he was about to impart a secret. "I truly would love to hear what you've been up to and all," he confessed, "but I'd also love to… well. I've got some time—I have no idea how long it will take me to tease out these glitches in St. Ben's servers, but it will probably be at least a week or two. I assumed I'd spend it skulking around my hotel room and feeling stupid sitting all by myself in restaurants, but spending some of that time with you would be infinitely more appealing." His tone—and the glint in his eyes—made it clear *exactly* what he was offering. "Dinner-dinner would be perfectly fine, of course, but I'd love it to be more than that."

He leaned in further, close enough Paul could smell the coffee and a hint of toothpaste on his breath, and ran one gentle forefinger over the vein in the back of Paul's hand as Paul clenched his cup. "I get that you'd rather keep your private life private, but I'm not exactly a co-worker," he murmured. "And after you were so absolutely breathtaking freshman year, I couldn't stop thinking about it for ages. Kept wishing we'd had the chance to do more. And if you've decided to never do anything like that again—in that case, I'd say it was a real shame. Because I've picked up a few tricks over the years, too, and I'm a pretty damn good teacher."

Oh God. Paul berated himself for each and every time he lay awake at night, fingers tracing over the outline of his cock, remembering back to how Brandon's confident hands had felt on him. They say you never forget your first time. Well, whoever "they" were, they *seriously* understated the situation. "You will obsessively replay the encounter over and over" would have been more accurate. And it would be so easy to lapse back into that memory, to give in and take Brandon up on his offer and try to recreate that one golden middle-of-the-night experience, but then where would he be? Alone again afterward, furious with himself and twice as miserable as before. A heroin junkie relapsing after staying clean for the last year and a half. *(Almost a year and three-quarters,* a voice inside his head pointed out.) Even if the physical sensations left him darn near rapturous, it wouldn't be enough to counterbalance the negatives.

He must have been quiet too long, because Brandon sat back again and made a big show of finishing his coffee. "Sorry," Brandon finally said. "I guess I forget what it was like, before. I didn't mean to make you uncomfortable."

"It's fine." Paul forced a smile. "And I'm flattered, really, I just... It's a no. I'm sorry."

Brandon nodded, a hint of disappointment on his face. "I understand. Come on; we should both probably get back to campus."

Chapter 2

Paul took his time packing a bag and loading up his car after work. Friday afternoons were always slow—nobody bothered stopping by for office hours when the weekend was so close—but it was late enough he really had no excuse to procrastinate any longer. He owed it to Danielle to get to their parents' house in time for supper, if only to stave off the disappointed lecture he'd receive otherwise. Danielle deserved to have her first day (well, evening) home be a no-nagging, no-grumbling zone. He couldn't guarantee their parents would comply, but he could at least do his best to not throw fuel on the fire.

The drive was tolerable, with not as much traffic as Paul expected. He spent most of it thinking about Brandon's offer. A no-strings-attached affair—was that even a real thing? Or just a product of wishful thinking and too much Hollywood? Back then, he and Brandon had both been new to the whole idea of mutual attraction, suffering through a semester of occasional glances and embarrassed looks before everything finally came to a head. So to speak. And look where that had gotten the both of them. *Cripes.*

* * * *

There was no lecture. Paul shouldered his little weekend duffel bag and gamely accepted hugs from his parents, then ran upstairs to dump it off in his old bedroom while Danielle finished setting the table and their mother got dinner the rest of the way ready. It was strange, how they lapsed so quickly back into their usual roles: Danielle chatted brightly about her adventures in France, their father interrupted with occasional warnings about the dangers of having fun, and Paul sat quietly and picked at his mashed potatoes. His updates were mundane compared to Danielle's and it wasn't like he could share his biggest piece of news either. *Gave a pop quiz to my freshmen today, have an important grant proposal due in a few weeks, and oh yeah, the guy who gave me my first sexual encounter showed back up and propositioned me and even though I turned him down, I'm really tempted.* Right, like *that* would go over well. Paul was well lost in his mental grousing when a change in tension at the table brought him back to the present.

"You never mentioned someone before," his mother was saying, worry in her voice. "This seems so sudden!"

"Not sudden at all," Danielle countered. "His name is Étienne and we've been dating for about six months now. I didn't say anything because I knew how you'd react." She turned to look directly at Paul and shrugged, a tiny gesture of apology. "Sorry, Paul—I was going to tell you last night, but I was still jet-lagged and it seemed easier to give the whole family my news all at once."

"It's fine." She'd undoubtedly tell him more later tonight anyway. He cast about for a suitable question and finally settled on, "How did you meet?"

Danielle's glance slid over to their father. "Totally by chance," she answered. "He moved into the apartment across the hall from mine about a year ago, and I kept getting his mail. Apparently his mother sent him letters once a week and had the wrong address. Or maybe she didn't notice she was writing it wrong. Anyway, after sliding them under his door a few times, one week I knocked and it kind of went from there. My French was good enough by that point, finally, which was lucky because his English is still terrible." Her eyes took on a bit of a dreamy look. "I mean, he's made a lot of progress since we started spending time together, but … yeah. That's how we met."

"He's French." The inflection their father put on the word would have been kind of funny if he hadn't looked so disgusted. "You couldn't find a good American boy?"

"Not in Paris, no," Danielle replied sweetly. "And he's only half French—his mother is Egyptian, although he doesn't get to visit her side of the family much anymore. I suspect they wouldn't approve of him dating an American any more than you approve of him. Luckily for us we're both stubborn like that."

It was nearly worth it, having to endure the drive and the tension and the almost-guaranteed guilt trip he'd be getting later on in the weekend, to see the look on their father's face. Egyptian was clearly several steps down even from French. Their father was wearing the same blank, uncomprehending look that Paul would probably get if he mentioned Brandon, as a matter of fact. Paul almost expected the meal to devolve into a shouting match—it had happened once or twice over the years, and Danielle was usually the culprit—but instead everyone retreated into stony silence.

* * * *

"I really am sorry I didn't tell you about him last night," Danielle said several hours later. They were sitting together on Paul's bed. Which finally had grown-up sheets without dinosaurs on them, a recent change, although the new less-garish matching blankets were nowhere near as comfortable to lounge on as the old ones had been. Danielle pulled her bare feet up so she could lean on her knees, the hems of her pajama pants riding up to expose a stubbly bit of her lower shin. "I had the whole plane ride here to figure out how to tell you all, but I kept trying not to think about it until I was literally on my way over from your place this morning." She sighed. "It went about like I expected."

"You could have told me earlier, you know," Paul said. "Like—oh, six months ago when you first started dating?"

"I—" She bit her lip. "Yeah, I guess I could have. But I honestly don't know what I would have said. 'Hey Paul, I met this amazing guy who makes me ridiculously happy and whom I've fallen head over heels for. I'm absolutely giddy for him. We're totally obsessed even though it's way too soon to see if it's True Love Forever but I don't even care. So how's the self-enforced celibacy going? Still in the closet?' I guess it kept being easier to wait."

Paul couldn't deny the pang of jealousy that ran through him at that. He could have brushed it off if there hadn't been so much truth to her words. Danielle read him easily and made a hasty sound of apology.

"Crap, you know I didn't mean it like that," she said immediately. "I respect what you're doing. Plenty of people choose their career over their personal life, and there's nothing wrong with it. I'm not judging, honestly—I get why you have to keep quiet. I'm just…" She ducked her head a bit to hide her twitterpated smile behind her pajama-clad knees, but Paul could still see the cheerful lines around her eyes as she grinned into the fabric. "Étienne is wonderful and the sex is fantastic and I'm thinking about him all the time. I really wanted him to come back to the States with me so he could meet you and see a bit more of the US besides what's on TV, but he's got a lot going on at work right now and trans-Atlantic travel isn't exactly something you do on a whim. Maybe for Christmas, though—I'm hoping I can get him to come back with me. Assuming we're still together by then."

"That's great," Paul said, and meant it. "I'd love to meet him. My French is almost definitely worse than his English, though."

She laughed. "His is getting better—we can usually get through a whole conversation now without either of us having to revert to our native language to translate something. I'm not telling Mom and Dad yet, but he's pretty much moved in with me in the last month or so. We're probably going to stop bothering with two apartments pretty soon. He hasn't told his parents about us either, so we'll have to get past that first. Although he's a few years older than we are—it's not like he needs permission."

"Sometimes you don't need it, but it's nice to get it anyway." Paul had never even *hinted* to his family that he and Christopher had been anything other than friends and apartment-mates—not that Christopher would have wanted anyone to know, in any case. Would telling the family have changed anything? *Probably not, other than giving me another source of things that make me feel terrible.*

Danielle sat up straighter, legs crossed and hands folded neatly in her lap. "Paul," she asked slowly, "is everything all right?"

"Why wouldn't it be?"

"You've been quiet today. Different than when I was crashing with you at your apartment last night. Should I shut up about Étienne?"

"It's fine." Paul flashed a quick smile and prayed it was convincing. "We've got all weekend. Tell me more about him?"

Chapter 3

Paul spent more of his weekend daydreaming about Brandon Mercer than he really wanted to. It wasn't intentional; it was just that Danielle was so darned happy about Étienne, and their parents were so ridiculously grumpy about Danielle and Étienne both that it seemed like everyone's "safe subject" was Paul's love life. Or lack thereof. Danielle at least had the tact to not say anything, but their mother was on a one-person crusade to inflict Paul on some poor woman. Nearly any woman would do, it seemed, as long as she was somehow connected with their social circle. Church on Sunday morning was a tense, awkward affair, punctuated by pointed comments about so-and-so's niece, wonderful girl really, studying to be a pharmacist, or so-and-so's daughter who recently finished a year teaching third-graders in an inner-city school and you know that my charming son Paul is essentially a teacher too, right?

By the time Paul got back to his own apartment that afternoon, he was more than ready to sink into his couch and play mindless videogames for the rest of the evening before scrounging up some leftovers for a late dinner and then falling asleep the moment his head hit the pillow. No matter how much he tossed and turned, though, he couldn't stop thinking about Brandon's offer.

Which had him thinking back to freshman year.

Brandon Mercer. God, it really has been forever. It hadn't happened entirely out of the blue—he'd noticed Brandon earlier that semester, and in retrospect it seemed that Brandon had noticed him too. The realization, though, the *oh God I'm now 100 percent positive I like guys instead of girls* moment, wasn't until the weekend before finals, at three o'clock in the morning, in their hall's shared bathroom. Even now, he could remember it all so clearly.

Too caffeinated to sleep and too bleary-eyed to study, Paul wandered into the bathroom to brush the coffee residue from his teeth for the third time that night. The hall wasn't entirely silent—Paul wasn't the only one cramming in every minute of study time he could—but all the normal daytime sounds were muted. He was in his pajamas—ratty Superman boxers and a plain white undershirt he wore so he didn't have to go half naked down the hall. Someone was showering in the bathroom when he got there. The room was warm, humid, the sound of water loud against the tiles. Paul spat his mouthful of toothpaste into the sink and looked up just in time to catch sight of a very naked Brandon cracking open the curtain and eyeing him speculatively—

Hell. Paul groaned and buried his face in his pillow. *I'm never going to be over him.*

* * * *

He got to St. Ben's bright and early Monday morning. There was no need to be anywhere near the psychology building yet, but Paul had snapped awake an hour before his alarm went off because his apartment felt suffocating. He'd dressed for work, not exercise, but when he got to St. Ben's, he wrapped his jacket closer around himself and resolutely plodded along the walking trail circumnavigating the campus until the strange sense of claustrophobia started to ease. The quad was practically empty except for a few hardy joggers and a handful of students. Perky morning people, probably. The barista at the campus coffee shop when he finished his walk—a rainbow-haired girl with a lip ring and a septum piercing—was almost offensively cheerful, and Paul had to exert effort to not growl at her. He took his coffee and morning muffin to the table farthest from the shop's built-in speaker system and spent a pleasant chunk of time fiddling with his phone and doing absolutely nothing.

"Hey, this seat taken?"

Paul managed to not jump, but Grace's hand on his shoulder did catch him by surprise. She was the closest friend he had at St. Ben's, but they didn't often see each other outside the psychology building. "No, help yourself. How was your weekend?"

"Quiet." She smiled at him over the rim of her cup. "First time in ages my neighbors in the apartment next door haven't been banging on the wall before sunrise on a Saturday morning. Still haven't figured out whether they're renovating something or practicing their tennis serves indoors."

Grace's neighbors were a safe topic, so she and Paul chatted about nothing in particular while he finished the last of his muffin and she drank her coffee. She'd always made no secret of the fact that that she'd have liked to be something more than friends, but so far Paul had been spared the discomfort of having to tell her yes or no. He thought back: they'd known each other for—*gosh, has it really been ten years now?* As freshmen, they'd ended up sitting next to each other in the very intro psychology course Paul and Grace both taught now. From there they'd become study partners, then tentative friends, then co-workers, and eventually somewhere between "friends" and "potentially awkward crush" at some point along the way. Grace was friendly and sweet and even though she not-so-secretly had a thing for him, he never asked and she never pushed.

"I take it your morning class went well today, then?" Paul asked when the topic of the noisy neighbors was exhausted.

"As expected," she answered with a little tilt of her head. "Half the class doesn't show up and the other half falls asleep while I'm talking. Next time *you* get the stupid-early section and *I'll* take the prime late-morning slot."

"You'll have to get better at Rock Paper Scissors," Paul countered.

She rolled her eyes, then suddenly sucked in a breath. "Oh, that reminds me, Dr. Kirsner is looking for you. Something that has to be yelled about in person, presumably. He only looks pleased like that when he's anticipating getting to annoy you."

"Oh Lord, shush, will you?" Paul scanned the coffee shop. There was nobody close enough to overhear, probably, but complaining about your department head still wasn't something that ought to be done in a public place. "Not that I'm saying you're wrong, but…"

"You're too paranoid." Grace shot him a mischievous grin. "What on earth have you done to make that man hate you so badly?"

Paul had a glib answer all ready on the tip of his tongue, but he settled for the truth instead. "He doesn't hate me; he hated Dr. Lancaster."

"And since he can't exactly complain about Dr. Lancaster retiring and practically handing him his job, he'll take it out on you. I guess that makes sense. You were practically Roy Lancaster, Junior for a while there."

Paul bristled at the implication. "It wasn't intentional."

"Oh, I know." She shrugged. "Face it, though—the man was a fantastic mentor for you. Your research is essentially built on his. And he's the one who fast-tracked you for tenure in the first place. Dr. Kirsner missed his opportunity to preemptively fire you by about a year and a half and he's never going to forgive you for it."

"He's still trying," Paul said. "Called me into his office on Friday to accuse my sister of being a prostitute."

Grace's eyes grew huge. "He *what?*"

"Danielle got back to the States a few days ago, and she slept off the jet lag at my place before heading out to see our parents this weekend. He saw me kiss her on the cheek Friday morning and assumed I had either a girlfriend or a prostitute spending the night with me. And then I…took her to work with me for some reason, I guess? He wasn't really clear about that part."

"Wow." She giggled behind her hand, looking more like a teenager than a colleague. "I mean—yeah. Wow. How does he expect you to ever meet a nice girl, anyway, if you can't be seen associating with one?"

This would be the right time to say something flirtatious, some buried part of Paul's brain piped up. *She's everything your parents would love to see in a girlfriend for you: she's pretty, she's Christian, she's* female, *and she's adorable when she laughs. You could do much worse.*

And yet she did absolutely nothing for him. Not in that way, anyway. She *was* nice, and he did care about her, but it was the same way he cared about Danielle. If he were truly a good person, he'd bring up the topic, let her down gently, and help steer her toward someone else.

Paul was not that person, though. He forced a silent smile, said his good-byes, and headed back toward the psychology building.

* * * *

"You wanted to see me?"

It was an awkward repeat of Friday morning, right down to Dr. Kirsner ignoring Paul hovering in the doorway until he'd deemed a sufficient amount of time had passed to prove his point. Finally he waved Paul to the seat across from him (one step up from a folding chair, hard and uncomfortable and a shade too low for the height of the desk) and leaned back in his much fancier leather desk chair. "I've got a task for you," he announced.

"O…kay?" Whatever this project was he certainly didn't look happy about Paul's involvement.

Dr. Kirsner steepled his hands over his lap. "I've been told to provide a 'departmental liaison' for a certain university-wide project," he said, the curl of his lip betraying how he felt about being ordered to do anything. "I don't know much about it, other than that every department is expected to participate fully and that the project is primarily electronic. Since you've got the lightest workload, I feel that this position should rightfully fall to you."

Lightest workload? Paul bit back the instinctive defense of his schedule— Dr. Kirsner knew *precisely* which sections Paul was teaching, how many students he was advising, and what his office hours were supposed to be. He had exactly the same number of classes as the other professors did, but Paul easily had 50 percent more students than most of his colleagues because he didn't shy away from the larger intro courses and—thanks to scheduling or just word of mouth—he had students *want* to be in his section. And even though he was still midway through the waiting part of the publishing process for his last research study, he was in the middle of drafting the next one. *It's not like I'm sitting around my office on my rear and twiddling my thumbs.*

Paul didn't have much of a leg to stand on when it came to complaining, though. It was well within Dr. Kirsner's rights to assign his little project to any faculty member he liked. Maybe if Paul made the psychology department look good, it could help his career in the future. Potentially. He cleared his throat. "What do I need to do?"

"You'll be meeting with the project organizer this afternoon—he can tell you all about it, I'm sure." Dr. Kirsner waved two fingers vaguely, as if the project wasn't worth the effort of lifting his hand the entire way. "His name is Brandon Mercer. He's some sort of consultant, and he'll be in your office at twelve-thirty."

* * * *

It was a good thing Paul had a pretty thorough lesson plan written out on paper, for once, because there was no way he'd have been up to winging it for his 11:00 Intro Developmental Psych lecture. Every relatively quiet moment between the summons from Dr. Kirsner and the impending meeting with "the consultant" seemed to be peppered with increasingly vivid memories of Brandon from that one magical night freshman year: the breathless sneak back down the hallway to Brandon's room, the sight of Brandon's head thrown back and eyes squeezed shut during a particularly loud gasp, the definition of muscles on his bare chest, how he'd kissed like he wanted to fellate Paul's tongue. And *Christ*, the feel of Brandon's erection rubbing against his own as they squirmed together on the bed. It had all been so overwhelming at the time, but somehow Paul's brain had managed to capture every single second in Technicolor.

And *none* of it was appropriate for Paul to be daydreaming about during class—or anytime while he was on St. Ben's campus. The cold shower would have to wait for when he got home, but in the meantime Paul bought a sandwich at the cafeteria as soon as his lecture finished, and hid in his office to eat. He really didn't need anyone around to ask how he could be "reading" psychology periodicals despite being distracted enough he forgot to turn the pages.

Brandon showed up right on time. The look of surprise on his face was almost—*almost*—worth the inevitable awkwardness which would follow. The momentary lapse was quickly covered by a cocky grin, though, as he came in and nudged the door closed behind him.

"So you're my departmental liaison. I had wondered."

Paul nodded, keeping his expression carefully neutral. Hopefully betraying no sign of what he'd been thinking about pretty much non-stop since Friday. "I was just let in the loop this morning—not told much about what I'm supposed to do," he admitted. "I don't know how much help I'll be."

"It's really not all that time-consuming." Brandon dropped into his chair with an easy grace. "St. Ben's has hired me to review a bunch of their electronic files, looking for irregularities. I won't necessarily know what I'm looking for, though, so I asked for someone in each department to act as my point of contact if I have any questions. Specifically, I need someone who's been here a while and knows everyone in their department fairly well—which it sounds like you do."

Paul nodded again. With those criteria, he supposed he was a valid choice. "What kind of irregularities?"

"Don't know yet." Brandon looked over the desk at Paul, a hint of teasing in his gaze. "The more of them I find the more I'll get to consult with you, so I'm not going to complain."

There it was again—that frisson of *something* between them, still there after ten years. Brandon was staring, now, perplexed by whatever he saw on Paul's face, but Paul couldn't look away.

"I'm about to be really forward again," Brandon said slowly, "but… Do dinner with me tonight? We can keep it to 'dinner-dinner,' I promise. It's just… I haven't seen you for ages. I know you're not interested in anything complicated, but I really would love to have the chance to catch up. I want to hear more about St. Ben's. And your research. And—well, anything really." Paul was astonished to see that Brandon was turning a bit red under his beard. "If you don't want to, it's fine. I'm just really not looking forward to sitting around my hotel room doing nothing all evening."

"No, that's—it sounds good. Nice." Paul cleared his throat. *Nothing too dangerous about merely having dinner, is there?* Some small voice in the back of his head started cataloging all the ways this was a horrible idea, but he ignored it. "Where do you want to go?"

* * * *

Even with the cold shower and a truly stupid amount of time spent staring at his closet and deciding what to wear, Paul showed up at the barbecue restaurant almost half an hour early. He ended up killing time sitting in his car and playing repetitive little games on his phone, glancing up every time anyone so much as drove through the parking lot. At ten minutes to seven, he finally gave up and went inside to get a table.

"Hey." Brandon slid into the chair opposite a few minutes later and shot him a bright smile, no trace of his earlier insecurity. "Damn, haven't been here in ages. I remember their okra was fantastic."

"Still is." Paul busied himself with looking over the menu, even though he ate here often enough he could have probably listed off almost everything on it from memory. Including prices. "I always get the fried catfish platter," he said instead of whatever stupider thing would have escaped his mouth if given the chance.

"Sounds good to me." Brandon shoved his menu aside. "So how was the rest of your day?"

Small talk was surprisingly easy, all the way through dinner and a slice of chess pie apiece. They'd never really been close enough freshman year to go out like this, just to spend time in each other's company, and it was nice. Novel. Brandon talked about his experiences at Georgia Tech and how he'd fallen into working for a digital security firm, and Paul outlined the basis of his doctoral thesis—the cognitive basis of human decision-making—and summarized the more interesting bits of his research. Before Paul knew it, their plates were empty and the check was sitting on the table between them and Brandon was regarding him speculatively.

"So," Brandon said quietly. "This was dinner."

"Yeah."

"It was good."

Paul swallowed and nodded. "Yeah, it was nice." *For the first time in forever, it feels like I have a social life.*

"Are you ready to go home now?" Brandon's question was simple, but the implied *alone* echoed over the table loud and clear. One last offer just in case Paul was interested. It felt like so much more than that, though. It was the only chance Paul was likely to get to *not* be that obedient son, the predictably boring professor. The final chance to indulge in more than what Grace—or any other nice, wholesome woman—could offer. Brandon was still pretty much the only face in most of his private little fantasies, and the chance to refresh that memory with actual sex…

"You could come over, if you want," Paul mumbled. "To—to hang out a bit, I guess? I mean—you don't have to, but if you were still thinking of... yeah. I might—maybe we could call it coming in for a drink? Not that I have anything alcoholic, I think, but if we...crap. I'm not making sense, am I?"

Brandon's smile was slow and smoldering and he bit his lip in what Paul could only call a sultry look. "Was that an invitation?" he drawled. "Because I very much like the idea of you taking me back to your place and letting me show you a bit of what you've been missing. I've certainly been missing you."

Holy crap. "It's... It's a maybe." Paul ducked his head, looking anywhere but at the gorgeously confident man across from him. "I...um. I don't know if I'm as ready as I—it would be mean to get your hopes up. I think I want to talk first. And then, possibly. I've been—I've been thinking about you a lot today. And I think maybe we can do something like that. Not everything, but...maybe some of it. If you want."

And *God*, Brandon's grin turned downright predatory. "I want," he murmured. "Oh, I want. Tell me what you want to learn, and I will be *happy* to indulge you."

Chapter 4

Paul gave Brandon his phone number and address before they left the restaurant, just in case, but with the light traffic they had no trouble caravanning back to his apartment complex. It wasn't the fanciest in town, but it was a step up from the apartments filled with partying students, and it was generally pretty quiet. His living room window overlooked the "pond"—currently more of a mud puddle—and the walking path at the front of the property. The complex's prime selling point had been that it was fifteen minutes away from campus, in the opposite direction from the apartment he'd shared with Christopher. Fewer memories.

"This must be convenient," Brandon commented as they got out of their respective cars and headed for Paul's front door. "Not much of a commute, I'm guessing?"

"Not with the hours I keep," Paul answered. "I'm hardly ever on the road during rush hour. Well, around here it's more like rush fifteen minutes." He let them both in and nodded toward the kitchen. "Um, coffee? Or a soda or something?" *God, I sound like an idiot. Or the hostess at a home Bible study.* Inviting Brandon back to his apartment was already feeling like a terrible idea. He didn't even know what he *wanted*. He wasn't sure if—

"You're adorable," Brandon announced, interrupting Paul's growing sense of self-doubt. He grabbed Paul's hand and tugged him over to the sofa. "I'm still stuffed full of chess pie and sweet tea, and so are you. I can see why that restaurant is your favorite. Right now, though, what I *really* want to do is—oh my God! Are these all yours?" He slid from the sofa into a graceful crouch in front of the entertainment center. And in front of Paul's ridiculously large collection of videogames. "Damn, I knew there was a reason I liked you."

"Um." *Because of course he had to notice those.* Could it have *been* more obvious that Paul was a sad, lonely bachelor? "I don't watch TV much. Those are...what I do."

Brandon was only half listening, already running a finger along the spines of the neatly-organized jewel cases. "This is amazing," he said. "And you've got excellent taste. Don't apologize. Maybe—"

Yeah, about that. Paul took a deep breath and tried to quell the butterflies in his stomach. "Brandon, about that... I want to say yes, but I don't know how much I ..."

To Brandon's credit, he picked up on Paul's shaky tone immediately and came back up to sit beside him on the sofa. "You're still not sure about this," he said matter-of-factly. "Tell me what you *do* want, then. Hell, there's nothing wrong with actual communication. Even if I would dearly love to pull you into my lap and let you ride me right now." That sly half smile slid back into place again. "You get the most adorable flush in your cheeks when you're flustered; did you know that?"

Oh God. Paul could feel himself blush further, but there was nothing he could do about it. "It's not that I don't want to, it's just..." *Christ, this is hard to put into words.* "You know when there's something you really, really want, but you know it's probably bad for you? And you'll regret it later?"

"I'm that something, I assume."

"Pretty much."

Brandon arched one eyebrow. "And you're already planning to regret this? Because that's not really the best start to a potential evening of wild sex."

Damn. Despite Paul's nerves, that sounded seriously tempting. Heck, *any* sex would be fantastic, given how long it had been since Christopher. But maybe it would be better to restrict the whole affair to a few good kisses—and even that would be pushing it. Surely a good make-out session with Brandon would be enough, wouldn't it? Not as rude as kicking him out of the apartment so soon after inviting him in, but it wouldn't be so...

Dangerous.

That's what it came down to: Brandon Mercer, with that wicked smile, that smoldering look, that deliciously tempting tone of voice. He was a serious threat to Paul's ability to convince himself that he'd be just as happy living a believably straight life forever. It was bad enough fantasizing over what Brandon had been like when they were both eighteen, but the current Brandon Mercer had an aura of confidence that was nearly impossible to ignore.

"You're worried," Brandon said aloud. He slid to the far end of the sofa, then stood. "Look, much as I'd like to have some sexy fun together,

I'm not the kind of guy who sticks around where he's not wanted. How about you let me know later, okay? Give me a call? We don't have to—"

"No!" *Crap, that came out sounding downright clingy.* "I mean—I do want this. Something. I just—I can't do casually gay. All my experience is built around 'guilty and closeted.' And I've got a lot to lose if this gets out, so you'll have to forgive me for being a little extra-cautious here."

"What, you think I'm going to go around announcing that we fucked?" Brandon rolled his eyes. "Christ—this is why I usually don't do this with closeted guys. Forget it."

"Stay."

"No—look." Brandon propped his hip on the arm of the sofa and crossed his arms. "I don't mind if tonight becomes your dirty little secret. I kind of expected that when I asked. I'm not going to go bragging about what you taste like or how you are in bed, and I wouldn't know anyone here to tell even if I wanted to. But I'm *not* going to be the focus of some Jesus-hates-me meltdown where you can paint me as some rainbow Typhoid Mary spreading gay cooties in my wake. If you want this, you've got to own it. I'd rather sit alone in my hotel room than be some big ongoing source of guilt for you to rail against. You want me? Then say it."

"I do want you." The words tumbled out all by themselves, but Paul realized he meant them. "I'm sorry I'm being a jerk about this and I wish I could...yeah." He sucked in a deep breath and let it out at a measured pace. "You're right. And I do have *some* experience. I'm not some blushing virgin or anything."

"Not anymore," Brandon countered with a wicked grin.

God. "I'm saying yes," Paul insisted. "I'm just not entirely sure what I want to say yes *to.*"

The smirk dropped from Brandon's face, replaced by a much gentler expression. "Want me to suggest something, then?"

Easier than me having to fumble through saying it. Paul nodded.

"Right, then—here goes." Brandon lowered himself back onto the sofa and slid an arm around Paul's shoulders. "First, we fool around and I show you a thing or two you may have been missing out on, your 'some experience' notwithstanding. And then we say screw it, curl up together here on the couch, and play video games together until we get tired. I'll either sleep on the couch or you kick me out. Deal?"

"Deal," Paul agreed. The promise of video games afterward was oddly soothing—made it feel like they were just hanging out and happened to be getting physical rather than the significantly more skeezy "hookup for the sole purpose of getting off." Not that he'd ever had someone over to hang out at this apartment anyway.

"Thank God." Brandon's eyes darkened. "Get over here." His hand slipped up to the nape of Paul's neck, warm and insistent, urging him forward.

Oh. Paul had seen the kiss coming, had expected it, but he hadn't predicted the sheer rush of sensation at even the first touch of Brandon's lips against his own. Not that Brandon was holding back—he knew what he was doing. His fingers cradled the back of Paul's skull, carding gentle tributaries through his hair and positioning him at the perfect angle to better steal every single thought from his head. Paul tried to keep up, but two seconds into the kiss he had to admit he had absolutely no idea how. It felt like every little nudge of Brandon's lips was a question and Paul didn't have the answers.

"Easy, easy," Brandon murmured, pulling back fractionally and pressing their foreheads together. "Too much?"

"A bit," Paul admitted. "I want to, but…"

"I get it." Brandon snuck a tiny peck against the corner of Paul's mouth, then another farther back against the curve of his jaw. His beard tickled Paul's neck. "Not gonna push you further than you want to go tonight, I promise. No matter how tempting you look when you're all flustered and overwhelmed." A third kiss, closer to his temple. "Tell me what turns you on the most, and I'll make it good."

Oh God. Paul sucked in a breath, the possibilities swirling in his head. There were a lot of possibilities, he knew, even if he hadn't personally tried most of them. Christopher had always harped on him for being a prude. And maybe he was, if Christopher's version was to be believed. Suddenly, admitting *I don't know what the choices are* felt like the most humiliating thing Paul could imagine. Why had he gone and bragged about having experience? Maybe he should make up something, pretend he knew more about—

"Want another suggestion?" Brandon murmured in his ear.

Paul nodded, his voice stuck in his throat.

"Here's what we'll do, then. You let me strip you out of that gorgeous hot teacher jacket and push you back right here in the middle of the sofa. We can unbutton each other's shirts as slow as we want, taking our time so we get all breathy and frantic as we're kissing each other. And then I'll unzip your pants and settle down right here between your thighs, and I'll absolutely blow your mind." One corner of his lips twisted upward. "And your cock."

Damn. If Paul hadn't already been hard, he was now. A completely unauthorized squeak escaped his throat.

"Is that what you want?" Brandon chuckled darkly, then licked a fat stripe up the side of Paul's neck. "After I've drained you so dry you're completely boneless, I'll drag you down on top of me on the floor and you can pull me off too. It won't take much after all that, I expect." A sudden wave of cool air against his neck. Brandon blowing on the skin he'd just licked. "Damn, I'm halfway there just telling you about it. I wasn't lying—I fantasized about you for ages, way back when. Still do, on occasion. So does that sound good to you? Or is that too far?"

"Hell yes." Paul blinked. "I mean, it sounds good. Isn't too much."

"Thank God," Brandon growled, and slid both hands between them to work on the buttons of Paul's shirt. Luckily they were large and easy to manipulate even without either of them looking, because it seemed like a good time for Paul to try initiating a kiss of his own. Brandon muttered something into the kiss, letting Paul take the lead but not backing down one jot. They only broke apart when Brandon finished and slid his palms over Paul's shoulders, wordlessly slipping the shirt free.

"Damn," Brandon murmured. "Your blush goes all the way down to your collarbone. I like it."

Paul wasn't surprised, but he couldn't find the voice to answer. Instead he extricated his arms from the sleeves and focused his attention on Brandon's own much smaller and finickier buttons. Brandon threw his head back as Paul worked, granting full access to his pale throat, and Paul couldn't resist the opportunity to taste in return. There was a vague shadow of stubble growing in below his manicured beard, barely enough to see but enough for Paul to feel against his tongue. He mouthed a sloppy kiss into the hollow under Brandon's jaw, and Brandon sucked in a ragged breath.

"God, that's—fuck. Okay, so forget what I said about this part being slow—I need our clothes to be off. Now." Brandon displaced Paul's fingers, tearing at his cuffs and tossing his shirt over his shoulder onto the floor. Paul used the opportunity to steal another taste of Brandon's neck, and ten seconds later they were bare chest to bare chest and locked in a dizzying kiss again. Everything was so much more intense now that there was more naked skin in play—Brandon's pectorals were pleasantly well-defined but not overly muscled, which suited Paul fine. The biceps were a step up from what Paul remembered, as was the hint of defined abs, and somehow Brandon gave the impression of being larger without having gotten physically taller. They'd both changed physically since freshman year and at least in Brandon's case it was for the better.

"Gorgeous," Brandon said, in between all but biting at Paul's lips. "Christ, it's criminal for you to be hiding yourself like this. I want to—here, lean back." He layered kisses along the edge of Paul's jaw again, detoured down his carotid, and eventually worked his way to the hollow between Paul's collarbones. "You taste fantastic," he whispered, and dropped to crouch on the floor between Paul's legs so he could press Paul back into the sofa and capture one sensitive nipple in his mouth.

"Oh God."

"Mmmm." Brandon swirled his tongue roughly, then gently, leaving Paul able to do little more than drop his head back against the top of the sofa and pant. "Tell me I can keep going—I need to taste the rest of you. Your stomach and your hip and your thighs and your cock and your balls and everything. Tell me that's not too fast."

"It's—*ah!*—it's good," Paul groaned. "This is… It's good." He buried a hand in Brandon's thick hair. Should he push? God, he wanted to push, to guide, to drag Brandon's gorgeous mouth down to where his erection was practically screaming for it. Brandon probably knew more than he did about blowjob etiquette, though, so Paul restrained himself. Barely.

"You like this, then?" Brandon laved a damp trail down Paul's ribs with his tongue, tasting each one in turn with little testing jabs before proceeding on to the next. When he reached Paul's navel, he gave it a filthy, sloppy kiss, darting his tongue in and out like he was slowly fucking the sensitive hollow of it, glorious enough to leave Paul moaning incoherently and his balls aching like mad. Paul had shifted himself forward on the sofa enough to create some delicious friction between his still-clothed erection and Brandon's naked chest. Brandon slid warm palms up Paul's thighs, massaging gently before continuing upward to bracket either side of his cock.

"Yes," Paul panted. "Touch me, please, just—"

"Shhh," Brandon murmured. He indulged in one more dirty swirl of his tongue in Paul's navel, then sat back on his heels and went to work on Paul's button and zipper. Paul nearly cried at the sudden relief as the extra pressure on his cock melted away and all that stood between him and Brandon's glorious mouth was the thin cotton of his boxers. Brandon's grin was blinding.

"Lift your hips a sec?"

Paul did, and Brandon slipped his pants and boxers down in one long sweep. Which was immediately fouled up by the fact that they were both still wearing their shoes. It took an awkward minute or two of frantic lace-unknotting before Paul could kick the offending footwear off—Brandon mimicking the movements as he shed his own—but then they were both wonderfully naked. Brandon was leaning over and breathing on him, and Paul had to close his eyes to avoid coming right there and then.

"I do still dream about you, you know," Brandon murmured. "Always regretted not getting to do this before." And he leaned over that little bit more so he could take the tip of Paul's cock into his mouth.

Holy hell. It was better than anything Paul could have imagined. Their freshman year fumblings had been wonderful, amazing, the highlight of his until-then-nonexistent sexual experiences, but neither of them had known what they were doing. And later, for all Christopher had been enthusiastic about Paul performing this particular activity on him, he had never been all that into returning the favor. Now Paul was five seconds into a blowjob and Brandon was already blowing his entire sexual repertoire out of the water.

"Your *mouth*, Christ, I...*nngh.*" There were other words, better ones, but Paul didn't have access to them right now. He couldn't see Brandon's face, but he could *feel* him hum in satisfaction before he sucked a bit harder and ducked his head a bit lower. And damn, even just the sight of Brandon's dark hair bobbing up and down was probably going to fuel Paul's masturbatory fantasies for years. The reality of the experience was well beyond anything he had expected.

Brandon did something with his tongue, a little flick timed to coincide with a particularly spectacular bit of suction, and all of a sudden Paul was *there.* It was all he could do to tighten his grip on Brandon's hair in warning before his orgasm hit him and he was reduced to incoherent half curses. Brandon pulled off and pumped him through it gently, just firm enough to prolong each wave, until Paul was completely and utterly unable to move.

"Gorgeous," Brandon proclaimed.

Paul opened his eyes—when had he closed them?—and looked down. Brandon's own erection was still hot and heavy between his legs. He caught Paul looking and smirked.

"Liked that, did you?" Brandon shifted his hips slightly, getting his balance, but then he grabbed Paul's hand and tugged him forward until Paul tipped off the sofa and fell over on top of him. "Gonna help me through it?"

"God, yes." Handjobs were easy—nothing new, in theory, although in this case everything was new because Brandon was amazing and not at all pushy about it. This was something Paul could be a bit more confident about, though. He may have been left reeling at Brandon's blowjob skills, but now his head was a bit clearer and he could focus on getting his own back.

Paul shuffled them around until they were side-by-side on the rug, facing each other, and he could get a nice firm grip on Brandon's cock. He was tempted to try for another mind-bending kiss, but at the moment it seemed more important to watch the way the head of Brandon's erection was peeking in and out from his fist as he worked it. Brandon was the one gasping and cursing, now, gorgeous and naked against the backdrop of Paul's boring beige carpet. They didn't have any lube, but Brandon was leaking copious amounts of pre-come and it was plenty to work with. Paul smeared it down as much of the shaft as he could and set to making Brandon moan.

It didn't take long. The groans and choked curses turned to full-on invectives and then a shuddering sigh as Brandon spilled into his hand. They both lay there for a few minutes, panting, absorbing the experience. Brandon rolled away first.

"Bathroom?"

Paul pointed out the appropriate door. While Brandon got himself cleaned up, Paul used the kitchen sink and some paper towels to wash up as best he could. Brandon came back out just as Paul was blotting the last of the stains off the sofa.

"Knew you'd be phenomenal," Brandon announced, leaning against the kitchen doorframe and looking absolutely at home despite being totally nude. "I'm so glad you gave me another chance."

"I don't recall having any complaints about what we did freshman year," Paul countered. *The lack of contact afterward, yes, but not the experience itself.*

"Still worth repeating, though, wasn't it?" Brandon winked and loped over to where his clothes had ended up in a messy pile. He looked nearly as sexy putting clothes on as he did taking them off. "Greatest regret of my life, not getting back in touch with you after we both went home for the summer. I'd pretty much resigned myself to living without knowing what you tasted like, and now I see I was missing out. I wouldn't be averse to trying something like that again soon, if you're up for it. I'll be in town for a few weeks yet." He paused, then nodded toward the rack of games. "You want me to hang around a bit longer tonight, or should I get going?"

Paul tried to get dressed as quickly as he could, not entirely sure what to do. Brandon was amazing, fantastic, incredible—and yes, it would be good to have someone to hang out with for the evening. Even though they'd had some spectacular orgasms in each other's company not ten minutes ago and his brain really wasn't going to be capable of processing that fact yet. "I'd love it if you wanted to stay," he finally said.

"Awesome." Brandon left his socks and shoes sitting next to the wall and came over to browse the row of jewel cases before planting himself on the floor next to Paul's leg. "I'm more of a PC gamer—which of these have a good multiplayer mode?"

"What are you in the mood for?"

Brandon laughed. "I just got off with the taste of you on my tongue. Believe me, I'm not feeling picky."

Chapter 5

I got off last night. With Brandon Mercer. Holy crap.

Paul put his head down on his desk and banged his forehead on the scarred wood, the noise echoing in his tiny office. *A freaking blowjob. And it was amazing.* This wasn't going to do anything to help him in the "staying in the nice, comfortable closet" department. And worse, the amazing part hadn't just been the physical aspect—the dinner had been great, the conversation had been interesting, and Brandon turned out to be pretty impressive at first-person shooters as well. The man was a walking pile of Paul's biggest turn-ons and he represented everything Paul couldn't have.

You can have him again tonight if you want to, a voice in Paul's head reminded him. They'd parted ways with one last lingering kiss and a promise to meet up for dinner (and implied orgasms) again the next evening. Paul didn't even want to think about how badly he was looking forward to seeing Brandon again.

It wasn't that big a deal, was it? Brandon was only going to be in town for the next few weeks. After that, Paul could go back to keeping his head down, to occasionally pulling himself off in the shower or safely hidden under his own covers, and nobody else would ever have to know. He could hold out for tenure and get that raise and work on funding his next research project and then the one after that and the one after that and if he was very lucky, he could stay in the closet for the next forty years until he was ready to retire.

And do what in the meantime? Should I find a nice, unsuspecting wife somewhere? Settle down and have a few kids? Christmas dinners with the in-laws? Or just be a "confirmed bachelor" for everyone to speculate about? It wasn't as if he had a whole lot of friends to be spending time with—his life had revolved around St. Benedict's for the last decade, and most of that was his student years. Now nearly everyone from his undergrad and grad school days had moved on. Paul had never been as enthusiastically Christian as his contemporaries in the psychology department, either, so his relationships there were mostly limited to chats about the weather and occasional campus gossip. The only exception was Grace, and anything more than friendship with her—however much it might fit what everyone expected him to want and however much she might have made it obvious she wanted him—would be built on a lie. No, Brandon Mercer was an anomaly, and it seemed the best thing to do would be to enjoy his presence while it lasted and then forget about it when he left. Best and safest. Paul would just have to *make* it not be a big deal.

Relieved to have talked himself through that particular minefield, Paul settled further into his chair and glanced at the clock in the corner of his computer screen. Forty-five minutes until class. More than enough time to catch up on some e-mail, tweak the wording on that proposal due next Friday, and look over his notes before he had to head downstairs to the lecture hall. Freshman survey courses weren't as much fun to teach as the sophomore and junior seminars, but Dr. Kirsner made a point of divvying up the large lecture classes among all the various non-tenured faculty. At least Paul hadn't gotten stuck with Grace's 8 AM section. He opened his grant proposal and university e-mail simultaneously, tapping his fingers on his desk while they loaded. Would be nice to finally hear back from the two juniors in his psycholinguistics seminar who hadn't chosen their spring paper topics yet...

The single new e-mail waiting in his inbox had no subject, no sender address, and—apparently—no recipient. Although it had still reached him, so maybe it was something official? There was no text, just a large image file which took a few more seconds to load.

When it did, Paul slammed his laptop shut and focused on just trying to breathe.

The picture was of him. Him and Brandon, but the only part of Brandon visible was the back of his head and the tops of his very naked shoulders as he knelt between Paul's legs. In Paul's living room. In front of Paul's sofa. And the man sitting with his head thrown back, fisting Brandon's hair as Brandon choked down his cock, was clearly Paul himself.

Fuck. Fuckityfuckityfuckfuckfuck. Paul didn't swear often, but right now it seemed completely justified. What was this—a warning? A message? Blackmail? He glanced toward the hallway to remind himself it was empty—even though his screen faced away from the door—and forced himself to open the laptop again. The picture was still there. It was still of him. He was making the kind of face he usually associated with bad porn, a scrunched-up gasping wince that made him look like he was possibly in pain and possibly just about to let out a moan loud enough to wake the neighbors. With a man giving him head. *Fuck.*

Paul's first instinct was to call Brandon and yell at him for ruining everything. Paul had been *very* clear that anything they did had to remain a secret, and this was pretty much his worst nightmare come true. That instinct only lasted a second or two, until his more rational mind pointed out that Brandon *couldn't* have taken the picture, seeing as he was otherwise occupied at the time, and thus someone else *had.* He hadn't closed the blinds before leaving to meet Brandon, and once they got back to the apartment the view had been the furthest thing from his mind. Had that someone else been out there waiting? Or had they just *happened* to have been wandering around in the dark and decided to practice some casual photography?

The someone else, whoever he or she was, wanted Paul to know he'd been seen. He took a closer look at the photo, trying to focus on the portions that weren't himself and Brandon. The picture itself was large, but the resolution was grainy. Cropped from a bigger picture, perhaps? Or a poor quality camera? The color was a bit washed out, but it didn't look like the kind of chunky grayscale security videos they showed on the news when a convenience store was being robbed. It seemed like a normal, albeit amateur, picture. The kind someone might post to Facebook, if the subject had been different.

Warning? If the photographer could send this to him, they could send it to anyone. Although as a blackmail overture it kind of lost something without any text. Threat, then?

It suddenly struck him that there was absolutely nobody he could ask about this. His parents didn't know he was gay, and anyone at St. Ben's was just as likely to report him as not. Danielle, maybe? But no—she was going to be spending her stateside vacation time with the family, and it wasn't like she could just leave to take a phone call so her twin brother could have a nice little freak-out. Plus if he told her about this, he'd have to tell her about Brandon, and she'd read *way* too much into that. Especially now that she was head over heels for Étienne.

Which only left Brandon himself. Practically a stranger, after all this time, barring their encounter the previous night. Paul wouldn't have to explain anything, though. Wouldn't have to come out to anyone to get help. And better yet, Brandon might be able to figure out where the e-mail came from. Paul was moderately tech-savvy, but no more so than most guys under thirty. From the tidbits Brandon had let drop in conversation the night before, he was head and shoulders beyond merely "tech-savvy." Closer to "tech god." If nothing else, he could be a sympathetic ear. Paul got up, closed his office door, and dialed.

Brandon answered on the first ring. "Thinking about me so soon?" There was a definite teasing note in his voice. "Thought you had class today."

"I do," Paul answered automatically. "I mean—I will, in a little while. But there's a bit of a crisis and I think I need your help."

All laughter immediately disappeared from Brandon's tone. "What's up?"

"I don't... it's..." Paul stared at his screen helplessly. "Someone sent me a picture this morning. Of us."

"Someone you know?"

"I'm not sure—there's no words. No sender, no subject line. Just the picture. It's, um." Paul forced in a deep breath. "Through my window. Of us together."

"Shit." There was a shuffling sound in the background, then the sound of a door closing and the background noise muffled substantially. Brandon closing himself into an empty room for privacy, presumably. "So. When you say 'together'..."

"Exactly what you're picturing."

"Shit."

"Yeah."

They both fell silent for a long moment.

"You want me to take a look at it?" Brandon finally asked. "Bring your laptop and meet me for lunch? I mean, you could forward it to me, but..."

Paul would happily do pretty much anything if it meant Brandon could fix things. "That's good. Lunch. Not on campus, though. I don't—"

"Hey, no, I get it," Brandon interjected. "You remember the coffee shop we went yesterday morning? I think there was a sandwich place next door—want to meet me there? They had free wifi, according to the sign in the window."

"I can do that."

"Good—let me know when you're ready to go and I'll meet you there. And Paul?" He paused. "Trust me—it'll be fine."

God, I hope so.

* * * *

"Let's see, then."

Paul pulled up his university e-mail, opened the photo, and wordlessly turned his laptop around so Brandon could see the screen. They weren't the only ones getting lunch, but they were the only ones not taking advantage of the beautiful spring weather to sit outdoors—which meant they had the entire small café to themselves. Brandon stared at the picture for several seconds.

"Too bad it's such a gorgeous picture of you," he finally said. "I would have loved a picture like that in other circumstances."

Not helping. Paul poked at his Reuben and forced himself not to scowl. "I knew it was a bad idea," he muttered.

"I seem to recall you enjoying yourself fine last night," Brandon countered, typing something rapidly without looking away from the screen. "Don't let your stalker taint what we both agreed was a fantastic evening."

Paul blinked and put down his sandwich. "You think it was a stalker? That sounds so melodramatic. Like a bad horror movie." *Although don't the guys who have sex at the beginning always end up getting killed off? Or does that only happen to beautiful blond cheerleaders?* His own hair was closer to tan than blond, not exactly Hollywood-worthy—

"I don't—hmmm?" Brandon glanced up and frowned. "Sorry, was trying to figure out how an e-mail with absolutely no metadata even got through the system. I didn't mean *stalker* stalker. Someone knew it was you and knew your home address, right?"

Paul nodded cautiously.

"So it's probably someone who knows you personally. They know you work at St. Benedict's, at least, because they sent it to your work e-mail. And there's a good chance it's either a student or a coworker; an outsider wouldn't have been able to do this." He turned the laptop so Paul could see the screen. It was open to an unfamiliar menu that seemed to be written mostly in computer-ese. "It's pretty easy to spoof the sender's address— which is why you sometimes get spam saying it's from PayPal or the FBI or whatnot. Even spoofed, every server the e-mail is routed through should be tacking on a bit of information. Instead, it's blank."

"Meaning the e-mail came from inside the house?"

Brandon's lips twitched. "From someone who has access to St. Ben's primary mail server, possibly. Although even e-mail sent from on campus should have *something* here." He tapped the screen. "Verification that it was passed on. Someone went to a lot of work to strip that out—if they wanted to stay truly anonymous, they could have bounced it through half a dozen proxies on the other side of the world and it would have said much less about them."

"Meaning they want me to know they're close by."

"You knew that anyway, since someone had to take that picture." Brandon let out a frustrated huff of breath. "Look, I'll see what I can uncover this afternoon—believe it or not, this does tangentially relate to what I'm at St. Ben's to do. There should be a *very* short list of people with this kind of access to the school-wide mail infrastructure. If this wasn't someone on that list, I need to know about it."

"Preferably before they send this to my boss?"

Brandon took a sip of his drink. "Right, so hear me out. I know you're pissed and worried. I am too, on your behalf. But nobody's come storming into your office threatening to fire you, right?"

Paul nodded cautiously. *Pissed* didn't even begin to cover it, but at the moment the paranoia was more than making up for it. "That's true," he admitted.

"So whoever-it-was probably sent it to you as a warning. Right now, there's no way to tell whether they're doing the creepy stalker thing or whether it's an acquaintance who happened to be walking past your apartment complex and recognized you and… Hell, I don't know. Wanted to warn you about the evils of being gay, maybe. Or to tell you to be careful about leaving your blinds open. The point is, they didn't send it to your boss, which means they might not intend to. And we won't know more until we figure out who they are and how they did it. Like I said, I'll take a closer look this afternoon. Okay if I forward myself the picture?"

"As long as it's not going to end up being seen by anyone else." It was *really* tempting to say no, to delete the whole e-mail and hope the problem went away, but Paul had already trusted Brandon with his biggest secret— heck, had trusted him enough to stick his cock in the man's mouth. And he was the perfect person to get to the bottom of whatever was going on.

It was a definite relief to know that Brandon was on his side.

Chapter 6

Brandon didn't bother with formalities; he just opened the call with, "So what do you feel like for dinner?"

"Hi? And I guess I don't care." Paul really didn't feel like eating, to be honest, but they'd made loose plans and he was dying to see what Brandon had found out about the mysterious e-mail. He was less enthused about the likelihood of Brandon wanting more sex afterward—it was hard to even think about getting off when there was a looming specter of someone watching them while they did it. Whatever "it" might be.

"Is that Thai place near the mall still open? I went there once freshman year, and I remember the food being pretty good."

Thai sounded no better or worse than anything else. "The mall itself is gone, but I do think the restaurant is still around. I don't remember ever having eaten there before."

"Cool." Brandon was silent for several seconds. "Actually... I'm going to make a wild guess here, but I suspect you're not feeling all that up to being out in public with me right now."

It sounded so bad when he put it like that. Paul scrambled for an answer that wouldn't be too offensive, but the pause told Brandon everything he needed to hear. "I it to be—"

"Hey, don't worry about it. It's totally understandable." Brandon didn't sound surprised. "I was just thinking... What if I stop off and pick up some takeout, and we hang out in my hotel room for the evening? It won't feel quite so much like someone is watching over our shoulders, and we can just eat and watch whatever's on TV".

Paul could practically feel him sorting through his stock of placating phrases.

"What I mean is," he continued once he found a suitable one, "that we don't have to do anything. Hang out. Chat. I wish I had more to tell you about what I've found, but at least I can show you what I've got."

That sounded perfect. Something in Paul's chest loosened. "I think I'd like that."

* * * *

Even just going from his car to the lobby of the hotel made Paul feel like he was in some sort of terrible spy movie. What if someone got a picture of him *there?* Going into a hotel to meet up with another man? Lord, Dr. Kirsner was bad enough when he thought Danielle had been doing something untoward; Paul didn't even want to think about what the man would do with photographic proof of what he and Brandon had been doing last night. *Being fired would be the least of my worries.* He slipped through the sliding double doors and ducked into the elevator as quickly as possible.

Brandon opened the door before Paul had a chance to knock. He'd changed out of his work clothes—instead of the crisp khakis and button-down he'd been wearing at lunch, he now sported a pair of faded jeans and a T-shirt proclaiming it provided "+2 to sexiness." It wasn't a lie—the shirt was just tight enough to show off the muscles underneath, in a cut a straight man would absolutely never wear. He looked fabulous. It took Paul a moment to realize Brandon was talking.

"Sorry, what?"

"Was asking if you wanted anything other than tap water—I'm going to go fill the ice bucket, but the soda machine's right there. I can grab something."

"Oh. No, water's fine, thanks." Paul got out of the way so Brandon could get past him to the door. "I'll just—um, these glasses here?"

"Yeah—food's on the desk. Help yourself. I'll be right back."

Brandon had gotten a good selection. Paul wasn't usually too picky when it came to what he ate, but they hadn't talked about what to order and it looked like Brandon had opted for a little of everything. It smelled fantastic. By the time Brandon got back with the ice, Paul had the desk set up closer to the bed so he could sit on the duvet and Brandon could sit in the desk chair and they could both reach everything. The arrangement had a sad ring of college life to it, eating takeout off the Styrofoam carton lids with flimsy plastic forks, but presumably nobody knew they were here and that made up for the rest of it.

"So I'm guessing you want to know what I found," Brandon announced. "It's not as much as I hoped, but it's at least a start."

Paul would rather not have thought about the e-mail at all, but ignoring it wasn't going to make it go away. "I'm assuming you can't—I don't know, 'un-erase' the sender or something?"

Brandon shook his head. "Not really, but I can track down the people who are supposed to have that kind of access to the server and work from the other end that way. I spent a fair chunk of this afternoon checking up on you."

"Me?" Paul swallowed wrong and ended up trying desperately to suppress a coughing fit. "Sorry. What'd you find?"

"That you're not the one responsible for data disappearing from St. Ben's." Brandon sat back in his chair and swirled the ice around in his glass, studying Paul carefully. "I'm not supposed to tell anyone here the full truth about what I'm doing, but screw it. I did some digging into your electronic trail today so I could be sure you weren't the culprit before I let you in on my secret."

Paul sucked in an exaggerated gasp of surprise. "Ooh, let me guess— you're Superman?"

"Right, I wish." Brandon rolled his eyes, but he was smiling. "Nothing quite so exciting. St. Ben's called my security firm because they suspect someone is mucking around with their system. Nobody really seems sure how long it's been going on, but there've been several incidents where someone remembered sending an e-mail that was never received, and when they looked later there were no traces of it ever having existed. Others had files stored on the university network revert to earlier versions, despite the owners swearing they backed everything up. Individually, they're all little things that could be chalked up to forgetfulness or human error."

"Except?"

Brandon nodded. "Except someone is also changing details *within* files. We think. And nobody should be able to do that. It's a potential PR nightmare for St. Ben's: if whoever-it-is is siphoning off interesting bits of data, they could pick out the most damning things they find and publish them. Or delete just enough to make it look like St. Ben's is trying, poorly, to cover up some big scandal. Or—hell they could be planting things too, for all I know. It's potentially really bad."

"Wow," Paul breathed. "I guess—could whoever it is delete the whole thing? Is that possible? Like, erase the student database or whatnot?"

"I think that's what the administration is worried about, but no, not really." Brandon crinkled his nose—and oh, that shouldn't have been so attractive—and speared another piece of chicken. "There are safeguards against *that*. Not to mention it would be really obvious if it did happen, which means IT could pretty easily restore everything from the last backup. It would be annoying and disruptive but fixable. No, what's worse is if something gets changed and nobody notices it and then it's overwritten on top of the old backups and no one knows how long it's been there, or whether it's supposed to be there at all. And—to come back to the original topic—chances are, whoever is mucking around in the mail server is using the same back door to get into the other systems as well. Which means it could be one person, or a group of people, or it could be a mostly-theoretical loophole that nobody else has discovered yet and all the inconsistencies are random. I've got to check all the obvious things before I start in on the wild conspiracy theories."

"Okay." Paul was mildly surprised to realize he followed all that, non-technical as it was. "So you came here because someone is poking around where they shouldn't be able to poke, and now that same person— maybe—sent that picture of us."

"Maybe," Brandon echoed. "Which is good, because it means my guys and I have another avenue to explore. Right now I need to find the overlap between people who would have a reason to send you that photo and people who have the ability to cause this kind of electronic havoc. Which admittedly doesn't help much yet, since I've really only just gotten started investigating, but it might help eliminate some possibilities down the road. Could save me some time."

"Or the stalker could escalate. Assuming it is a stalker."

Brandon blew out a long breath. "Or that," he admitted. "Look, I didn't mean to come in here and cause you trouble. Once I saw you again, I latched on to the idea of catching up, of finally getting to do some of the stuff we both wanted to do freshman year but didn't have the chance to, and…shit. If I don't take some downtime from work, I go crazy, you know? Sex is good for that, and getting you into my bed would be—hell, it would be fantastic. And long overdue." He flashed a rueful smile. "I get that you've worked hard to keep your personal life and your professional life separate, though, and I understand why. I may not agree with how you're doing it—hiding in the closet really does a number on you after a while, and I've got enough friends who've lived through that to know what I'm talking about—but that's your choice and I'm not going to preach. If you want to tell me to fuck off and only want me to deal with you as a fellow professional, I will."

"Bit late for that, isn't it?" Paul couldn't stop the words coming out of his mouth, and he immediately felt like kicking himself. "Sorry, that was rude. And it's not your fault. I mean, my first instinct was to call you and cuss you out for ruining my life, but really we should have at least closed the curtains or something."

"Oh, I don't know," Brandon drawled. "Could have gone the other way—rented lights and a disco ball and blasted some cheesy porn music. Then any evidence would disappear into the mass of dreck on Redtube and no one would ever find it again."

Paul opened his mouth, closed it again, and finally let out a shaky laugh. "I really don't know how to respond to that."

"Don't take it as a serious suggestion," Brandon said with a smile.

"Want to put this all aside until tomorrow?"

"Yeah, okay." Paul took a deep breath and let it out slowly, letting the moment drain away. "Let's just—let's just eat. And ignore it for a while."

* * * *

They finished their Thai while chatting about nothing in particular— memories of freshman year, the St. Ben's basketball team's abysmal season, the latest embarrassing news from the Georgia state legislature. Paul told Brandon a bit about what it was like to grow up with a twin sister who was always too observant by half, and Brandon reciprocated with horror stories about what it was like to have three older brothers. They avoided saying anything more even vaguely dealing with computers, or the e-mail, or the utterly fabulous blowjob from the night before. Eventually they had worked their way through about two-thirds of the Thai, and Brandon let his anecdote about a family car trip wind down into a vague joke about Atlanta drivers.

"So what do you want to do now?" he asked after a few seconds of awkward silence.

Paul wished he had an easy answer, but there wasn't one. "Um."

Brandon studied him for a long moment, then nodded and stood. "Right. I'm going to start by ferrying the leftovers to the trash bin at the end of the hallway so they don't stink up the room overnight. And that will give you a few minutes to decide whether you want to go home now, or stay and hang out with me for a bit and *then* go home, or stay the night. Not pushing you," he clarified. "If you want to crash here with me, I'm not going to take it as some big declaration or anything. We can make this just casual or just friends or neither and whatever you choose is fine by me."

Paul nodded automatically, his brain trying to sort everything out without being shouted down by input from his cock. Brandon didn't seem to expect an immediate answer, though, so Paul sat on the bed and tried to ignore Brandon bustling around collecting Styrofoam containers.

Did he want to stBut *should* he stay? That was trickier. If he stayed, was that implying he wanted actual sex? That seemed to be the expected outcome of spending the night at a guy's place, based on everything he'd heard. And Brandon had been kind enough to go slow with him the first time, but the idea of having anything up his rear end (or sticking anything in someone else's rear end) was...all right, not quite as awful with Brandon as it would have been with anyone else, but it still didn't sound fun. Did that amount to "some big declaration?" Because if so, Paul was pretty sure he'd rather go home early and deal with the jumpiness of being at his apartment alone than have to explain that he was a kinda-sorta-gay man with a pathological aversion to anal intercourse.

"Thoughts?" Brandon lowered himself onto the bed beside him, reclining onto the pillows and looking absolutely gorgeous with the hem of his T-shirt riding up and showing an inch-wide stripe of pale skin.

Paul tore his eyes away and shrugged.

"In that case, I'm going to see what sorts of movies we can get on this thing." Brandon grabbed the remote, the muscles in his shoulders bunching pleasantly, shirt riding up a bit more as he stretched up over his head to reach the nightstand. *Stop it, stop it, not thinking about that.* Brandon waded through the menus on the TV. He kept his eyes on the screen, but Paul could feel the weight of his attention like a physical touch.

Hell, I want to stay so I'm going to. Why not. "I'm not much for horror movies," Paul admitted, "but anything else is good."

"Careful, or I'll make you watch some terrible children's movie. In Claymation." Brandon settled on a recent superhero-type action movie. "Seen this one already?"

Paul shook his head no. "Meant to, though."

"Me too. Let's give it a shot."

* * * *

It was pretty good, if totally implausible. Brandon rolled his eyes at how easily the hero hacked into the secret government database, and Paul scoffed at the cheesy mind-control pseudo-science explanations, but overall it was perfect for two totally normal guys to watch while happening to share a mattress and hiding from a stalker in a hotel room. Nothing wrong with that. Brandon stayed on his side of the bed, fingers laced behind his head as he leaned against the headboard with his legs stretched out in front of him, and Paul sat cross-legged on the other side with a good foot of space between his knee and Brandon's thigh. Two friends watching a movie—

"You ever dream of doing something like that someday?"

"Hmmm?" Paul tore his gaze away from the credits rolling on the screen.

"That." Brandon waved in the direction of the TV. "The superhero stuff. Ever feel the need to go start some fights and prove you're a badass just because you can? I mean, he could have gotten into the compound with his magical hacking skills; he didn't really need to knock out every bad guy personally. When I was a kid I spent half my free time chasing imaginary villains and showing them who's boss. I'm curious about your take."

Paul frowned down at his own not-terribly-athletic physique. "I'm more like Captain America before the super-soldier juice. Or Spider-Man before the radioactive spider bite. Not really built for brawling."

"Oh, I wouldn't say that." Brandon rolled to his side, ignoring the movie in favor of giving Paul a hot once-over. "I bet you're stronger than you look. And you'd out-think the enemy—I knew you were brilliant even when we first met. Thought your braininess was sexy even back then."

There it was again—the casually smoldering look, Brandon undressing him entirely with his eyes. Paul swallowed hard and abandoned all pretense of following the plot of the movie. "Brandon, I..."

"Not gonna pressure you," Brandon murmured. "But I'm going to appreciate the view here." He smirked. "And in case you're wondering, my answer is *yes*, I'd love a repeat of last night. No big coming out needed, just some safely-on-the-down-low mind-blowing sex between friends. If you're interested."

"I don't know."

Brandon pushed himself to a sitting position and turned so they were facing each other. "That's honest, at least. Did I do something to turn you off, or it is just the whole gay thing? You wanted one last time to see how it was and you're done with being gay now?"

"It's not you," Paul replied immediately. "I don't mean for it to sound like that. I know I'm not very good at this. At"—*not going to say sex*—"at the physical stuff. And for all that we're technically in bed together at the moment—"

"More *on* bed," Brandon interjected.

"Fine, *on* bed together. But it still boils down to the fact that I'm in the closet. I *like* my closet. It's cozy and familiar here. And coming out is scary." Paul dropped his gaze down to where his hands were clasped tightly in his lap. "I know that makes me sound like a whiny kid, but it's true."

"No, I get it," Brandon said, a surprising lack of judgment in his voice. "I had a wonderfully supportive family and I was still scared shitless when I had to come out to them. You've got a lot more riding on you keeping your sexuality a secret, and I can completely understand why you're still hiding." He grabbed the remote and muted the TV without looking at the screen. It was starting on some show Paul had never heard of anyway. "Want to talk about it?"

Hell no. "Um, not really?"

"Okay, up to you—let me know if you change your mind." Brandon tossed the remote into Paul's lap and stood with a yawn. "I've got Thai breath, so I'm going to go brush my teeth and change for bed. Like I said, you're more than welcome to stay here tonight if you want. I don't usually snore."

Paul couldn't hide the surprise he knew was written all over his face. "You're still offering, even if I don't want to get off with you right now?"

"Doesn't change the fact that having someone spying on you is creepy as hell. I wouldn't want to sleep at your place tonight if I were you, either." One corner of his mouth twitched upward. "I think we'll both prefer you here," he added. "Indulge me."

"Oh." They didn't know for sure that it *was* a stalker, or what the e-mail was even supposed to mean, but Brandon was right: if Paul went home right now to his unguarded little ground-floor apartment, he wouldn't be doing much sleeping. "I didn't bring anything for staying over."

"Hotels are good for that kind of stuff." Brandon nodded toward the room phone. "Tell them you're me and you forgot your travel kit—housekeeping will send one up. And you can always sleep in your boxers, or you can borrow a T-shirt if you want. I brought plenty. I can never stand wearing my fancy 'impress-the-bigwigs' work clothes one minute longer than necessary, so I came prepared."

"Thanks." The thought of sleeping in Brandon's T-shirt was strangely comforting. *Not going to examine that too closely*, Paul thought with a mental grimace.

"No problem." Brandon dug out a shirt from his suitcase and tossed it onto the bed. "You'll want to go home in the morning to freshen up and change before work, I'm sure, but I wasn't lying before—if you weren't here, I'd be sitting by myself watching crappy TV and browsing the Internet. It's nice to not be going to bed alone." He grimaced. "Ah, not that I'm planning to molest you overnight, just saying—"

"It's fine." Paul forced a tight smile. "And thanks. I really do appreciate this."

Chapter 7

Paul woke up at dawn with someone else's palm loosely splayed over his chest. It took a minute to remember what the heck was going on. Brandon shifted on the mattress next to him, snuffling softly into his pillow, then tightened his arm momentarily before going limp again. Paul lay on his back and stared at the diffuse light of sunrise peeking around the edges of the curtains and had a small freak-out.

I'm in bed with Brandon Mercer. Somehow the situation felt so much more intimate than the blowjob from before, even though they both spent the night in T-shirts and boxers and hadn't touched at all before falling asleep. It brought back memories of collapsing into bed with Christopher, sometimes spooning up together and letting Christopher's longer limbs envelop his own and other times just lying next to him and listening to him breathe. Paul winced and shook his head, shoving those memories aside. They were too tightly linked with everything else—Christopher being a controlling dick, the constant feeling of inadequacy in bed, the fights and the sulking and the passive-aggressive reprisals whenever Paul didn't do exactly what Christopher wanted him to. *I don't miss him at all,* Paul realized, *but I do miss this.*

Beside him, Brandon murmured something and rolled to his stomach. The motion shifted his arm off Paul's chest and onto the mattress between them. It was Paul's chance to get up without waking him, so he slid carefully out of bed without disturbing the covers more than absolutely necessary and tiptoed into the bathroom so he could close the door and safely turn on the light.

He looked like total crap, especially for someone who had enjoyed a good night's sleep. His hair was sticking up in weird tufts, his forehead had a red mark from where he had been lying on his own hand for a while, and his overnight stubble practically made him look homeless. Plus it itched. Absolutely nothing about the reflection in the mirror said "sexy" or "desirable" or "the kind of man Brandon Mercer would give two fucks about."

And there I go—I know I'm wallowing when I start swearing in my head. Paul groaned aloud. *Shit.*

A glance at his watch showed the time to be a quarter past six. Late enough to get up—especially since they had both fallen asleep surprisingly early—but early enough to give him plenty of time at the apartment to shower and change (and *think*) before he had to get to campus. Would it be polite to wake Brandon before he left? Or was it better to sneak out and let him sleep?

The question turned out to be moot because Brandon was sitting up when Paul got done in the bathroom. He flashed Paul a drowsy smile and stretched his arms out to the sides with an audible *pop.*

"G'morning," he said, his voice still scratchy with sleep. "Have a good night?"

Paul nodded and tried not to think about how deliciously rumpled Brandon looked in the mornings. Rumpled and warm and touchable and kissable and all those other things he couldn't afford to let himself get used to. "Thanks again for letting me stay."

"No problem." Brandon rolled his shoulders and tilted his head from side to side a few times before finally standing up. "We can do it again tonight, if you're up for it—bring your laptop or PlayStation or something and we can shoot bad guys for a while. It's good stress relief."

And a good excuse to spend more time together. All of Paul's excellent reasons for why he had to avoid Brandon and stay in the closet wavered at the thought of having someone to relax with. To eat and chat and game with and to maybe possibly work back up to the possibility of more sexual encounters in the future.

Damn it.

Brandon just stood there and watched what had to be an illuminating parade of emotions over Paul's face. He waited for several seconds, long enough for Paul to give the flippant, casual answer the conversation required, but Paul still couldn't get past the fact that—when faced with the possibility of having an actual real-live *friend* there to hang out with—he didn't know what on earth to *do.* That, more than anything, drove home how utterly depressing his had been. Christopher had *been* his life, his only social contact with the world outside the psychology department, and once that was gone he'd pretty much gone into seclusion.

The silence stretched, long past the point when Paul should have replied.

"Hey," Brandon said in a low voice. "It's just an offer, okay? Not a command appearance. I'll keep trying to track down the source of that e-mail whether or not you want to come over. And whether or not you decide you want anything more than simply hanging out. Solving this is part of my job, and I promise you I'm really damn good at it. Anything else you want to do is a bonus." He blatantly dragged his gaze up and down Paul's body and one corner of his lips twitched upward. "A very *nice* bonus, I'll grant you, but an optional one." His confident smirk was interrupted by a yawn. "God, sorry. I can't do sexy banter before I've had my morning coffee. I'm going to hop in the shower—feel free to stay as long as you want, but I should probably get moving." He went to brush past Paul, then paused and pressed a firm but close-mouthed kiss to Paul's lips. "For what it's worth," he murmured, "you inspire some very nice dreams."

And he winked before shutting the bathroom door behind him.

* * * *

Paul closed all the blinds and curtains and double-checked his locks before undressing to get in his own shower. It was a stupid, paranoid thing to do—it's not like one anonymous e-mail suddenly meant there was a peeping tom at his windows 24/7—but the idea of getting naked with a creepy stalker watching was just too much. He took the world's fastest shower, shaved, changed into clean clothes in record time, then took nearly ten minutes trying to talk himself into being able to walk into his living room without feeling like he had to hide his face.

It's fine. Nothing's been moved, nobody's been here, nobody's watching. And yet. Paul growled aloud and slammed the box of cereal onto the kitchen table. *I hate this—hate it, hate it, hate it.*

Where had the picture been taken from? Outside, but where? Probably somewhere along the walking path around the mud pit masquerading as a pond—nobody walked there this time of year, not with the marshy smell of pond scum in the air. That meant someone could lurk about in the dark and watch his living room window without anyone noticing. What were the chances one of his neighbors would happen to be looking outside at exactly the right time?

Paul took a deep breath and pulled aside his living room curtains. The sun was still low enough in the sky to leave everything casting long morning shadows, but it was daylight. And there was no one there. Paul sat at the window for several minutes, alert to any sign of movement. A couple of birds fluttered around the trees along the trail, but that was it.

What did you expect? Paul let the curtains fall closed again and finished getting himself ready to go. As an afterthought, he threw a change of clothes, a toothbrush, and his deodorant in the spare compartment of his laptop bag. Not that he was *planning* to spend the night with Brandon again, but it felt good to be prepared. Just in case.

Still twenty minutes before he absolutely needed to leave. Paul got as far as throwing his laptop bag in his car, then looked over at his living room window again. Not the right angle from the parking lot, but if he could match it…

There really wasn't any point in wandering over to the pond. It's not like seeing the exact spot the stalker stood would really shed light on who the culprit was or what their motivations were, but Paul couldn't resist the chance to look. The details of the photograph was practically burned into his brain: a little farther along, nearly head-on looking into the window, maybe a bit higher up—

Paul stumbled and nearly brained himself on the nearest tree limb. *Higher.* If the angle didn't match someone standing on the path, it had to correspond to someone sitting in one of the trees. They were some sort of ornamental species, looked like apple trees minus the apples—not easy to climb up to the lowest branches, but not impossible unless you were unusually short. And once there, you could probably clamber around the rest of the tree fairly easily. It was still early enough in the spring that the buds were just starting to turn into leaves. They wouldn't provide a lot of cover if you wanted to hide yourself, but they wouldn't get in the way of a photograph either. If you assumed the vertical angle came from about halfway up the tree, the horizontal angle corresponded with…*gotcha.* Paul walked up to the next tree in the line and studied it. The lowest limbs were barely within reach—with a bit of a jump and a lot of agility, he could probably haul himself up. He checked his watch again. It really was time to get going, but now that he was here it would be a shame not to try.

He got a good grip on the second attempt. *Haven't done this since I was a kid—weird how muscle memory works.* The bark was mostly smooth, enough texture to grab on to but not enough to catch at his pants legs as he swung his feet up and locked them around the branch. A fair amount of wriggling and upper-arm-strength later, Paul was crouching on the lowest branch and could see his living room window clearly from inside the tree. The curtains were still closed, but the angle looked about right.

He tested the next branch with his foot before putting weight on it, grabbed the center trunk for balance—

The texture was different under his hand. Paul carefully skirted around to the other side of the tree, bringing him face-to-face with the odd spot. The whole tree was relatively smooth, but a two-foot strip of bark along that side was totally, completely missing. The wood underneath felt like it had been practically sanded and polished. He looked down at the branch now under his feet—there was a worn section there, too. And it was about the width of a person.

Paul stared blankly at it for a long moment. Things like this didn't just *happen* to trees, did they? Danielle had always been the more adventurous one, between the two of them, but they'd both spent their fair share of time climbing various things in their neighborhood. Including a lot of trees. He couldn't remember ever seeing damage like that to a tree they'd climbed, though, even when they'd both been clambering around for a while. If this was caused by a person sitting on the branch and leaning against the trunk, they'd had to have been there for *ages*. Hours at a time? Several times a week? Both?

It didn't take rocket science to figure out how the stalker got the photo, at least: the angle would have made it easy to take pictures without being too easily seen. The bulk of the parking lot was on the other side of the building, and the land sloped downward from there—as long as the walking trail around the lake remained more mud than trail, there was no reason for any passers-by to be on this side of his living room window. After dark, it probably wouldn't have mattered anyway.

It was also blindingly obvious that this little viewing perch was for him. His upstairs neighbors almost never opened their curtains—anyone sitting here was watching *his* window, *his* living room. Paul rarely kept his blinds closed in the evenings—why bother, when there weren't any neighboring apartments close enough to see in? That was the whole point of having a unit with a view. All those hours he spent playing video games on his sofa... His stalker could have been watching him the whole time.

Hell, damn, shit, motherfucking... Paul's mental lexicon of curse words was a bit rusty, but he ran through them all the same. There wasn't anything he could do about the picture his stalker had already taken (*not without Brandon's help*, a voice in his head pointed out), but the fact that there was visible evidence of someone having been there meant he wasn't just going crazy. That minor bit of relief wasn't much but it was something.

He called Brandon as soon as he got back to his car and could use the hands-free feature.

"Hey, what's up?" Brandon asked.

"I found where he was hiding," Paul said without preamble. "I'm really creeped out right now, honestly. There's a tree down near the pond outside my window with a worn spot like someone's been camping out there. A lot. It could have been there for *years* and I'd never have known."

"Probably not years—how long have you lived there?"

Paul had to count the months. "About a year and a half now. Give or take."

"Okay." Brandon wasn't laughing at him, which was something at least. "And what do you mean by a worn spot? Like, a rope thrown over a branch and digging into it or something?"

"More like a hunter's perch, about halfway up the tree. Bark rubbed off pretty much exactly where it would be if someone were spending a lot of time leaning against the trunk and staring into my living room. The only reason I found it was because I was trying to figure out where the picture was taken from and I had the bright idea to climb a tree. The angle of the photo looks normal, but the ground slopes downward a bit the closer you get to the pond—I figured the picture had to have been taken from higher up, if it was from that far away."

"Well damn." Brandon was silent for several seconds. "This really isn't my area of expertise, but I can take a look at it later if you want. Although maybe not tonight? I really feel like you ought to stay over again, at least one more time. I don't like the thought of you home alone when we don't know what your secret admirer wants."

"Secret admirer? What happened to stalker?"

Brandon snorted. "I was trying to be diplomatic. Whichever one convinces you to stay with me again tonight."

Stay with me. Paul wave of emotion at the phrase. "Yeah. Yeah, I will."

Chapter 8

The take-no-prisoners tone in Brandon's voice during their phone conversation went a long way toward helping Paul un-panic before his first class. It helped that nobody showed up for morning office hours. That wasn't unexpected, since there weren't any major tests or projects looming for any of his classes, but the free time meant Paul had that much more opportunity to work himself back up again.

How the heck had he never noticed someone watching him before? He almost never bothered closing the blinds unless the sun was interfering with his ability to see the TV screen... But he never looked out the window. So much for an apartment with a good view. Paul put his head down on his keyboard and groaned. *I was practically asking for it. How could I have been so blind?*

The knock on the open door caught him by surprise. When he picked his head back up, Grace was giving him an odd look.

"I was dropping by to say hi and ask how you're doing, but I suspect you'd lie to me." She came into the room, then reached up and pressed the back of her hand to his forehead before he could react. "No fever?"

"Grace." Paul pulled back—not enough to cause offense, hopefully, but he never did like her touching him and she did it way more often than was strictly necessary. "I'm fine."

"No you're not. You're very clearly not fine."

"Grace..."

She sucked in a long breath, but held her hands up in surrender. "All right, but I get to say 'I told you so' when you come down with the flu or something. You should go home and get some rest."

"I'm *fine*. Really." *And the last thing I want to do is to go home.*

"If you say so." She clearly didn't believe him, but darn it, he *wasn't* sick and Grace's mothering wasn't going to do him any good. Dr. Kirsner's sudden appearance at Paul's office door felt like a reprieve.

"Productive use of office hours, I see," Dr. Kirsner said, ignoring any need for a polite greeting.

"I'll just go," Grace murmured and fled, leaving Paul to deal with Dr. Kirsner alone. *Thanks.*

Paul sat back up, already feeling his cheeks turning pink. "I, um. Most of my students prefer to e-mail. I try to be flexible." *There, that didn't sound quite as stupid as it could have.*

Dr. Kirsner nodded, clearly not listening to a word. "I decided to stop by and make sure you touched base with that consultant. I assume you have everything worked out?"

"Yeah, it's going great." Brandon was the *last* thing Paul wanted to discuss with his boss, especially given how even hearing Brandon's job title in casual conversation seemed to inspire a great number of unwanted thoughts. Or perhaps they were "wanted" in a very different context, but not while Dr. Kirsner was present. "From what he said, I think he needs me for confirmation more than anything else—sounds like the project won't take too long anyway."

Dr. Kirsner frowned. "Confirmation of what? I was given very little information about the initiative, which is usually a bad sign. Something I should know?"

"Um." Paul tried to remember how much had Brandon said in confidence and how much was public knowledge, but ended up opting for a middle ground. "The project has something to do with data security, but it sounds like he just needed people familiar with the last several years' worth of department staff and university policies to verify his findings as he works. He's doing this for every department. I'm sure there's nothing to worry about."

"Previous staff—is this a legacy of the esteemed Dr. Lancaster, then?"

Darn it, walked right into that one. No matter how much he denied it now, Dr. Kirsner would fix the blame on his predecessor and there wasn't much Paul could do about it. Worse, it was possible the issue *did* stem from something under Dr. Lancaster's reign, although that didn't explain the strange stalker-ish perch and the mystery culprit's obsession—was that the right word?—with Paul. If they were even related. It was quite literally a no-win scenario, and he'd stepped right into the middle.

"Can't talk about it?" Dr. Kirsner said, a hint of disdain in the quirk of his lips. "Please do remember that you work for me now; any lingering loyalty would be entirely misguided."

"Yes, sir." Paul ducked his head in a polite acknowledgment, although all he really wanted to do was to push the smug asshole out of his office. "Anything else you need from me?" he added.

"If I find a use for you, I'll let you know." Dr. Kirsner flashed a patently insincere smile and nodded a crisp dismissal.

Right. Paul waited until the department head's footsteps had receded to the stairwell before opening his e-mail again. Intellectually he knew there'd been no chance for his stalker to snap another photo of him in a compromising position, but the feeling of apprehension was still there and he darn well wasn't going to run the risk of opening a second mystery e-mail with his vindictive, homophobic boss lurking in the hallway. When the inbox revealed nothing worse than a handful of departmental memos, Paul let out an actual sigh of relief.

* * * *

The 11:00 AM freshman lecture took forever. Either the students were abnormally thick or Paul was uncharacteristically snappish, but every single point on his outline seemed to be punctuated by stupid questions that interrupted the flow of the lecture. It didn't help that this historical recap section was Paul's least favorite aspect of teaching the course. Granted, they were just starting the section on behaviorism and it was important to know the historical roots, but that didn't mean most of the early research was relevant anymore. Half of it was common sense—things any parent or dog owner could tell you—and the other half was outdated, disproved science. And yet. His students all seemed to be stuck on "How did Skinner know the pigeons were learning?" *That was the entire point of the study!* Or "What makes the unconditioned response unconditioned?" *It wasn't conditioned yet?* Or equally inane questions which demonstrated they not only hadn't done the reading, they hadn't been paying attention either. For the entire semester. Paul was tempted to give a pop quiz, just to make them panic a bit.

He didn't, of course. It was the whole situation with Brandon and the anonymous e-mail that had set him on edge, and it wouldn't be fair to take it out on the freshmen. But he really, *really* wanted to. When the end of class came, Paul was practically the first one out the door.

The afternoon seminar was much better. He only had eight students, all but one of whom seemed to care about the subject, and they were all dedicated enough to do the assigned work and bring their questions to class. Teaching consisted of gently guiding the discussion whenever it threatened to get sidetracked. Beyond that, Paul was able to let the students take the lead. It was a nice contrast. The minutes still ticked by too slowly, though, and Paul was more than happy to skive off as soon as his actual obligations on campus were finished.

Which left a dilemma: go back to his apartment and sit around feeling creeped out until he could meet up with Brandon later, or find somewhere else to be? There probably was something telling about how *not* seeing Brandon didn't even feel like an option anymore, something worth noticing and thinking about and stressing over, but Paul ruthlessly pushed that observation to the back of his mind. He had his change of clothes already in the car, he had his laptop, and he had two hours to kill. He just didn't have anything to *do*.

After a few minutes of sitting in the parking lot and second-guessing himself, Paul finally settled on driving around until he felt like stopping. St. Benedict's wasn't exactly in a bustling urban area, which left plenty of space to just *be*. He found himself twenty minutes later at the trailhead of a small out-of-the-way county park, somewhere he and Christopher used to go walking sometimes. The forest was thin, the underbrush mostly dead and withered over the course of the winter and the leaves finally starting to come back in, but the ground was dry and the weather was finally warm enough to be comfortable without a jacket. Plus walking gave his feet something to do. Paul determinedly aimed himself toward the closest trail and started wandering.

The exercise helped. He kept at it until his thighs hurt, then stopped for a drink at the public water fountain near the trailhead and started a second loop. The park was practically deserted—of course it was, at four in the afternoon on a Wednesday—but the quiet suited Paul's mood perfectly. Nobody around meant nobody watching him. Nobody to question what the heck he was doing with someone like Brandon Mercer when he was supposed to be happily single and unquestionably straight and a perfect Christian role model for all the impressionable students at St. Benedict's. Nobody to tell him what a big fat liar he was.

So what do I do now? It's not like Paul was *completely* new to the concept of a relationship with another man—the whatever-it-was with Christopher had become some sort of relationship, if not exactly a healthy one. Something not platonic. Christopher had been more comfortable with it than Paul had been, although he'd been adamant that they not let anyone guess they were more than roommates. *"I want you all to myself. I can't stand the thought of sharing you. You're mine."* And Paul had gone along with it, had gone along with the whole ridiculous not-technically-a-relationship-because-Christopher-said-so, up until the point where he couldn't ignore the problems any longer and they had their epic fight and he'd stormed out like a petulant five-year-old and left Christopher behind. And then he'd gotten his own apartment and Christopher had eventually gotten a new job, not on campus, and that had been that. Over. Finished. The capstone of Paul's romantic experience, after which he'd assumed he'd end up staying single forever.

Brandon was different, though. He wasn't asking for a commitment, for one thing. More the opposite—he was really only interested in sex, and anything else was a distant second. *I'm only a worthwhile distraction while he's here because he finds me slightly less boring than the Hallmark channel.* The really awful thing was, even if that's all Brandon wanted from him, Paul was desperate enough to take the deal. Casual or not. Because he was truly that pathetic. *Crap.*

He took a few moments to glare at the empty path ahead of him.

Boredom wasn't the entirety of it either, though. Not really. Paul finished the second loop of the trail and collapsed back into his car. Brandon wanted him around because they'd felt something together, once. It had been just a possibility, a hint of a different future waiting for them, but it was a *something.* And then Brandon had left and they hadn't kept in touch and that was that. Maybe this "week or two" of him being in town wasn't about some star-crossed lovers reconnecting—maybe it was merely a convenient chance to explore a bit more of that *something* without having to come out to anyone who didn't already know his secret.

A chance which was rapidly approaching, Paul noted as he started the car and saw the clock on the dashboard. He'd walked longer than he thought—rush hour traffic (such as it was) should have died down already, and the sun was now getting low on the horizon. He put the radio on the first not-terrible station he could find and headed back toward town.

* * * *

"I brought pizza—you like sausage and black olives, right?"

Brandon blinked, surprised, but his lips curled upward into a slow smile as he held the door open wider. "Don't tell me you just guessed that."

"We ordered pizza once as a hall freshman year, and I remember you mentioning it. Mostly because it's my favorite combination, too, and I never get to order it because someone else is always grossed out by either olives or Italian sausage." Paul set the box down on the desk (which Brandon had already dragged into place at the foot of the bed, he noticed) and tossed his laptop bag into the corner next to the air conditioner. "I brought napkins, but I forgot to steal some paper plates from the break room at work today. We're going to have to make do."

Brandon shrugged, the smile never wavering. "I'm amazed you remembered that—flattered, actually. What do you want to drink? I'll be right back."

The pizza was good. One of the lesser-known perks of working around college students: you always knew where all the best independent pizza joints were. Paul didn't indulge much anymore, because there's only so many days in a row you can eat leftover pizza and there's always a lot of leftovers when you live alone. But it was nice to not have to compromise on toppings for once. Between them they demolished most of it. Eventually Brandon leaned back in his chair with his Coke and rolled a kink out of his shoulders in a way that immediately focused Paul's attention on the way his biceps peeked out from under his sleeves.

"So." He cocked his head to the side, regarding Paul with an assessing frown. "You want to talk about that thing with the tree you found today, or ignore the whole mess for a bit longer?"

Ugh. That. Paul put down his third slice of pizza, no longer hungry. "Is there anything to talk about?"

"How about, do you have any thoughts on who might have done it? Student with a crush? Co-worker? Total stranger you ran into at the mall one time who creeped you out?"

"God, how would I even know?" Paul knew he was one of the younger faculty, which meant he did get the occasional overture from a female student hoping to look past the few years' age difference between them, but only one had needed more than an oblique rejection. "There was a Tiffany something last year, I guess, but I did finally tell her directly I wasn't interested in dating and I don't think our paths have crossed since. And I don't really see her as the stalker type. Clueless, yes, stalker, no."

"We don't know that it was a stalker, not for sure." Brandon put his Coke down and leaned forward, forearms on his thighs. He really did have nice arms. "I'd like to swing by your place sometime to take a look at what you found, but don't panic yet."

Paul knew he was right and they should both shrug off the photo and hope it was just some poorly-handled attempt to anonymously shame him into staying in the closet, but logic and anxiety didn't always correlate well. He was going to worry and obsess and keep picking at it in his mind until he couldn't face even the idea of going back to his own apartment. And there was nothing he could do—

"Hey." Brandon came around the table and sat on the bed next to him, nudging Paul's shoulder with his own. Their legs were touching from hip to knee, but Brandon didn't say anything so Paul didn't either. Even that much contact felt oddly calming.

"There's no point in stressing out," Brandon reassured him. "This kind of thing is what my company does, and believe me when I say I'm one of the best there is at it. Disgruntled people with grudges and inappropriate access to administrative accounts are my bread and butter. I don't know why whoever-this-is is targeting you, but I promise I'll get to the bottom of it. I know it's terrifying and invasive and *wrong*, but this happens to people every day and all you can do is to persevere and fight back. We'll both fight."

It was a nice speech. Not terribly effective, but nice. And it was good to know that Brandon cared enough to bother. "I appreciate the pep talk," Paul admitted.

Brandon ducked his head, but he was smiling. "Sorry; that was a bit *Braveheart*, wasn't it? But I did mean what I said—I promise I'll see this through, and I *am* good at it." He stood and started clearing up the remains of their meal. "In the meantime, I noticed you brought your laptop?"

* * * *

The hotel wi-fi was on the slow side, which meant the terrible framerates knocked most first-person shooters out of contention, but luckily they had similar tastes in video games and Brandon had a stunningly broad array of choices on Steam. Several of which were also in Paul's collection, even though he did most of his gaming by console. They settled on Portal 2— they'd both played through it when it first came out, but neither had tried the multiplayer. Brandon ended up sprawled across the bed with his laptop on the table and a pillow under his elbow so he could use his external mouse without too much strain on his arm. Paul took the small desk and chair. Even with a laggy connection due to the substandard wi-fi, they managed to blow through about half the co-op campaign in three hours. It was nice, getting to game with someone in the same room—they couldn't see each other's screens, but it was refreshingly easy to just *say* "Go to your right" or "Watch out!" instead of having to worry about typing or microphone issues. They took a break at the midpoint of the game by mutual consensus, Brandon flopping back onto the mattress and grinning at the ceiling.

"You're good at this," he said aloud. "I usually hate one-on-one co-op gaming because so many other people are annoying idiots."

"These aren't exactly the world's hardest puzzles," Paul admitted. "But I am having fun. And it's good to keep my mind off things."

"Mmmm." Brandon rolled to his side and shot Paul a look through heavy-lidded eyes. "I'd be up for more, if you want. Different kind of playing together."

It was on the tip of Paul's tongue to do the rational thing and say no—he'd already botched everything enough already, and doing anything more with Brandon was probably asking for trouble. But he was already in a much better mood after just playing a silly video game together, and Brandon looked *so* gorgeous sprawled out over the bed like that. Paul couldn't help but visualize a whole slew of interesting scenarios Brandon might suggest. He swallowed back his insecurities and nodded.

Hell, he's worth it, isn't he?

"Yes," he finally said. *Don't ask me why; I don't know either.* "You are offering what I think you're offering, right?"

Brandon grinned and patted the mattress. "Come over here and find out."

Chapter 9

Paul approached slowly, but Brandon didn't seem to mind. Seemed content to watch, even as Paul's knees hit the edge of the bed and he faltered a bit.

"I've been fantasizing about you all day," Brandon murmured. "Hoping you'd been thinking about this too. Pretty sure I lost a good twenty-minute chunk of time this afternoon, staring at my computer screen and remembering what you tasted like the other evening."

"I…" Paul drew a complete blank for how to respond to that. "I've daydreamed about this too, but I don't have a lot of experience. I don't know if the things I've been imagining are too much. Or even if they're physically possible."

"That's okay." Brandon rolled smoothly up to his knees, shuffling forward so he could grip Paul's hips lightly. The warmth of his palms burned, even through the fabric of Paul's clothes. "It isn't about experience—it's about what feels good, and what we both want to do. Experience doesn't matter." He tugged Paul closer, close enough to lip at what little of his collarbone was visible through the V of his button-down shirt. "You tell me what you like, I'll tell you what I like, and we'll both enjoy it." His hands tightened fractionally on Paul's hips. "Trust me."

Paul closed his eyes and took a moment to adjust. "I will," he whispered.

"Anything come to mind?" Brandon kept it up, little licks and kisses, but his hands moved from Paul's hips to his shirt and started undoing the top button. "I want to—hell. Just tell me what you want. I'm feeling pretty damn generous right now."

Lots? "I haven't… I don't want actual sex." *Hopefully that was clear enough, without sounding too pathetic?* "I mean, I don't *know* that I don't like it, but—"

Brandon's fingers stopped moving. "Define 'actual sex,'" he said in a quiet, controlled voice.

Oh God. "Um." Paul knew he was flushed bright red, but there was nothing he could do about it at the moment. "You know—anything with...penetration."

"Anal intercourse."

"Yeah. That." Paul closed his eyes, praying Brandon wouldn't try to make him define it further. "That guy—a while back—he always wanted to try it, but I don't think I want to."

"Hey," Brandon said gently. He sat back on his heels, putting a few vital inches of space between them, but nudged Paul's face up with one fingertip under his chin so Paul couldn't avoid eye contact. "You know that we've already had 'actual sex,' right? What we did the other night was sex. So was what we did freshman year. Sex doesn't have to involve someone's cock in someone else's ass to count as real. It just means two people together, doing something that feels good, until one or both of them get off. No anal necessary."

The honesty in his expression was enough to dry up any more embarrassing babbling Paul would have otherwise done. Paul swallowed back his instinctive refusal, the urge to duck his head and back out of the conversation entirely. "That's not how Christopher made it sound," he finally managed to say.

"No offense, but from the bits you've let drop, it sounds like Christopher was kind of a dick." Brandon swiped his thumb softly over Paul's cheek. "Believe it or not, plenty of guys don't like anal. It's not like there's some hazing ritual or checklist you have to try before you can get your gay card. Anal sex feels wonderful when done right and horrible when done wrong and even guys who generally like it don't necessarily try it with a new partner right away. It's not a deal-breaker here."

Paul felt a hesitant smile break through on his face, one he had no control over. *He still wants this. Wants me.* "I don't even know what to ask for," he admitted. "But we should do something. If you want."

Brandon's reply was a nearly feral growl. "Oh, I want." He grabbed Paul's hips and tugged. Paul probably could have resisted, but instead he let himself be overbalanced onto the mattress. Brandon immediately went to work unbuttoning the rest of his shirt.

"I want to see you naked again," Brandon announced, not slowing his fingers for an instant. "I want to take you right up to that edge and watch you when you come. I want to be right there with you. Tell me that sounds good."

"It sounds good," Paul echoed. Heck, it sounded *fantastic.* "You should be naked too." He tugged ineffectively at the hem of Brandon's T-shirt, scrunching it up over his chest and exposing his lean stomach. The angles were all wrong, with Paul mostly reclining and Brandon mostly kneeling next to him, but Brandon seemed to approve of Paul's attempt. He broke away from his task long enough to whip his shirt off over his head, then popped Paul's last few buttons free and spread his palms greedily across Paul's chest.

"I love this," Brandon murmured, trailing his fingers through the wisps of dark blond chest hair. "Enough here to enjoy but not so much that it hides the skin beneath. I can still touch you—and taste you." He ducked his head and pressed a firm kiss to Paul's sternum, square in the middle of his chest. "You smell good, too," he added with a tiny smirk.

"I sme—*oooh!"* Paul lost his train of thought completely as Brandon pinched sharply at his nipple.

"You do," Brandon murmured against his pectoral. "Some of it's soap or body wash or something, but you've also been exercising today. I can taste the salt on your skin." He licked a broad, flat stripe over Paul's other nipple, which absolutely *should not* have been as erotic as it was. "Very masculine," he added.

"You're saying I'm sweaty."

"In the very best of ways." Brandon's face was hidden, but Paul could sense the smug satisfaction in his voice. "Trust me, that's a turn-on. I want to absolutely *devour* you."

Paul found that he didn't entirely object to the idea, mostly because he was feeling very much like he wanted to be devoured. He couldn't see all that much of Brandon now, other than the top of his head, but that quick flash he'd seen of Brandon kneeling over him, peeling his T-shirt off... *damn.* Brandon wasn't thin, not really, but he was casually in shape the way you can only achieve through good genetics and not really caring about your weight one way or the other. The overall effect was acres of smooth lines, the gentle angle of his collarbones arrowing down to the little dip above his sternum and the line of his lower ribs sloping upward to delineate his chest from his stomach. He had almost no chest hair to speak of, just a few dark curls which only highlighted how pale his skin was. *The anti-tan of a computer geek.* It fit him.

"Hey." Brandon gave no other warning, just lowered his head and bit at the lower edge of Paul's ribcage.

"Christ!" The bite didn't hurt—more of a nibble, really—but between Brandon's teeth and the way his hands were roaming all over Paul's chest

and sides, it was hard to even think straight. They were both still half dressed, and Paul was already harder than he'd ever been in his life.

"Mmm," Brandon breathed. "Delicious. Where else do you want my mouth?"

God, anywhere. But... "Not quite so hard."

"Mmm. Kisses, then. Licking." Brandon trailed his tongue inward, swirling it over and around Paul's navel. "Sucking." He scraped his teeth over the sensitive skin of Paul's abdomen. "Tell me—where?"

"Everywhere."

"Oh, you've got to be more specific than that." Brandon pulled back and pressed a surprisingly tender kiss to the tip of Paul's nose. And then scooted down to dot a second kiss on the point of his left elbow, and a third to the crest of his hip, and a fourth to the side of his calf right above the top of his sock (which required some awkward shuffling to get his pants leg out of the way). "Like this?" he asked, moving back up for a final brush of lips back over Paul's navel.

"You know very well what I mea—*oh.*"

Brandon sat back up with a smirk, but he didn't remove his hand from where it was now, slowly fondling Paul's cock through the fabric of his khakis.

"Eager, aren't you," he growled. "And oh so lovely when you're at my mercy like this. How long do you think I could keep you hard like this? Until you're completely incoherent? Until you're *begging* me to let you come? I could suck you until you're right on that edge and then—" He tightened his grip around the base of Paul's cock, just to the edge of pain, but Paul was beyond caring because that tight grip was probably the only thing keeping him from already coming in his pants like some helpless teenager. "What do you think?" Brandon asked. "Want me to draw this out?"

Yes. No. Paul groaned, loud and raw, no longer caring about how he might sound. "Want to come," he gasped.

"Now?"

"Not..." Paul sucked in a breath. "Want to see you, first. Want to taste you. God, Brandon, I'm so close right now—"

Brandon let go abruptly, then backed away until he was standing next to the bed and looking down at Paul's sprawled form with undisguised lust. "Take a second, then, and get us both naked. I'll wait."

A second. A second is good. Paul closed his eyes and focused on breathing, in and out. He ran through his mental list of erection-killers: bio lab dissections, his childhood piano teacher, the time his scout troop went camping and the port-a-potties were nearly overflowing. After a minute or so he was able to sit up and adjust himself without exploding.

He kicked off his shoes, letting them thump one at a time on the floor as they fell, then peeled off his socks and khakis. He hesitated a second over taking off his boxers, but *hell, it's not like Brandon hasn't seen it before. And fondled it. And tasted it.* He wriggled out of those, too, until he was completely nude and kneeling at the edge of the bed in front of Brandon in a reversal of the position they'd started in.

Brandon was both silent and patient as Paul removed his shoes and socks. Brandon raised his feet one at a time to brace against the mattress and dropped them on the floor to join his own. He was just as hard as Paul was—the evidence was kind of difficult to miss given their positions. Paul obediently maneuvered around to tug Brandon's jeans and boxers off, though, and didn't comment. There was something incredible about *being* there, stripping Brandon down to his skin, and it felt like speaking would ruin the moment.

Brandon's thighs were muscled much like his chest. Nothing defined, nothing *deliberate*, but they were still long and powerful and Paul couldn't help running his hands up and down one and then the other, enjoying the feel of the crisp hairs against his palms. Brandon let out a little sigh and spread his feet wider. Paul replaced his palms with his nose, trailing up the inside of Brandon's leg—

"Holy hell," Brandon breathed. "You know, for someone without a lot of experience at this, you're really damn good at that."

"I didn't say I've never done *anything*." It was true—whatever kind of messed-up relationship Paul and Christopher had eventually stumbled into, the physical aspect had become more and more present as time went on. And the interludes had grown increasingly intense. They'd never talked about it, but Christopher had been very good at making his needs known. If he hadn't kept trying to bully Paul into doing one more thing and one more thing and one more thing, they'd probably have bumbled along together contentedly for quite a while.

Actually, that wasn't true—Paul had started to get frustrated with Christopher long before their troubles in bed. And now he was practically nuzzling at Brandon's groin and *what the heck is wrong with me? I'm thinking about my ex while about to go down on someone else!* Paul sat back on his heels and scrubbed his hand over his face.

"Something wrong?" Brandon twined his hand into Paul's hair, then slid it down to caress his cheek. "I was enjoying that, if it wasn't already blindingly obvious. You're welcome to keep going. Unless…?"

"Nothing's wrong." Paul grabbed Brandon's hips and tugged him forward again. Into tasting range. "Weird thought brought me out of the moment, is all."

"Oh. I see. In that case…" Brandon leaned in and barreled forward, rolling as he pounced, until Paul ended up landing with a huff and an incredulous little laugh squarely on top of his chest. "I was hoping we could come up with something else we might enjoy." Brandon shifted his hips, pressing the hard length of his erection against Paul's, and *oh* it felt amazing. He smirked at the expression on Paul's face and repeated the motion, slower. He stretched up to kiss Paul gently on the lips, just once, then let his kisses trail down over Paul's jaw and along the side of his neck to his ear. He didn't pull, didn't hold Paul down, but Paul plastered himself to the warm body below him anyway as if he had.

"Want to do it like this," Brandon breathed in Paul's ear. "You on top of me, our whole bodies skin-to-skin. Tell me that sounds good."

"Nngh." Paul practically gave a whole-body shudder at the suggestion. "God, yes."

Brandon nipped at Paul's earlobe. "I put my lube in the nightstand drawer next to you—can you reach it?"

Paul peeled himself off Brandon's chest far enough to yank the drawer open. A small bottle of lube and a Bible. The sight brought him a moment of hesitation—*this is pretty much everything a good Christian shouldn't be doing*—but Brandon's body was shifting silkily beneath his own as he ran his hands up and down Paul's sides and then it didn't matter. God versus gay was a personal crisis Paul had been living ever since freshman year. In all these years he'd yet to come up with a good answer and the dilemma would still be waiting for him tomorrow. Brandon was gorgeous and waiting on him *right now,* though, and Paul had no intention of letting the opportunity pass him by. He grabbed the lube, slammed the drawer shut—having enthusiastically gay sex with the Bible right there seemed disrespectful somehow—and pressed the bottle into Brandon's hand. "Show me?"

Brandon rolled them so they were on their sides facing each other, then warmed a dollop between his palms and reached down to slick up Paul's cock with both hands. The pressure was perfect and Paul didn't realize he was moaning aloud until well after Brandon had stopped and repeated the motion on himself. They were both rock-hard and—if the take-no-prisoners look on Brandon's face was anything to go by—both desperate for this. Brandon nudged his hips forward, barely brushing the head of Paul's cock with his own, and they both gasped.

"Oh, yes," Paul moaned. "*Do it, please!*"

Brandon didn't give any warning before attacking, he just launched himself forward and landed on Paul so they were pressed together chest-to-thighs. The momentum carried them over and all the way around, until they had rolled to the very edge of the bed and Paul was on top again and their erections were slotted together against each other's bodies.

Paul groaned and dipped his head to kiss whatever parts of Brandon's neck he could reach. "Feels amazing. Want you." *God, please. Don't stop.*

"Tell me." Brandon rolled his hips forward, sliding their cocks against each other, making Paul groan. It was less a noise and more a rumble vibrating through both their chests, and from the way Brandon groaned back, he clearly appreciated hearing it. "Tell me what I feel like," he commanded.

"You're—*oh.*" Paul blinked a few times, taking a second to catch his breath and form his thoughts into some semblance of words. "I love how you feel against me," he admitted. "How your beard scrapes my skin when you kiss me, the way your hips move. The way you—*oh God.*"

Brandon repeated the thrust, slowly, and anything else Paul might have intended to say disappeared.

"Christ, you're gorgeous like this," Brandon declared. "I want to watch you come apart—see those blue eyes go to almost all pupil and then slam close as you come. Want to feel your breathing stutter and freeze and then all the air escape your lungs at once as you finally collapse on top of me." His hands trailed down Paul's back as they thrust against each other, palms coming to rest firmly over Paul's rear. "Want to feel these muscles tense up and quiver right before you fall over that edge and come all over my stomach. I want that feeling to be what tips me over. Yes?"

"God, yes." Paul thrust harder against him, desperate but unable to move much with Brandon's hands restraining his movements. The slick slide of their cocks against each other was incredible, the warm pressure of Brandon's abdomen underneath him, nothing except *Brandon* but oh, it was enough. It was going to be enough. Paul tilted his head back, giving Brandon better access to where he was currently kissing and sucking and nibbling and Christ, it felt amazing. Brandon was rocking faster now, too, an unyielding rhythm sliding against him, a counterpoint to his own frenzied movements.

The world went white around the edges. Paul fought against the rush he knew was coming, wanted to memorize how Brandon's eyes and mouth were both wide as he thumped his head back against the mattress, but then that familiar hot rush washed over him and nothing else mattered. He was vaguely aware of Brandon stiffening below him and calling out, and then they were both sagging against each other. Brandon was grinning up at him like the Cheshire cat.

"Fuck," Brandon said.

Paul nodded silently, unable to conjure up enough words to return the sentiment.

They stared at each other for a long moment. And then Brandon snickered. It was a happy sound, and it was infectious. *What the hell are we doing here?* Paul stared down at him for what felt like forever, totally at sea, but something about Brandon's complete inability to suppress his laughter caught something inside himself, and then he was laughing too. Which only made Brandon laugh more, until they were both splayed on the formerly-clean hotel duvet and getting come everywhere and giggling their heads off at the absurdity of the whole situation which wasn't really that absurd, not truly, but laughter was the only release they had left.

"I don't even know what's so funny," Paul choked out when he could finally breathe properly.

Brandon's eyes twinkled. "Me neither, but—oh Christ—that was incredible. *You* are incredible." He gathered Paul in his arms and planted a deliberate kiss on his lips. "Damn. I don't want to get up now."

"So don't."

"This is going to get uncomfortable eventually." Brandon gestured down to the sticky mess covering both their stomachs and the random smears on the bedspread. "Rock paper scissors you for who has to go get a washcloth?"

Paul lost. When he came back after wiping himself down in the bathroom and moistening another washcloth to bring back, Brandon had the covers thrown off and was lounging naked—oriented correctly for the first time that evening—in bed.

"I want to sleep with you again," Brandon announced.

Paul tossed Brandon the washcloth, which landed with a wet *slap* on his belly. "I don't know about you, but I *do* have a refractory period. Let me recover from that last round first."

"No, I mean…" Brandon braced himself on his elbow and swiped away the mess on his skin with a few efficient strokes. "Actual sleeping. Last night was the first time I've ever tried that, and I want to do it again. It was nice." He tossed the washcloth in the general direction of the bathroom door and dropped his head back onto the pillow. "Never mind—it wasn't entirely a coherent thought. I'm still a bit muddled."

First time? Paul turned off the room light, leaving only the bedside lamp on, and climbed silently into the bed next to Brandon. *It's been nearly ten years since that awkward night freshman year. Surely he's dated since then, hasn't he?* Paul tried to remember whether Brandon had ever mentioned someone. He clearly knew what to do in bed, but...

"You've never spent the night with anyone?" Paul asked after a long, awkward moment of silence. It felt awkward to him, at least. "I assumed you'd have had more than a few partners by now. And I think it's pretty obvious you're more comfortable with sex than I am."

Brandon didn't answer, just leaned over to switch off the lamp. The two of them lay side-by-side in the darkness, both still naked but not touching, for several minutes.

"It's never meant anything," Brandon finally said.

"You mean the sex?"

"Any of it." Paul could hear Brandon shifting around, rolling to face him, not that it did any good with the lights off and the blackout curtains pulled. "I had a few hookups at college—after leaving St. Ben's—and after that I got into the club scene. It's easy to find sex when you're young and willing and you say upfront you're not looking for anything serious. I mean, I always use a condom for anything penetrative and I still do get tested regularly, out of habit. I've never really 'dated' someone, not the way you mean."

"Never even taken a guy home overnight?"

"The whole point of an anonymous fuck is that you don't have to deal with them in the morning. Nobody's ever asked and I've never offered. I've always liked it that way."

"Oh." Paul stared at the ceiling in the dark and let that sink in. What would it be like, to share this sort of intimacy with a complete stranger? One who makes it clear right off the bat they don't care about you and don't ever want to see you again afterward? *Is that what being gay and single is supposed to be about?* It sounded terrifying. And yet, they'd had sex and Brandon had made it clear he was offering something with no strings attached. "But you're letting me sleep here already. Because of everything..."

"I invited you. I still don't want anything complicated, but it's different. With you." Brandon's hand found Paul's in the darkness, squeezed. "I've got a question," he added.

"Sure?"

"Back during freshman year. When did you..." Brandon broke off and sighed. "I guess I'm trying to ask when you first noticed me. Or how that all came about. And yes, I fully realize how much I sound like a moony teenage girl, but I want to know."

"First day of second semester," Paul answered immediately. *Like I'd ever forget.* "We'd all just gotten back from Christmas break and a bunch of us were sitting around in the second-floor commons room. You walked in and you were wearing this T-shirt that—I don't even know what it was about the shirt, honestly, but it fit you really well. And I had a bit of a silent freak-out right there in the middle of everybody, because I thought you were absolutely gorgeous and I didn't know where the heck that thought had come from."

Brandon *hmm*ed thoughtfully. "You didn't know you were gay?"

"I'm not sure, honestly." Paul grimaced. "If I did, I'd tried very hard to not admit it. To not think about anything even vaguely related to that. It was the first time I'd truly felt *lust* for someone I knew in person, and it threw me for a loop."

"You didn't say anything, though."

Paul shrugged, even though he knew Brandon couldn't see it. "How could I? Being gay was—*is*—a sin. And was—*is*—grounds for getting kicked out of St. Ben's. I wanted so desperately to not feel that way. To not deal with it. I'm sure I saw you around before that, during our first semester, but that's the first time I remember really being bowled over by how attracted I was to you. After that it became an absolutely ridiculous crush." Another pause. "What about you?"

Brandon's hand squeezed once more, then stilled. "For me it was back at the beginning of freshman year. I was pretty sure I was at least bisexual by that point, but both my parents went to St. Ben's—they met there—and I had already applied and been accepted and all, so when I finally got everything sorted out for myself that summer before, it felt like it was too late to go to a more gay-friendly school. I figured I could just go and make the best of it, like I did all through high school. But then I got here and there were so many gorgeous guys and I realized pretty quickly I had signed up for my own little personal hell."

"Makes sense." *I lived it too. Still do.*

"I saw you at one of the orientation things, though, and I remember being excited that you were in my dorm. Nervous, at the same time, that I'd do or say something to give away the fact that I found you attractive. I think I avoided you most of that first semester to be safe."

"If you did, I don't remember."

Brandon huffed out a quiet snort of laughter. "It must have worked, then."

"So what changed?" Paul had been asking himself that every day for the last decade, but never could come up with an answer. "How did we go from being afraid of each other to... Well, you know. How did that happen?"

"To a middle-of-the-night mutual hand job in the shower?" Brandon made a contented noise and snuggled closer, curling one long arm over Paul's chest. "Couldn't control myself any longer. And I hoped that you wanted me too. After you saw me naked, the way you looked at me… It didn't take much to convince me, after that."

"Oh." It came out sounding strangled, but Paul couldn't manage much more with Brandon's naked body now pressed against his side. There wasn't anything overtly sexual in how they were touching (apart from the somewhat telling lack of clothes), but the proximity was having an effect on his sympathetic nervous system. Paul forced his residual libido back down, his muscles to relax, and made himself lie still under Brandon's arm. "I wish you hadn't left," he admitted softly.

"I wish you had come with me," Brandon whispered back, lips nearly brushing his ear. "I've been waiting for this for a long, long time."

Chapter 10

Can't do dinner tonight—have a conference call for another client at 5. Will probably take hours—client is woefully indecisive.

Paul really didn't like to think about how much Brandon's text disappointed him. It's not like they'd even made plans for dinner, really—they'd both woken up happy, but neither of them had been in a talkative mood. Words were unnecessary. Even the half-dozen sentences they had exchanged were mostly in the vein of "do you see my other shoe?" and "can't think, need coffee." There'd been no mention of dinner, together or otherwise, but there had been copious snuggling. After three nights of eating together and then sleeping together, two of those with sex in between, Paul realized he'd been thinking of another night as guaranteed.

Condolences on working overtime, he texted back. *I assume you're going home tomorrow for the weekend?*

His phone rang a moment later.

"Sorry," Brandon said. He sounded like he really was. "Completely forgot about the semi-monthly status update meeting—being here feels like a totally different world, as if it's disconnected from everything back at the office. I would have told you earlier if I'd remembered."

"It's fine," Paul assured him. "I mean, I've been fending for myself for years; I won't starve or anything if we don't do dinner. And we hadn't talked about it."

"Sure, but we both know what we'd be doing tonight otherwise."

No point in denying that. Paul tried not to think too hard about what, exactly, their activities would have entailed—work was not the place to daydream about sex. Heck, there really *weren't* a lot of places which counted as "the place" for that, but St. Ben's was off the list.

There was silence on the line for a long moment. "Right," Brandon finally said. "So tomorrow's Friday, and then I've got the weekend off. I assume you do, too. If it's not too weird to ask… Want to get out of town with me?"

Paul blinked. "Like a vacation?"

"Sorta? Come back to Atlanta for the weekend. We can go out and do tourist stuff or stay in and watch movies or whatever you want." He paused. "Normally I work a bit on Saturdays," he confessed, "just to get a leg up on the next week, but if I get all my non-St. Ben's stuff done tonight I won't have to. My apartment isn't huge, but it's big enough we won't be tripping over each other. And it would be a change of scenery, at least."

It sounded incredible. Paul closed his eyes and nodded. And belatedly remembered Brandon wouldn't be able to see it over the phone. "Yeah. That would be great. Thanks."

Sleeping in his own bed alone that night sucked. Paul hung his spare blanket over the bedroom window, just in case the blinds weren't thick enough.

* * * *

Friday dragged by, a pattern that was starting to become distressingly familiar. Paul's only class was his mid-morning developmental psych lecture, which was nominally followed by office hours. "Nominally" because not a single student had bothered to use his Friday office hours all semester, but Paul still had to be there and ready to answer questions. He ate a turkey sandwich at his desk and focused on the grant proposal due the next week instead.

The work did help. Securing research funding wasn't all that exciting, but it was hugely important to any long-term career in academia and thus demanded a fair amount of attention. Which meant he didn't spend *every* second involuntarily daydreaming about Brandon—what was he doing, what was he working on right that very minute, was he wearing that sexy little half smile he'd had on his face when they woke up next to each other yesterday morning? *Blast it.* Paul went back and re-read the last two methodology paragraphs because he hadn't taken in a word the first time around.

Brandon had been sweet, really. Sluggish and still a bit rumpled from sleep and his hair had been sticking up like some strange alien terrain, which had only made Paul want to smooth it down and kiss him more. And they did kiss, lethargic and gentle, neither of them wanting to face the day yet. When Brandon had finally rolled away with a groan and a vague "ugh—need my shower," it was all Paul could do to let him go and not just tackle him and beg him to stay in bed. He was so gorgeous nude, the way the muscles in his shoulders shifted as he scrubbed his fingers through his hair and how his spine twisted as he stretched. Even more than twenty-four hours later, after a hellish and sleepless night in his own bed, that particular movement was emblazoned into Paul's mind.

It hadn't been like this with Christopher. Sure, they'd slept next to each other more often than not by the end, but Christopher was very *not* a morning person. He barely became human until after his second cup of coffee. Okay, *that* part was eerily similar to Brandon's morning routine. Waking Christopher up in the mornings had been like poking a hibernating bear, even when Paul let the alarm blare away practically in his ear. He'd never been interested in long morning cuddles or just lying in bed with no expectation of sex.

And darn it, there I go again, staring off into space. Paul let out a long breath and closed his eyes. Still hours yet before Brandon would be ready to leave for their stolen weekend together. It was tempting to go home and wallow for a while, but it was good to be seen in his office even if he wasn't getting much accomplished work-wise. *Which I really do need to do. No matter how much I'd rather daydream.*

Darn it.

* * * *

Paul managed to stay until slightly after two o'clock through sheer force of will. With the door open, he sat at his computer, tweaking the research proposal and his next week's lesson plans. It was well past his required office hours, but it felt good to know he *could* be professional if he wanted to and ignore the distraction known as Brandon Mercer. That all went out the window when he got a text from Brandon at 2:05.

Finishing around 4 - where do you want me to pick you up? This is gonna be fun - can't wait to show you my little corner of Atlanta :-)

Right, the heck with professional. Paul closed down his laptop and grabbed everything he needed to take home over the weekend. Or in this case, everything he needed to leave at his apartment while he was enjoying a very not-professional, not-heterosexual weekend away with Brandon. Two hours was enough time to go home and pack, take another shower, and have a nice private freak-out before Brandon showed up.

"Paul?"

He literally jumped at the sound of Grace's voice from his office doorway.

"Sorry, I didn't mean to surprise you. Were you heading out?"

"No, I ..." Paul let out a long breath and closed his eyes. "Okay, yeah, you did catch me off-guard. But I was daydreaming a bit, there. My fault. What's up?"

"Nothing important, I promise." She bit her lip, suddenly looking shy. "I just—I was wondering if you'd have some time free this weekend. I've got some new bookshelves being delivered this afternoon and I don't know who else to ask. I'm pretty sure I can get the boxes up the stairs by myself, but I'm terrible at assembling furniture like that and it's always easier with two people. I could make you dinner to say thanks?"

Normally he'd have jumped at the chance to socialize—and to see Grace's apartment in person, after all the stories he'd heard about her neighbors—but Paul couldn't summon the enthusiasm to pretend. "I wish I could," he lied. Sort-of lied. "It'll kill me to miss your cooking. I'm headed out of town in a little bit, though. Maybe if you still need help by Monday?"

"Oh." She returned his fake smile with a brittle-looking one of her own. "I hope you have fun, then. Where are you going?"

"Atlanta. To see a friend."

"Oh. Good. I'm sure it'll be nice to get away from home for a bit." She took a deep breath and nodded. "Okay. Well I'm sure I can manage. Have a wonderful weekend?"

"You too," he answered mechanically. "And let me know Monday if you need my help—I really wouldn't mind."

I'm just planning a much more wonderful weekend in bed with Brandon.

* * * *

"Is that it?" Brandon tossed Paul's bag in his trunk, slammed the door closed, then jerked his head in the direction of the trees lining the apartment complex's walking path. "Do you mind showing me what you found?"

Paul led him down to the sad-looking lake and along the path to the correct tree. "You can see the worn patch on the trunk if you stand over here—it's more obvious up close."

"I see it." Brandon backed up and cast an assessing look at the lowest branches. "Mind giving me a leg up?"

Oh Lord. Middle of the afternoon. Someone was bound to see. "Do you really have to—"

"I want to take a closer look," Brandon interrupted. "You know—check to see that there's not a torn piece of monogrammed fabric stuck up there."

"I'd say 'if only we were so lucky,' but nothing about this situation feels like I've been having good luck." Paul did sink down on one knee, though, and let Brandon use his thigh as a springboard to get up into the tree. Which he did with surprising agility—much more gracefully than Paul's attempt the other day. An agility that also showed off how well his black jeans molded to his backside as he scrambled up to a sitting position and then to standing.

Brandon maneuvered himself around until he was standing on the next branch down and could touch the smooth patches for himself. "No smoking gun here," he called down. "Not that I expected one, but you're right that the whole thing is pretty damn creepy. We're just going to have to solve this the old-fashioned way."

"What's that?"

Brandon grinned. "Copious amounts of data-tracking, electronic manipulation, cyber-spying, and you and me sleeping together whenever the opportunity presents itself."

"Right, *that*'s the old-fashioned way?" Paul raised an eyebrow at him.

"Maybe not, but it's my plan." Brandon shrugged—not looking the least bit repentant—and gestured back toward the car. "Shall we?"

* * * *

Metro Atlanta wasn't all that far away when measured in miles, but that didn't account for rush-hour traffic. They were going into town while nearly everyone else was coming out, which helped, but I-285 was still a parking lot.

"This right here is why I've never moved to a bigger city," Paul said, craning his neck to see what the cause for the complete standstill was. "I thought the point of a ring road was to *conduct* traffic?"

Brandon snorted, making it clear what he thought of *that* assumption. "Believe it or not, my commute is usually only about twenty minutes. My apartment isn't all that close to downtown, but neither is work. Haven't you been here before?"

"Of course." Paul's hometown was slightly past St. Ben's, an hour farther out into the middle of nowhere. Atlanta was the only real city of note anywhere within driving distance, and it was impossible to grow up in Georgia without having been there at least a few times. "Never for fun, though. And I've never driven it myself."

Brandon arched an eyebrow. "Not even for the touristy stuff?"

Paul thought back and ticked off fingers one at a time. "Middle school band competition, state finals. Some Christian pop concert for a singer I'd never heard of, but it was a church youth group outing. Um, something at the downtown Marriott for some reason, I've forgotten. Oh, and helping my sister look for a prom dress."

"You went shopping for a prom dress."

"I mostly held her friends' purses and coats, but yes." Paul leaned back against the headrest and tried to figure out how to explain. "Danielle and I... I can't remember, did I ever tell you my sister and I are twins?"

"You've mentioned it." Brandon glanced over at him, an amused smirk on his lips.

"Not identical, but we do look a lot alike. Her hair's a slightly darker blond and she's got a smaller build, but any idiot can tell we're siblings." *Maybe not* any *idiot—Dr. Kirsner was caught by surprise.* Paul caught his reflexive snicker at Dr. Kirsner's reaction before it could escape. "I'm told we've got a lot of similar mannerisms and verbal tics, too, even though we haven't lived in the same house for over a decade."

"Where does she live now?"

"At the moment, France. She's been there for the last two years, but she's planning to move back to the States soon."

"That's a long way away."

"Yeah, but she loves it." *Raved about it all weekend, when she wasn't rhapsodizing about* Étienne. "She's in advertising—some big firm most laypeople wouldn't recognize but is apparently *the* company to work for in the advertising world. She asked to be transferred to the Paris office for a while so she could pick up some skills to help prepare projects here before they're passed to the international department. Dunno if that excuse was totally made up or not, but her French is fantastic now. She's back in town for the next few weeks. I don't get to see her much, but we both went home last weekend and it was nice. She's doing a whirlwind tour of the East Coast right now, visiting some of her other friends. Hopefully we can catch another day or two together before she heads back."

"You're close, then."

"We are," Paul agreed. "She's the only one I've ever come out to." Paul never wanted to relive *that* conversation again. Danielle had come around eventually, was a huge proponent of LGBT rights now that she'd spent so much time in France, but the initial revelation had been painful for both of them. "It's good, now, to know that at least one person knows that about me, but it was hard at the time."

"How old were you?"

"Summer after freshman year." *About a week after you made me realize a lot of things about myself I had been avoiding and I decided I couldn't hold it in any longer.*

Brandon made a bit of a strangled noise. "You didn't..."

"It was all very general, no mention of any particular inciting incident." Paul snuck a glance at Brandon out of the corner of his eye. "I did eventually tell her that it wasn't entirely theoretical, but that was a few years down the road. Once she got more comfortable with the idea of me being gay. And once she was over her initial issues. I still didn't say anything specific, but she's good at reading between the lines." He shifted in his seat, slipping the seatbelt a bit farther down his shoulder and away from where it was starting to chafe. "Reading me."

"I can honestly say I've never had anyone like that," Brandon replied. "Three older brothers, remember. All I got when I came out was some good-natured teasing. But that kind of connection ... It's not the same. They still treat me like the baby a lot of the time."

"I've heard that's the lifelong curse of being the youngest." Paul dared a more direct look, watching Brandon's profile as he kept his eyes on the slowly moving traffic ahead of them. "So they were supportive of you all the way through? Parents not lamenting the loss of future grandkids or anything?"

Brandon shrugged. "My oldest brother is married now. He and his wife have been together since high school. Grandkids were inevitable from them. I've got a four-year-old niece and a two-year-old nephew. Who are adorable, by the way. My other two brothers have had long-term girlfriends for ages, and things are looking like they'll tip toward marriage soon." He shot Paul a sideways glance, too quick to interpret. "Being gay doesn't mean you necessarily have to give up the idea of getting married and having kids, you know. If you want them."

Paul knew intellectually that Brandon was right, but he'd never put much thought into it before. "You want children someday? If you get the chance?"

"Do you?"

God, yes. Paul was, instinctive response. *Where did that come from?* "I never really thought about it," he said slowly.

"Because you're planning to stay single and closeted your whole life."

Paul clenched his jaw to keep from saying anything and looked out the window instead.

"That was an asshole thing for me to say," Brandon said after a long moment, "and you deserve an apology. It's kind of a pet peeve of mine. People assuming that because I'm gay, I must only care about musicals and the club scene and fashion and have no interest in being a dad. What if I want to settle down eventually? Do the whole house-in-the-suburbs thing, maybe raise some kids? No reason I shouldn't be allowed to want that."

Something in his voice pled for reassurance, and Paul's heart went out to him. "No reason at all," he agreed.

"I shouldn't jump on you for not making the same choices I did. It's your life."

Paul took a deep breath and let it back out again. "You're right. About the whole closet thing. Until this week, I just never thought I could do anything else. I've got no interest in musicals and the club scene and fashion, and even though I knew there was more to being gay than that, I never really...*knew* knew, you know?"

They caught each other's eye and both snickered a bit, the awkward wording clearing some of the tension in the air.

Brandon was silent for a long moment, staring blankly at the back of the car ahead of them. "It took me a long time," he finally said.

"For what?"

"To realize I don't like most of that stuff either."

"Ah." Paul watched him, not saying anything more, not wanting to interrupt as Brandon gathered his thoughts. Traffic stalled again.

"I told you I used to go clubbing," Brandon said suddenly. "It was more than that—I really jumped into 'the scene' with both feet after college. *During* college actually. When I transferred to Georgia Tech, I joined the Georgia Tech Pride Alliance almost immediately. Got involved in all the political activism stuff, pierced my ear, checked all the boxes for the gay college student stereotype." He grimaced. "I didn't date, really, but I did pick up a lot of guys. I went a bit wild."

Paul nodded firmly, determined to not sound like he was judging. "What about after you graduated?"

"I got the job I'm in now and I fell into the club scene. I stayed friends with a bunch of the guys from Pride Alliance, so it wasn't like I was out partying all alone, but the core group of them are still just as flamboyant as I was back then. We still see each other sometimes, but everything we usually do together seems to involve glitter and drag revues and musicals. Which is great for them, they love it, but I kind of drifted away."

"Decided that wasn't really you?"

Brandon shrugged, but there was too much tension in his shoulders for it to be a nonchalant gesture. "Eventually I realized I didn't have to be a stereotype to be gay. I took out the earring and let the hole close up. I started dressing more professionally during the week and saved the tight clothes for our nights out. I focused more on work than clubbing and I stopped picking up those kinds of guys. Lots of people love the club scene, of course, but I finally admitted I wasn't one of them."

"And yet you picked me up anyway." Paul didn't mean to say it, it kind of popped out, but it felt good to get it out in the open. *Am I just one of a long string of one-night-stands, one of which happened to stretch out for a week, or is this different?*

Brandon's quiet smile was one part sad, one part sweet. "What can I say? You were irresistible."

Paul didn't know what to say to that, either, so he looked out his own window and they puttered through the traffic in silence.

Chapter 11

"So this is it." Brandon swung the door open and waved Paul ahead of him into the apartment. "I wasn't really planning on company, so forgive the clutter."

Paul looked around, taking it all in. It really was *Brandon*, for all he knew of him: comfortable-looking sofa, modern glass coffee table, giant TV on the wall, three gaming consoles of varying ages, several good-sized bookcases, and not much else. The room had a practical, professional feel. "It's nice."

"Thanks," Brandon replied. "I can give you the grand tour, if you want: living room and kitchen here, bedroom's that door there, and the bathroom's down the little hallway. Thus endeth the tour. It's nothing fancy, but it's close to a MARTA stop, it's gated, and it's got parking."

It was cleaner than the usual state of Paul's apartment—no clutter to speak of, despite Brandon's apology. And it didn't look like it had been furnished entirely from Goodwill, which was another point of contrast. "It suits you."

They brought their bags in from the car, which consisted of a weekend duffel for Paul and the week's dirty laundry for Brandon. Brandon tossed Paul's bag on the queen-sized bed without a word. *Guess I'm not going to have to make do with the sofa, then.* Paul was about to suggest dinner when Brandon's stomach rumbled loudly.

"Damn," he muttered. "I don't have much to eat in the fridge—didn't know how long I'd be gone, or whether I'd get back home this weekend or not. What are you hungry for? None of this 'I don't care' crap; give me three choices that sound good to you."

That certainly seemed like a more efficient way to choose. "Chinese, barbecue, or burgers," Paul said, trying not to overthink it.

Brandon grinned. "Burgers it is. You, my friend, are missing out on the experience that is Soulburger."

* * * *

Soulburger turned out to be a hole-in-the-wall restaurant about five minutes from Brandon's apartment. A short black woman in a flowered apron stood behind the counter, taking orders and yelling them back to the kitchen in a thick Georgia accent. It was so ridiculously, stereotypically southern that Paul had to fight the urge to look around for hidden cameras.

"Hey, y'all! Welcome. You been to Soulburger before?"

Brandon's eyes flicked to Paul. "I have."

Paul shrugged. "First time."

Her whole face lit up. "Everybody, we have a virgin!" There were answering whoops and what sounded like a large dinner bell ringing from the kitchen area. Several of the people in the cramped dining area turned and clapped.

Paul glared at Brandon, who was snickering and looking unforgivably smug. "I'm going to murder you," Paul said not quite under his breath.

"Not after you try their onion rings, you're not." Brandon grinned broadly and ordered the "Don't Go Bacon My Heart Burger." Which was one of the less cheesy puns on the menu. "Seriously, go for the onion rings and then tell me you don't hear angelic choirs proclaiming their perfection."

"You could have warned me," he said, mock-kicking Brandon's ankle.

"I could have, but then they wouldn't have all gotten to yell. That's half the fun of coming here—seeing the newbies freak out and wonder what the hell is going on. Well, that and the terrible burger names. It's mortifying when it's you, but it's hilarious when it's anybody else."

There was really no point in fighting it, after that. Paul went ahead and ordered a burger with the onion rings on the side. He was only slightly mollified when they got their food and it was confirmed that yes, they were probably the best onion rings on the planet.

"I still hate you, you know," Paul grumbled, but there was no heat in it. He was hungrier than he'd thought. So was Brandon. Between the two of them they polished off everything they'd ordered, down to the crusty bits of fried batter at the bottom of the grease-spotted paper bowls. Finally Brandon sat back and tilted his head to the side, studying Paul with a tiny smile on his face. "So."

"So," Paul echoed.

"Ready to head back?"

"Sure."

"What should we do tonight?"

Is that a hint that he expects us to jump straight in bed together when we get back? Paul shrugged and busied himself collecting their trash onto the shared plastic tray. "No particular preference."

"You say that and I might just drag you out clubbing," Brandon retorted, his smile widening.

"I thought we both established that wasn't really our scene?"

"Yeah, we did; that's why it was the perfect threat." Brandon swiped the tray away from Paul and tipped the contents neatly into the trash can. "Better idea—how about an evening swim? My apartment complex has a really nice pool, and it's open until eleven. We'll probably have it all to ourselves—nobody comes after dark. Even though it's pretty well lit."

Some sort of exercise sounded heavenly, as well as the chance to see Brandon shirtless and wet. "I didn't exactly bring a suit."

Brandon's flicked his gaze down Paul's front and back up again. "We'll figure it out," he said, and nodded toward the door. He wore a carefully controlled expression, but he couldn't entirely hide the heat in it. "Ready to go?"

* * * *

There was a brand-new swimsuit in a box at the back of Brandon's closet. He yanked the tag off and tossed it to Paul, leaving the box on the shelf. "Christmas gift from my friend Lito—it was kind of an inside joke. I already had one I liked so I've never worn it. And I don't swim as much as you might think, considering the pool's right there. Hopefully it fits—I'm guessing we're about the same size."

It did. Together they made their way through the chilly night air to the pool area in the middle of the apartment complex. It was a beautiful indoor-outdoor affair, with a long, curved arm running through an outdoor deck area and connecting to a rectangular indoor lap pool, separated by a sheet of Plexiglas that came down to just under the surface of the water. As he had said, the entire facility was empty. Brandon let them into the building with his key, set his towel down on one of the lounge chairs, and launched himself into the water with a splash.

"Warmer in here!"

Paul eased himself in, but the pool really was warmer than the air and it felt wonderful after the long car ride and the greasy dinner. The deep end of the pool wasn't all that deep—neither of them could stand, but it wasn't enough to dive. Paul to settled in and did a few laps while Brandon leaned back against the wall and watched. The air in the indoor pool area was humid with a chemical tang and the air outdoors was positively frigid when compared with the warmer pool. The contrast back and forth was interesting, and Paul let himself be distracted by cataloging the differences as he swam.

"You make that look graceful," Brandon said when Paul stopped for a breather just inside the Plexiglas divider.

Paul didn't feel particularly graceful, but the full-body exercise was helping counteract some of the tension from the last few days. "I've always liked swimming," he answered. It's not like he'd had anything much beyond the lessons from when he was a kid. "I don't get to do it often, but it feels nice to stretch muscles that don't usually get stretched."

"Looks nice, too." Brandon grinned and grabbed at Paul's waist below the water. "I can help you stretch some of those new muscles," he growled in his ear.

Dang. "Brandon, I…"

Brandon huffed softly against his neck. "Embarrassed to kiss me here?"

"Yes, if you must know." Paul pulled back, putting a bit of space between their bodies. That had come out a bit more snappish than he'd intended, but it was true. "Sorry, it's a lot to take in, all at once. And I'm not ready to do, um." He gestured from his own bare chest to Brandon's. "*That.* Where anyone can see. The light's on and we're right next to a giant window."

Brandon's expression was startled, then contrite. "Sorry, I wasn't thinking."

Crap. "It's fine, I only meant—"

"No, I was being a jackass." Brandon turned away and shook his head. "I'm trying to give you space, but sometimes I'm an idiot and I forget that not everyone flirts quite as aggressively as I do. It's not like you haven't told me."

"To be fair, I suppose I never did specifically say 'no kissing or groping in a pool in the dark.'" Paul thought about offering his hand, in truce, but Brandon wasn't looking. He splashed Brandon's back instead. It was absolutely worth it for Brandon's stunned reaction, which morphed into retaliation in about three seconds flat.

"I assume pool wars are acceptable, then?" Brandon asked between well-executed lunges, forcing short shocks of water up over Paul's head to rain down on him. "Because I'll warn you, I'm good at these. Older brothers, remember."

"Yeah, yeah—twin sister. She's deadly at this." Paul interlocked his fingers with each other and shoved the heels of his hands outward, directing a spectacular jet of water right at Brandon's chest. It hit dead-center, splashing up into his face and—judging from his sudden startled snort—directly up his nose.

It only devolved from there, the two of them chasing each other around the indoor portion of the pool like ten-year-olds and splashing every chance they got. They were both a bit out of breath by the time they called a truce. Brandon looked fantastic when dripping wet, his beard and hair even darker than usual. The individual droplets running down his arms and chest only drew attention to the subtle ridges and furrows of his musculature. Paul knew he was staring, but Brandon seemed to be staring at him just as much so he didn't bother to hide his appreciation.

"You're thinking," Brandon said.

"You know," Paul answered quietly, his voice barely carrying over the water, "'not here' isn't the same as 'not now.' I may not be an exhibitionist, but that doesn't mean I'm not ready to take you somewhere significantly less public and let you find out *exactly* what I'm thinking about."

"Oh. *Oh.* I suppose that could be arranged." Brandon bit his lip. "And," he purred, his eyes smoldering, "you really need to see my shower. It's surprisingly large, given the size of the apartment. Would fit us both, easily." He drew closer, not touching but close enough to murmur directly into Paul's ear. "I know what else I want to do tonight," he breathed.

They were out of the pool and back to Brandon's apartment in record time.

Chapter 12

Paul waited until the door closed behind them to whirl Brandon around, press him up against it, and kiss him breathless. Brandon only resisted for an instant, probably out of surprise, then let Paul tease at his mouth until they were both moaning softly. He didn't try to reclaim control of the kiss—Paul was proud to be doing quite well at that, thank you—but when they finally broke apart he followed it up with an even more scorching kiss of his own.

"Eager, are you?" he murmured into Paul's mouth.

"Desperately." Paul was quite certain that if he didn't get Brandon's hands on him *that very instant* he might very well explode. He reached for the hem of Brandon's swim trunks, but Brandon twisted away and smacked his hand playfully.

"Patience, grasshopper." Brandon thumbed Paul's nipple, sending goosebumps chasing over his skin, but he very carefully kept their lower bodies apart. "I promised you a shower first. Then I'll let you maul me to your heart's content."

"Don't wanna wait." Paul reached for Brandon's hips again.

Brandon pinched Paul's nipple, lightly but firmly, and Paul nearly bit through his tongue. When Brandon smirked and turned to go lead the way to the bathroom, though, some devilish impulse prompted Paul to land a brief retaliatory swat to Brandon's rear. It was a somewhat damp swat, since Brandon's swim trunks were still sopping, but it made Brandon jump anyway and then shoot him a bemused expression over his shoulder.

"What's gotten into you?" he asked with a little laugh.

"I don't know." It was the truth. "It hit me, you know? Any other Friday night, I'd be sitting at home playing video games. By myself. And now I'm staying with this sexy guy in Atlanta for the weekend, and he's wet and shirtless and flirting with me and he's interested in doing all sorts of amazing, depraved things to me. And I can barely believe it."

"*With* you." Brandon grinned at him and pursed his lips in a parody of a kiss. "I want to do amazing and depraved things *with* you, not *to* you. Important difference."

"Oh?" Paul grinned back, helpless to do otherwise. "Are you going to elaborate on that?"

"Sure—once we're in the shower." Brandon sauntered through the living room and down the short hallway, sashaying slightly and swinging his hips in an utterly mesmerizing manner. He turned on the light in the bathroom and started the water, all without looking back, but Paul could sense Brandon's full attention on him the entire time.

The shower stall was astoundingly large in comparison to the rest of the bathroom: tiny sink, tiny vanity area, tiny linen closet, tiny square of tiled floor to stand on, a normal toilet, and a big freaking amazing shower/tub combo. Paul shucked off his wet swim trunks and ran them under cold water in the sink to get out some of the chlorine. Their knees collided a few times as Brandon stripped behind him, but that was fine because they were both halfway hard already. Brandon caught him looking—they locked eyes in the mirror, then Brandon smirked and ran a hand slowly over his own naked chest. He didn't say anything, but then he didn't have to. Paul could figure out perfectly well what the raised eyebrow and the jerk of Brandon's head toward the shower meant. Chlorine-soaked swim trunks were immediately forgotten.

The warm water felt heavenly, washing away the pool residue and the fatigue of the long car ride. Brandon maneuvered them around so they could rinse first and get their hair thoroughly wet without elbowing each other in the face. Paul hadn't thought to bring his own shampoo, but Brandon had a bottle of something expensive-looking and if it smelled anything like what Brandon had been using for the last week, Paul was all for it.

"Come here." Brandon poured a little pool of the pearly liquid into his palm and stepped back, giving Paul space to find a comfortable angle under the spray. Paul had to duck a little, but the first touch of Brandon's fingers on his scalp sent a shiver throughout his entire body. *Good grief,* it felt amazing. Brandon laughed at his reaction, but he kept up the gentle massage until Paul's entire head was tingling and his eyes had drifted closed.

"I want to make a joke about your magic fingers," Paul mumbled with his chin against his chest, "but I'm afraid if I do you might stop."

"Oh, I want to be touching you much more than this." Brandon slid a shampoo-slicked hand down Paul's torso, tweaking a nipple and coming tantalizingly close to his now-fully-erect cock before pulling away. "First you have to tilt your head back to rinse your hair, and then you can do me."

Paul let Brandon turn him this way and that under the spray, washing the shampoo out. There was perhaps more caressing than necessary, but naked like this it was obvious they were both enjoying the moment. He eventually got Brandon to swap places with him, so the water was cascading down Brandon's shoulders and back in thick rivulets that twisted and bent with the lines of his body. Brandon closed his eyes and submitted to Paul's fingers on his own scalp. He didn't moan out loud, but he might as well have—they both knew exactly where this was leading.

Oh yes, I could get used to this.

As soon as Paul finished his hair, Brandon twisted around and yanked their bodies chest-to-chest. He barely gave Paul a chance to react before closing the gap in a near-violent clash of mouths, nudging Paul's jaw open and tangling their tongues together. Paul scrabbled desperate fingertips against his back, melting against him and relaxing into the kiss. Eventually it gentled, turning exploratory, until Brandon pulled back with a hint of a sigh and planted a chaste peck on the tip of Paul's nose. "You bring out the caveman in me," he said with a hint of a rueful smile.

"I like the caveman in you," Paul answered honestly. "You have no idea how much." *Rather have a bit of your caveman in* me. Paul grimaced inwardly. *Right. Not the time, and heck if I'm going to ruin the mood with terrible jokes. Or the reminder that I'm not able to give him all the variations of orgasms he probably wants from me.* He kissed Brandon back instead, playful but short—or it would have been, if Brandon hadn't caught him by surprise with a sneak encore of tongue action.

Brandon eventually let out a long groan and stepped away, running a blatantly lustful eye over Paul's entire body. "Right, finish washing," he declared. "Then I can ravish you up against the wall."

"Oh?" Paul didn't even pretend to hide how his cock jumped at that. *Caveman, indeed. Dang.* "You did promise some amazing, depraved plans."

"Oh, yes. Those." Brandon sighed dramatically in mock disappointment. "Unfortunately, elaborating would give away the surprise. Plus I keep seeing you from new angles or with a new expression—my plans have to keep growing to encompass all the wicked things I want to do with you. It's become a race to see which of them happens first."

"Oh." Paul felt a little dizzy at even the promise of whatever "wicked things" Brandon might be interested in. "You've inspired me to wash fast." Paul stepped around Brandon to peek into the shower caddy for something resembling soap. "Whoa, a loofah? Seriously?"

"Hey, we're gay—it's allowed. Although I'm pretty sure we have to just call it a 'scrubby thing,' since we're both such manly macho men." Brandon very pointedly slid his wet chest against Paul's arm as he leaned in to pull out a pump-top bottle of body wash. At least it had the label printed in block letters instead of flowing pink cursive with flowers. "Got to be some advantages to being gay and naturally fabulous, after all."

Paul choked on what would have probably come out as a giggle. "I don't think I've been 'fabulous' a day in my life."

"Oh, me neither, and I even tried it for a while. Takes a surprising amount of effort. And hair product. Turn around." Brandon dragged the soapy loofah slowly over Paul's shoulders and back. It should have tickled, having someone else wash him like this, but the teasing scrape over his skin had Paul breathing faster and leaning back into Brandon's touch. Brandon braced him with a warm palm against his hip, anchoring him in place. "None of that; you'll fall over."

"Then at least one of us would be horizontal. It's a start."

Brandon huffed, his grin audible in the sound. "Seriously, what's gotten into you tonight? Not that I'm complaining, mind you, you're just being extra-flirtatious." His hand drifted around to Paul's waist, brushed higher to settle flat and heavy against his stomach. "After I was such an idiot in the pool…"

"Mmmm." It was a fair question, but Paul didn't really have an answer. Everything was wonderful at the moment: All the trouble at St. Ben's was worlds away, he was warm and comfortable, and he was being buttered up by Brandon Mercer, of all people. For sex, which they'd already had twice. And which had proved to be significantly more amazing than anything had been with Christopher.

"Should I assume you've got your own amazing and depraved plan, then? You might be able to persuade me to be indulgent."

Ooh, yes. That. "I think, if you're going to play it *that* way…" Paul turned to face him, so Brandon's empty hand was pressed against the small of his back and the loofah was squashed between their two bodies. "Tonight I want to be the one to make *you* lose your train of thought. I want to touch you all over. With my hands and with my mouth and with my body. And I want to make you drop the 'scrubby thing' on the floor of the tub because your muscles have all but given out on you and you can't concentrate enough to hold it anymore. And then I want to make you come, right here, with the water raining down on both of us. Sound good to you?"

"Well, fuck. Look who's gone all toppy now?" Brandon dropped the loofah immediately and leaned back against the wall of the tub, maneuvering them sideways so the spray warmed them both. "I suppose it's only fair—turnabout's fair play and all that."

"Oh, I thought so too." Brandon's head was angled back, exposing the underside of his jaw, so Paul stepped in and took advantage. Brandon tasted like clean skin and warm water and nothing else and it was absolutely marvelous. Droplets of water gathered on his beard, glittering and smearing against Paul's cheek as he moved his head. *Fantastic.* Paul let his mouth slide lower, down Brandon's neck to his collarbone and his chest, until finally Brandon surrendered with a low grunt and tangled his fingers in Paul's wet hair. "Christ," he breathed.

"Your vocabulary diminishes, the closer my mouth gets to your cock."

"Don't need words," Brandon groaned. "Need—*oh fuck.*"

Paul's own erection jumped at how responsive Brandon was to just that single fingernail up the underside of his shaft. "Should I do that again?" he murmured against Brandon's sternum.

"Fuck." Brandon was clearly making a serious effort not to wrap his hands deeper in Paul's hair and yank his head down to the right height, but his fingers were twitching and it felt good. Very good. "I think I can"—Brandon gasped as Paul repeated the motion—"I can put up with you having the depraved plans every once in a while."

"Mmmm." Paul could feel Brandon's hands practically trembling against his scalp as he lowered himself to his knees. From this height the spray of the shower was coming from almost directly overhead, tickling his face and running down his neck, but the close-up view of the gentle waterfalls cascading down Brandon's torso more than made up for the annoyance. Brandon moaned, loudly, and shifted his hips forward in a blatant request.

Hell yes.

Someone somewhere once said that giving a blowjob was like riding a bicycle: Once you learn, you never forget. It may have been ages since Paul had last tried this, but he was pleased to discover it came completely naturally this time around. The best way to angle his neck, the way to hold his mouth so his teeth wouldn't cause a problem, how to flick his tongue against the slit with just the right amount of force—it all came back to him. Brandon was swearing again, somewhere far above him, but for right now the world consisted of Brandon's cock in his mouth and Brandon's hands in his hair and the warm water cascading down over both of them. It was absolutely marvelous.

"Touch me," Brandon said, his voice barely more than a whisper. *"Fuck*, just—touch me and touch yourself. Get yourself right to that edge. I want to hear you."

The moment Paul's hand closed over his own length, the tension in the rest of his body ratcheted up tenfold. It was like all the sensations had been separate, disjointed, and they'd all suddenly found a home at once. He groaned around Brandon's cock and Brandon banged the back of his head a few times against the shower wall again in appreciation. And when Paul let his other hand close over the base of Brandon's erection, covering all the parts his mouth couldn't reach, Brandon groaned louder. "God, so fucking amazing. *Fuck*."

It was heady. It was incredible and astounding and it felt so *powerful* to be the one making Brandon tremble like that. Paul realized he could have happily stayed there all evening, just doing this, being together. Being the kind of person that everyday, boring, effectively-closeted Paul Dunham never got to be. He executed a particularly luscious maneuver with his lips and tongue and was rewarded with a not-at-all-muffled shout from Brandon. *Hell yes.*

"So damn close," Brandon breathed. "I want you to come too—but I want to do it. Don't you dare get yourself off until I can get my hands on you. Oh, Christ."

Paul hummed acceptance around Brandon's cock, just to make him jump and shiver, then backed off enough to give him a moment to come back down from the edge. Tiny kisses, up and down his shaft. One hand gently rolling Brandon's balls back and forth and the other on his own. "Where should I touch you?" he murmured between kisses.

"Want your fingertip inside me." Brandon let out what could only be described as a whimper. "Want to come with a little bit of you in me. *Please*."

Paul sucked in a breath. Anything anal had always been his hard line with Christopher, the one thing he absolutely wasn't comfortable doing. But this was his big chance, wasn't it? In the shower, perfectly clean, feeling ridiculously turned on but still mostly lucid, with Brandon all but gone already above him? He couldn't let himself think about it too much—if he thought, he might chicken out. Instead he let go of his own cock and brought both hands between Brandon's legs, thumbs caressing the insides of Brandon's thighs. Brandon immediately shuffled his feet a bit wider, sucked in a sharp breath—

There. Paul pressed one forefinger gently against Brandon's perineum and traced upward and back. He couldn't see, not with the head of Brandon's cock still in his mouth and his other hand blocking his view, but he didn't really need to. The skin was soft under his fingertip, lightly dragging against his cuticles on either side, smooth changing to textured in the middle. Brandon bucked and twitched his hips, clearly trying not to thrust so hard

Paul would gag but having a hard time holding still. Unable to control himself. Paul passed his fingertip over Brandon's hole again, light enough to be considered teasing, then nudged it inward slightly and sucked hard.

And Brandon came apart with a long groan and a shiver. Paul pulled off and stroked him through the aftershocks with his free hand but kept his fingertip right there where Brandon liked it. The shower washed all the evidence of orgasm away immediately, except for the taste already in Paul's mouth, but that was fine. More than fine—he was about ten seconds from coming himself, just from seeing, hearing, feeling, tasting Brandon shake apart. He started to get to his feet but Brandon tackled him halfway through and knocked them both down to the floor of the tub.

"Not done yet," Brandon growled in his ear, practically lying on top of him, water raining down on his back. "My turn—you want my mouth or my hand?"

Oh yes. God, anything. "Both?"

"Done." Brandon grinned and nipped a slightly-too-sharp bite at Paul's earlobe, then scooted backward and flailed blindly over his shoulder to turn the water off. The sudden silence was startling. Paul didn't have much time to adjust, though, because Brandon zeroed in on his cock with a vengeance and less than thirty seconds later, Paul was arching his back and groaning nearly as loudly as Brandon had.

They lay there on the wet tub floor for a few minutes, bodies tangled together, both catching their breath. Eventually Brandon stood and offered Paul a hand up.

"Suggestion: We turn it back on for a super-fast rinse off, then we go crash in bed and spend all night enjoying being naked together with nowhere to be in the morning. Acceptable?"

It sounded perfect, and Paul told him so. And if every little comment and gesture between there and the bedroom felt infused with more meaning than it would have had before... Well, Paul didn't need to mention it.

Chapter 13

"What time is it?"

Brandon rolled over and stared blearily at the clock. "Fuck-it early. It's a Saturday. How are you awake?"

"Bladder." Paul rolled out of Brandon's bed and stumbled his way to the bathroom. The overhead light hurt his eyes, but he couldn't find the nightlight without it (there was one in the socket under the mirror, he noticed eventually) and by the time his eyes had adjusted well enough to see the nightlight it didn't really matter. He relieved himself, scrubbed a hand through his hair, brushed his disgusting morning breath away, and went to climb back into bed. When he got back in the bedroom, though, the lamp was on and Brandon was awake enough to seize him from behind and tug him back under the covers in a limpet-like grasp.

"Thought you were asleep," Paul said.

"I was. Then you left and your side of the bed got cold." Brandon grumbled something against the nape of Paul's neck and pulled him closer, throwing a warm leg over Paul's own and pressing a hard, recognizable shape up against his rear. "It's all your fault, you know—I didn't know what I was missing until you let me sleep next to you. I had no idea I would be a morning cuddler."

"When I don't have to pee, I don't mind a bit." Paul let himself relax further, shuffling back and letting Brandon tighten an arm over his chest. "It's one of the few things I miss about living with Christopher—he was terrible at waking up in the morning, but I was never cold."

Brandon exhaled, a soft huff of laughter which ruffled the hair at the back of Paul's neck. "Demoted to portable space heater. Thanks a lot."

"Oh, come off it." Paul nudged a shoulder backward into Brandon's. "You know what I meant."

"Not really," Brandon said, his voice still a bit rough but sounding more awake than he had been a minute ago. "Like I told you before, I never stick around for the sleeping part. I always assumed sharing a bed with someone would be like when we went on vacation and I had to share a hotel room with my brothers—we usually ended up having to draw straws for who had to sleep next to Jordan. He liked to 'vent a toe' in the middle of the night when he was hot, then plaster his cold foot against your back when he rolled over. Maybe he still does; could be why he's been dating his girlfriend for six years now and they're not engaged yet."

Paul hid his smile in the pillow. "Jordan's the next oldest?"

"Eric, Marshall, Jordan, then me. Six, three, and two years older than I am, respectively. Marshall and Jordan both live out of town—Marshall's in New York and Jordan's in Virginia—but Eric's still in Atlanta. He and his wife, Anita, have me over to eat sometimes." Brandon nuzzled a kiss against the nape of Paul's neck. "They're kind to take pity on me, the lonely bachelor who can't cook. They're both fantastic at it."

"Mmmm." Paul grabbed Brandon's arm to keep it in place, then rolled so they were chest-to-chest and wrapped in each other's embrace. "I'm jealous. Danielle and I Skype a lot now that she's in Paris, but she's never been able to come home all that often. There've been a lot of times I wished I could talk to her in person and couldn't."

"You said she's the only one you've come out to?"

Paul couldn't help planting a quick kiss on Brandon's cheekbone, just above the edge of his beard. "Not including our thing freshman year, since we never quite got around to words. You make number two."

"Plus your ex?"

How had that happened, exactly? "Not really sure how that came about. I know I never told him I was gay, so I don't think it counts."

Brandon drew back, a confused wrinkle between his eyebrows. "You just, what? Accidentally fell into bed together one night?"

"You really want to know?"

"If you're willing to tell." Brandon's gaze darkened, but his eyes were full of concern. "You've mentioned him a couple of times now. And it sounds like he was pretty instrumental in creating your mental picture of what 'being gay' is supposed to be. I'm curious."

Paul finally gave in and pressed a second kiss to Brandon's lips. This one wasn't quite as chaste—more of an acknowledgment of emotions. Heck if he knew which ones. *His fault for being so kissable, anyway.*

"We were roommates first. Well, study partners first." Paul had to sort out how the whole Christopher thing started. "We had an advanced statistics class together senior year; pretty sure that's where we met. I had already been accepted to the psych PhD program and Christopher was graduating with a job offer from St. Ben's under his belt. We got to talking about it while studying together one day and decided we'd make good roommates. We found an apartment together that summer—tiny rooms, but it was a two-bedroom and it was better than what either of us could have afforded alone."

"Did you know he was gay at that point?"

Paul shook his head. "We never talked about it. Our friendship really was just a friendship for a long while—I taught and worked on my degree, he got a promotion to better hours and better pay. I think we were living together for a good year or so before it tipped into anything more than platonic. It's just...neither of us dated. At all. And eventually you start to wonder. Or he did, anyway."

"You didn't?"

"I figured it was wishful thinking." That rankled a bit, now. It would have been nice to say he'd never been attracted to his roommate like that until Christopher made the first move, but that would have been a lie. "I didn't really have a lot of experience with any of it, other than you."

Brandon interrupted him with a sneak attack kiss, one which took several minutes and involved quite a bit of full-body maneuvering against each other. When they finally pulled apart, Paul was panting.

"Sorry to interrupt," Brandon said.

Yeah right. "No you're not."

"Okay, I'm not." Brandon grinned. "But you were talking about wishful thinking, and I was wishing I could kiss you. And I realized I could and you'd probably let me."

"Twit." But Paul couldn't keep the smile off his face. "Anyway. I don't remember exactly how it happened, but we kind of gradually moved from 'platonic roommates' to sharing a bedroom and using the other one for a makeshift home office. We never really talked about it; it just ended up that way."

Brandon's grin faded. "See, that's the part I don't get," he said. "How do you go from both pretending you're straight to sleeping together? In either the literal or the idiomatic sense?"

If I knew that, I wouldn't have been so crap at deflecting him later on. "If you knew him, you'd understand."

"Try me."

Paul rolled onto his back and closed his eyes—this was hard enough to explain without Brandon's expressive face being six inches away from his own. "Christopher was a lot to take in. He's a hard guy to say 'no' to. Most of the time he was pretty easy-going, but every once in a while he got something in his head and it was usually a heckuva lot easier to just let him have it." He let out a long breath. "In my case … He probably figured out I liked guys, I guess? I have no idea how. It started out with lots of innuendo and little insinuations, comments I didn't know what to do with. And then he kissed me one day, and it wasn't awful, and he was convenient, and he already knew about me anyway, and … I don't know. It just happened."

"But he never told you he was gay."

A short bark of laughter escaped before Paul could rein it in. *Hardly.* "He pretty regularly insisted he was straight. Even while he was in bed with me. He'd say it was 'my fault' I was so tempting—it was always kind of teasing but kind of not. At the beginning I thought I knew what he meant, but by the end I realized he might have believed it." He turned to look at Brandon again. "You joke with me about me being in the closet, but Christopher was much worse. At least I know I *have* a closet."

"I've known guys like that," Brandon said darkly. "They come to the gay clubs and want anonymous blow jobs in the bathroom, but they're ready to kick your ass if you imply in any way that getting a gay blowjob in a gay bathroom at a gay club might somehow indicate they're gay."

"I don't think he went *that* far." Gay bars would have been too public for Christopher, even gay bars as far away as Atlanta. "And I don't want to make it sound like it was totally on him, because I was pretty eager to give it a go at first, too. My only experience had been—well, you—and for the first time since then, *someone wanted me.* It was nice."

"Nice but not perfect?"

Paul shrugged, hoping it looked more nonchalant than he felt. "It got to be too much."

Brandon levered up on one elbow, so his face appeared in Paul's field of view as he stared at the ceiling. "He's the one who said it wasn't sex if you weren't doing anal, I'm assuming."

"Yeah." God, this was hard to talk about, but it was only fair that Brandon know. "It built up so gradually, but after a while it hit me that we were always doing what *he* wanted. Almost never the things I liked. He was always a bit too demanding in the bedroom, but he'd go all passive-aggressive and snippy if I dared to call him on it. That's why we broke up—he kept harping on me about why wouldn't I have actual sex with him, but *that*—"

"You can say it, you know," Brandon interrupted.

Paul mock-glared at him. "—Fine, *anal intercourse*—was a step too far for me. I told him I didn't want it but he kept pushing. Eventually I didn't have a glib excuse and I was sick of his shit. Sorry. His nonsense."

"Holy fuck, you swore!" Brandon grinned, but the look in his eyes was still slightly pained.

"Screw you." Paul aimed an open-handed swat at his shoulder, not hard enough to knock him down but enough to make him sway a little. "I only talk like that when I'm really pissed off."

Brandon's laugh that time was real.

"*Any*way. We split up after about six months of not-gay not-dating, I moved out, and it was another whole semester before he got downsized— or fired or something, I wasn't keeping track at that point—and I didn't have to see him around St. Ben's anymore. It was a whole big bundle of awkward for ages—he was the only IT guy on call during off-hours, so when I had problems with the intranet or the grading software or whatever I usually waited until the next weekday so I could deal with one of the other tech crew instead."

"He was in IT?" Brandon went very still. "What's his full name?"

"Christopher Aaron Kluterman." Paul pulled back, out from under where Brandon was looming over him, and scrambled to sit up against the headboard. "Why?"

"IT employee, worked at St. Ben's for some number of years, and did on-call troubleshooting so he presumably had access to at least some portion of the tech offices. And the server room. Unsupervised, if he came in during the middle of the night. And he was either fired or downsized, which means he may have been feeling less than charitable about the university when he left." Brandon rolled out of bed in one smooth motion—still naked, although he didn't seem to care—and grabbed his laptop off the small work desk in the corner of the room. "I hadn't gone back that far yet because I was still focusing on current and recently-fired employees, but it's possible the security holes have been lying dormant for a year or more. I need to follow up on this."

"Holy ... You think he's the source of the data issues?"

Brandon pinned him with a sharp look. "Passive-aggressive ex who 'won't take no for an answer?' Who won't admit he's gay, but presses you for sex and was the dump-ee in your relationship? And who was 'awkward' for months afterward? Tell me, can you picture him spying on you from in that tree?"

Shit. The mental curse didn't feel like enough, so Paul repeated it out loud. Brandon didn't laugh.

"Okay, yes, I can, but I don't want to think about it," Paul admitted. "He was mad when I moved out, but not…You really think it could have been him?"

"I think he's worth investigating," Brandon said, not looking up from where he was already typing something. "Not much I can do today, unfortunately, but if I get a few e-mails out to the right people I can hopefully be ready to jump in with both feet first thing Monday morning."

The shift from sleepy-cuddly-Brandon to awake-and-working-Brandon shouldn't have been so sexy, but it was. Especially since he was now sitting at the very edge of his desk chair, foot twitching, typing madly, and still didn't have a stitch of clothing on. He looked like a businessman's version of the Emperor's New Clothes. It was the first time Paul had ever seen him functional in the morning without coffee, too—which probably said something reassuring about how seriously Brandon was treating the whole issue. Paul closed the distance between them and pressed a gentle kiss into the curve of his shoulder.

"You do what you need to do and I'll see if I can rustle us up something to eat for breakfast. Also some coffee and maybe some underpants."

Brandon grinned at the screen, then caught Paul's arm and tugged him down for a quick open-mouthed kiss. "You're a mind-reader."

Chapter 14

"You all finished?" Paul asked, suddenly aware of Brandon looming in the doorway.

Brandon sank down beside him on the sofa in a loose sprawl. "As much as I can get done from here, yes," he answered. "Sorry to ignore you like that—not a very good host of me, I know. Thanks for breakfast." He'd finally gotten dressed in a pair of dark jeans and a ring-necked T-shirt that showed off his arms, but his feet were still bare. Which was more erotic than it really should have been, considering the mess Paul was in.

"If it's helping you keep Christopher—or whoever—from threatening or blackmailing me in the future," Paul said, "ignore me all you want. And it wasn't 'breakfast' as much as scrounging for edibles in your kitchen. You weren't kidding when you said you don't cook, were you?" He turned off the TV that he hadn't really been watching anyway and twisted so they were at least partially facing each other. "What now?"

"Now I take you out to experience something fun in Atlanta, because apparently you've lived in Georgia all your life but haven't done anything here. And we enjoy our weekend because there's absolutely nothing we can do about anything at St. Ben's until we get back there tomorrow evening." Brandon grimaced. "I know you're probably eager to charge back and go dive in, but I've got to get the formal go-ahead from a few higher-ups before I go chasing after an individual employee, and they're not going to be checking their work e-mail until Monday at the earliest. Even if we went back now, I wouldn't have access to the databases I'd need. Waiting sucks, I know."

"It's not that bad." Paul was surprised to realize, as he said it, that it was true. "We're here and the rest of my life is there. It's freeing, in a way. I'd rather be here with you than sitting around my apartment, worrying.

Sorry, that probably doesn't make sense—but yes, doing something touristy sounds good. And a real lunch at some point would be nice, too. Pickles and fried eggs and coffee are technically food but they're not exactly part of a balanced breakfast, you know?"

* * * *

After some back-and-forth—and a little more making out and a lot more frantic gasping and a truly spectacular mutual handjob—they ended up at the Georgia Aquarium. Brandon swore he hadn't been for years and Paul had never been at all. The Saturday morning crowds were a bit daunting at first, but once they got inside the entryway the press of bodies dispersed and there was a bit more room to breathe. Brandon handed Paul an exhibit map and waited, lounging casually against the wall, while Paul glanced through it. Nothing stood out as more interesting than anything else.

"I'm just following you." Paul took Brandon's nearer hand without thinking about it—then froze, their hands clasped together. In public. "Sorry, I—"

"It's fine." Brandon squeezed their joined hands and smiled, a tiny little private smile for Paul's eyes alone. "There's nobody you know here, nobody you'd give a shit about who can judge you for the sin of wanting to enjoy a bit of a day off. And I kinda like the idea of wandering around the aquarium holding hands—neither of us really got to do that as teenagers, did we? This is our chance."

They held hands. No one commented. A few people did give them the side-eye, as they wandered down the giant underwater tunnel in the ocean exhibit, but it was easy to ignore the funny looks when they were surrounded by the incredible aquatic panorama outside the tunnel walls.

"This is ridiculously huge," Brandon murmured quietly, leaning in so his breath tickled Paul's neck. "I assumed I just remembered it being big because I was still a kid when I was here last, but yeah—it's actually that big."

"I wonder if they pay any attention to us at all." Paul watched a manta ray float slowly overhead, its body easily twice the length of a person. "We may be the closest thing these poor critters get to a TV."

Brandon nudged Paul's arm and nodded toward a small boy, not much past learning to walk, who was absolutely fascinated by the fish outside. He stumbled along the edge of the tunnel, hand on the glass, staring out at the tank. His mother ambled slowly in his wake, nose buried in her phone, not even watching the scene outside. Maybe they were regulars and she'd seen it all too often to be impressed anymore, but it seemed like a waste of a beautiful moment. Paul caught Brandon's eye and squeezed his hand, understanding without speaking.

* * * *

The only truly awkward moment was when they went to the dolphin show. Brandon warned that it was a bit corny, but Paul countered with *how the heck can you pass up dolphins?* He caught Brandon around the waist and mock-dragged him toward the auditorium. There was a fair crowd there already, fifteen minutes before the doors were set to open, but the press of bodies in the waiting-area-slash-gift-shop just meant Paul had ample opportunity to step back against Brandon and nestle his spine against Brandon's chest as they staked out an out-of-the-way spot in the room to wait.

"I always hated seeing couples get all snuggly like this," he said softly over his shoulder so Brandon could hear. "Silly teenage PDA. But now I want to pull your arms around me and bask in it. I'm feeling giddy. It's like puberty all over again."

"Without the awkward voice cracking and the bullying at school," Brandon murmured in his ear. "I'm not going to pull you around and kiss you right here, but you should probably know that I want to. Very much."

"Just as well you don't—I'd probably kiss you back. And we'd scandalize some of the parents here."

"Look at you. Last night you wouldn't kiss me out in the open with no one around. Today, PDA." Brandon let his hands rest on Paul's hips. Nothing indecent, nothing sexual, but it let him pull Paul even closer and rest his chin on Paul's shoulder. Paul could feel Brandon's chest rise and fall with each breath. "For the record, though, their kids wouldn't care."

They stood like that, barely moving, until the doors opened and the assembled crowd started filing into the auditorium. Brandon snagged them two fantastic seats, slightly off to the side but near the front, just out of range of the "splash zone." They settled in, holding hands and sitting slightly angled in their chairs so their shoes touched. Brandon's eye caught Paul's and they both froze, grinning inanely at each other. It was the most ridiculous thing, Paul knew, but he couldn't tear his attention away from the sheer surprised happiness on Brandon's face. As if he couldn't believe his luck. The cheesy music Brandon had warned about was already well underway, but it didn't require any effort to ignore. Everything was fine until a dark-haired woman with two children in tow tapped Paul on the shoulder.

"Could you not do that?" she asked.

Paul blinked at her. "Sorry, do what?"

"All that in public." She settled her children into the two seats on either side of her—directly behind Paul and Brandon—as she spoke. "My boys want to sit close enough to watch the show, but I don't want them to witness any funny business when we're just here for the dolphins."

Paul was suddenly thrust into the uncomfortable position of realizing he was probably supposed to say something in response, but having absolutely no idea what. He opened his mouth, but no sound came out. Frantically he looked over to Brandon, unsure—

"Sitting next to each other?" Brandon asked, his voice deceptively calm.

The woman frowned. "Just…you know." She gestured vaguely toward the space between Brandon and Paul. The only part of them touching were their palms. "That."

"Hmm. This?" Brandon twined his fingers in Paul's and lifted their joined hands together so she could see. "The exact same thing you were doing with your sons only thirty seconds ago?"

"It's *different*," she snapped. "My boys shouldn't have to see that."

"It's only different if you tell them it is," Brandon retorted calmly. "And they're only going to be more curious now that you've made a big deal of it."

The older of the two boys was indeed watching their conversation with interest, something the woman only gradually seemed to realize. With a huff, she grabbed her children and stalked off to find another seat. Somewhere with a larger buffer against sinners, presumably.

Brandon tracked her with his eyes for several seconds after she left, then let go of Paul's hand reluctantly. "Sorry—didn't really ask if you minded me using you to make a point."

"It's okay."

"Is it?" Brandon twisted a bit to look at him face-on. "I always try to stay calmer than they are—it makes them look that much stupider by comparison—but it drives me crazy how people seem to think that just by existing I will somehow give their children gay cooties. Like I'm some sort of gay plague vector. I could deal with them thinking that quietly, but the pushy ones always seem to want to tell me about it."

"I didn't mean *that*, you twit." Paul nudged Brandon's foot with his own. "I agree that she was being ridiculous. I meant what you did. I didn't mind being a prop." It was fun, in a tweaking-someone's-nose kind of way. "Kind of exciting too—my first bigot! Well," he amended, "the first one to say something to my face who didn't assume I was also straight and just commiserating with them about the evils of sinners these days."

"You get that a lot?"

Paul rolled his eyes theatrically enough to get a tiny smile out of Brandon. "I teach at St. Benedict's—of course I get it a lot. Every darn day."

* * * *

They spent almost three hours at the aquarium. It was long enough to work up a thorough appetite, for food as well as for more chances to touch each other, so they finally left to go find somewhere for lunch. They found a Greek hole-in-the-wall a few blocks away and ended up getting their gyros to-go so they could backtrack to Centennial Olympic Park and eat there. The spring weather was only recently warm enough for local families to bring their kids out and play in the fountains, so the center part of the park was filled with loud and enthusiastically damp children. Paul and Brandon wandered the paths for a bit afterward, enjoying the sunshine, but by late afternoon Paul could tell Brandon was ready to head home. They made their way back to the nearest MARTA station and walked the six blocks to Brandon's apartment.

"Now what?" Brandon asked. "I'm ready to get away from other people's children for a bit, but we can go out again this evening if you want to. Today's for you."

Paul leaned in and pressed a quick kiss to Brandon's lips in response. "You may not have noticed this about me, but I'm kind of an introvert. I was thinking …maybe some video games? And then we can order a pizza or Chinese or something that delivers, and we can stay in our pajamas all evening, and if at some point we happen to end up *out* of our pajamas again…"

The answering predatory grin would have been worth the trip to Atlanta all on its own.

* * * *

Brandon may have generally preferred PC games to console releases, but he still had a nice selection of multiplayer options. "I do occasionally have my friends over," he explained with a bit of a shrug when Paul asked him about it. "Most of them aren't really gamers, not the way you and I are, but we can't go to drag revues and gay bars *every* night."

"You are kidding about all that, right?" The idea of getting dragged along to an environment like that was terrifying.

"Oh, I'm totally serious—I don't think I'd have that kind of stamina. We can save that for tomorrow afternoon, though." Brandon managed to hold a straight face for a full two seconds before cracking and bursting into totally undignified giggles. "Sorry, you just looked—I'm sorry," he panted between snickers. "I mean, I don't go out to those with them as much anymore because I finally decided I'm not into all that, but it's not like we *never* see each other. We usually still get together once a month or so and do whatever. Sometimes it's a bar, yeah, but sometimes we just sit around each other's apartments and gripe about our week. They're all out at a drag show tonight, but I would probably have sat out anyway. My friend Lito has another friend who's performing, but I've only met her once or twice. She won't care whether I'm there to cheer her on or not."

Paul heaved a theatrical sigh and flopped himself backward onto the sofa, pretending he was thoroughly disappointed in Brandon's answer. "I don't think I'm ready to be gay enough for that."

"I understand. It can take some getting used to." Brandon sank onto the other side of the sofa and lifted Paul's legs into his lap. "Like I said yesterday—I spent a couple of years trying to fit in with that world, but it's really not me. Some of the guys got really into the drag scene a few years ago and I love seeing them get so excited about it, but the whole thing never resonated with me the same way. I still go along every once in a while because I like to see my friends, but I'd be just as happy if we all did something a little less..."

"Extroverted?"

Brandon snorted. "Yeah, pretty much."

"Good, because that takes us back to some nice macho alpha-male-fantasy video games." Paul lifted his legs off Brandon's lap and gave his hip a little shove with one foot. "Go pick something out for us. I'm pretty sure I've been too ridiculously happy all day. It's not manly. I need to either shoot things or blow them up."

* * * *

"How the hell are you so good at this?" Brandon dropped his controller into his lap in mock-disgust and stared at the screen, where his character was getting exploded in slow-motion by one of Paul's grenades. "I'm used to either playing online with opponents I assume are mostly twelve-year-olds or playing with Lito and the gang who are all terrible. I *like* being the videogame expert."

"It's because I have no life." Paul kept his character moving long enough for their team to formally win, then tossed down his controller too. "Want to try a racing game instead? I'm awful at those."

Brandon snorted and shook his head, a smile blooming on his face. "It wasn't a complaint. Well, not really."

"Still." Paul went over to the cabinet and pulled out a driving game he recognized but had never tried. "I like the idea of competing against each other and the computer instead of a bunch of strangers. This way we have no one else to blame when we lose."

"What's this *we?*" Brandon asked with a laugh, but he waved toward the console. "Fine, fine, go ahead. But I'm upping the stakes."

"Oh?"

"As long as we're acting like giddy teenagers today, we should add in an element of truth or dare. Winner of each round gets to ask the loser a question. Absolutely anything."

Paul thought it over as he swapped out the discs, but nothing *bad* came to mind. Brandon already knew the big secret he'd been keeping from everyone for so long—what else was there to hide? The always-cautious part of his mind yelled that this was a *terrible idea*, that he was going to ruin what was turning out to be a very good thing, but there was always the possibility that he'd get to ask Brandon something too. "I guess I'm game."

They dove into the game with way more gravity than the bright cartoon graphics would have suggested. Brandon waited until he had thoroughly trounced Paul at the first race before admitting, "by the way, this is the one the guys and I play the most. If you were curious."

Paul flipped him off. It was a novelty; he'd never done *that* before, as far as he could remember, but it was turning out to be a week of firsts. Brandon smirked and leaned back against the cushions of the sofa.

"So. Question. We'll start off easy—how did you come out to your twin sister, and how did that go? It sounds like it would be an awkward conversation no matter what, but you said yesterday she took it badly."

"It was. And she did." Paul thought back, trying to remember their exact words. "It was the week after finals, right after I got home. Her school finished before St. Ben's, so she'd been back a few days already. Mom and Dad were both at work, I think. Danielle and I were sitting around on her bed, just catching up, and she asked me if I'd met any pretty girls."

"And you told her girls weren't your thing."

"Not in so many words." God, it was still awkward to even think about. "I admitted I'd kind of met someone, and she got all excited and started peppering me with questions, and I remember wanting to say it was you and just not being able to get the words out of my mouth. Danielle has always been able to read me better than anyone else—she picked up on it. I'll never forget the look on her face."

A touch on Paul's wrist startled him. Brandon was covering his hand with his own, present but not pushing. "What was it?" he asked.

"Pity." Paul closed his eyes, the memory still fresh in his mind. "She looked at me and asked if I was gay. It took me forever to form the word 'yes.'" He sucked in a deep breath. *Right.* "And then she asked if I was sure, if I'd...if I'd tried it with a girl. I said no, but I knew, had known for ages. And she nodded and we didn't talk about it again for months, until Thanksgiving break. Didn't talk about anything much. Things were strained. By then she'd come around a lot—she gave me a hug and said she was sorry for not being more accepting and she's been my biggest champion ever since. She'd like you."

"I'm sorry it didn't go better for you." Brandon rubbed his thumb over the back of Paul's hand, back and forth. Hypnotic. "Everything is hard enough without adding an unsupportive family."

"It's gotten better," Paul amended. "I mean, there's still no way I can tell my parents, but Danielle spent most of the past weekend gushing about this French guy she's dating and lecturing me on how I need to find a nice boyfriend and settle down." *Bit awkward to bring that up now, with him looking at me like that.* "She's totally gung-ho about being an ally."

"That's good." Brandon let go and picked up his controller again. "Another round?"

He won again, of course, but not by as huge a margin this time. "Second question: Why did you stay at St. Ben's? Even if you didn't want to come out to your family, you could have transferred to a different school."

"Like you did?" It was a valid question, but with a complicated answer.

Brandon grimaced. "Not necessarily... I didn't mean it that way. Not saying you were wrong to stay; I was just curious."

It was only natural, Paul supposed. In retrospect, St. Ben's probably wasn't the healthiest college environment for a probably-gay-but-very-closeted guy, but it had been the path of least resistance. "I guess I wasn't ready to change," he finally said.

"Wasn't ready to accept that you were attracted to other men? Or wasn't ready to deviate from the trajectory you'd already planned out?"

"Definitely the latter. But it was more than that." Paul leaned back against the cushions, letting himself stare at the ceiling for a minute while he tried his best to put it into words. "My parents are pretty conservative—not as strict as some, I wasn't homeschooled or anything, but they always did see the world in black and white. Still do. Even if I never told them why I wanted to transfer, I would have still had to wrestle with the idea that I was giving in to this compulsion for sin inside me. As long as I stayed at

St. Benedict's, as long as I kept all my lustful thoughts to myself and tried very hard to pray myself straight, I wasn't a failure yet."

Brandon made a choked sound, which drew Paul's attention back down to him. He was sitting very still, his jaw clenched. "Do you think of yourself as a failure now?"

"Not now, no." It had taken a long time to get to that point. Years, even before the thing with Christopher. "I did a lot of thinking. A *lot* of praying. I accept that I'm gay, that I can't do anything about that and there's no point in trying. And I can't…I just can't believe that God would make me gay, give me this biological drive, and then punish me for it. If you're going by the Old Testament prohibitions, it's all a sin: masturbating, thinking lustful thoughts, premarital sex, all of it. But by the same token, so is divorce and birth control and refusing to force your dead brother's wife to marry you. So why do divorce and masturbation and birth control get a pass from almost everyone, but being gay doesn't? Even if I keep it hidden? I finally decided that if God loved me, He was going to accept me as I am, imperfect and all, and it was making me miserable to second-guess what He wanted me to do. All I can do is try to be a good person and a good Christian and pray that it's enough. I do still get this feeling of residual guilt sometimes, but I *am* gay and that's not going to change."

Brandon swallowed and nodded, closing his eyes. "That's … That's good. What you're doing. That you've thought it through. And I can respect that, even if you're coming at it a bit differently than I did."

He looked so concerned. Paul put down the controller and stood up. "Me next—can I request a dare this time?"

Brandon looked up at him with confusion. He didn't point out that—according to the rules of their little game—Paul needed to win something first.

Because he needs this just as much as I do. "Here it is: I dare you to come to bed with me. I want to hold you for a while and think. I need to do some more thinking tonight. A lot of it, I suspect. I'm sick of second-guessing myself, but you deserve better than me floundering with self-doubt. And I do too."

Brandon smiled slightly and took Paul's outstretched hand. They got ready for bed in silence. And when Paul finally fell asleep, it was with Brandon spooned up around him.

Chapter 15

"Wake up, sleepyhead."

This time around, it was Paul's turn to blink blearily up at Brandon. Who was awake enough to have gotten out of bed, thrown a bathrobe on, and magically produced two cups of coffee from somewhere in the distant recesses of the kitchen. Paul propped himself up against the headboard and accepted one of the mugs gratefully. "Coffee make awake go," he joked with a straight face. "Paul un-function no caffeine."

"Har har har." Brandon settled back into bed next to him, careful not to jostle the mattress too much and cause either of them to spill. "Yes, this is my second cup, which is why I'm capable of complete sentences. And I know you're more of a morning person than I am, but I've seen you drink it before so I know you're not opposed to a little help."

"Not complaining." It was pretty good coffee. Brandon had gotten the half-spoonful of sugar and the brief slug of creamer almost perfect. Paul shot a pointed glance at the clock and arched one eyebrow.

"Fine, so it's earlier than I'd usually choose to get up on a weekend," Brandon admitted with an eyeroll. "I wanted to show you something, but we need to get moving sooner rather than later."

Paul adopted a dramatically suspicious accusatory look. "It involves getting out of bed? After you kept me up so thoroughly last night?" The languid cuddle at bedtime had been fantastic, but somewhere around two in the morning they both found themselves awake again and the languid cuddle transformed into a silent but heated exchange of kisses and then blissfully slow handjobs. Sleepy-snuggly-sex wound up replacing shower sex as Paul's favorite erotic memory of Brandon sometime in the last several hours. Which was decidedly wonderful: The more memories to choose from, the better.

"I only claim half responsibility for that, you know." Brandon smirked and stretched his free arm over his head, blatantly showing off the triangle of chest currently displayed beneath his bathrobe. "Mmmmm. I call dibs on the first shower, since I doubt you'll be budging until you've finished your coffee."

He was right, so Paul didn't bother with a response. Although he did get sidetracked wondering whether Brandon had boxers on under that robe or whether he was totally nude.

"We've got about forty-five minutes before we need to leave, so I'll be quick. Wear whatever you've brought; it's fine." Brandon drained the rest of his mug, leaned over to press a quick kiss to Paul's stubbly cheek, then hopped off the bed to go put it in the sink.

* * * *

"Where are we going?"

"You'll see when we get there." Brandon zipped through the Sunday morning traffic with the ease of someone who was used to driving in Atlanta and taking no prisoners. "It's a good surprise, I hope."

That doesn't sound promising. "You hope," Paul echoed.

Brandon's confident smile turned a bit fragile. "If you don't want to go, it's no big deal, but after last night I thought you might be curious. Here we are."

Paul caught a glimpse of a large signboard advertising service times. Then they were pulling into the parking lot of a large church built in some sort of modern style, all sweeping curves and elegant landscaping. Brandon shot him a look and pulled into the nearest parking space.

"So here's the thing," he said, turning off the car and twisting in his seat to face Paul. "You've been at St. Ben's for, what, a decade now? And everyone there has made this big deal about how you must be a bad Christian and a terrible role model if you're gay. But there are plenty of places you can go that don't treat you like a second-class citizen for being LGBT, and I wanted to show you mine." One side of his mouth twitched upward a bit in a tiny self-deprecating smile. "Okay, more accurately it's my brother's, but I don't really have a 'home church' and everyone here has always been more than welcoming to me. Even when I was in my glitter-and-musicals phase. I'd love for you to see what it's like for *all* of you to be welcomed somewhere, not just the not-gay parts."

A gay Christian is a contradiction in terms. Paul's father's favorite rant echoed in his head. His parents both had rather strong views about what should or shouldn't be acceptable for a "good Christian," and homosexuality was near the top of the *shouldn't* list. Another reason Paul had never really thought about coming out of the closet. Still, though, for Brandon to be willing to share this … "This is the oldest brother, right?"

"Yep – the married one with two kids. You'll meet my sister-in-law and niece and nephew today, if they're here this morning." Brandon shrugged awkwardly. "I didn't want to tell them we were coming, in case you decided you'd rather we just go back home, but when I'm here we usually sit together for the service and then do lunch afterward."

"Ah." Even beyond the whole church aspect, this felt like a huge step, something like *MEETING THE FAMILY* in giant flashing marquis lettering. Brandon was willing to share this, even though it meant he'd undoubtedly be the butt of some serious teasing if and when he and Paul went their separate ways.

Wait, when did that "if" sneak in there?

This was about more than just reconnecting with an old friend and enjoying some consequence-free sex. Brandon was offering him this, an unexpected solution to his ongoing identity crisis. And Paul would be the biggest jerk in the world if he turned it down.

He met Brandon's slightly nervous gaze, nodded, and got out of the car.

* * * *

"You said this wasn't your church," Paul murmured to Brandon as yet another sharp-eyed older woman spied them from across the communal gathering area and descended with the clear intention of acquiring a hug. "So how does everyone know you?"

"I'm Eric's prodigal brother, who shows up on occasion when not traveling for work," Brandon murmured back. "And who is perpetually single. I swear half the church has tried to set me up with friends and coworkers and recently-out grandsons at some point. People hear 'gay' and immediately start matchmaking. It's their way of showing their queer friends and family that they're supportive, I suspect."

Paul thought about his parents' own church. And his mother's attempts to set him up with the daughters and nieces of all her friends. "It's not that you're gay," he said. "They'd be equally bad if you were straight. You're just a darn good catch."

Brandon shot him a private little look—one which was *way* too hot to be appropriate for a church hallway—but then they were swept up with the social niceties of Brandon introducing his "friend" Paul once again. The little old lady currently in front of them reacted as if Brandon had just announced they were engaged—"We're all so glad to see you back, and with a *friend!*"—and practically rubbed her palms together in excitement. "We're always happy to have you here, you know. Eric and Anita's pew looks so empty when you're gone." She shot a glance over Paul's shoulder. "Speaking of whom—Eric, you didn't tell us your brother was bringing a *friend* this morning!"

Paul turned around and found himself face-to-face with a slightly older, clean-shaven version of Brandon. Eric looked at Paul, then Brandon, then Paul again, then finally remembered his manners and offered his hand. "Eric Mercer. And my little brother never tells me anything, so I apologize we didn't come over to say hi when we first came in. Anita!" He waved over a short woman carrying a toddler and casually transferred the little boy to his own hip. "My wife, Anita. This is Liam and the girl spinning in circles over there near the bulletin boards is our daughter, Kimberly. It's really nice to meet you."

Anita was a gorgeous woman of indeterminate ethnicity, with a long black braid almost down to her waist and beautiful brown eyes. Liam had her eyes, but his shock of dark hair was almost a mirror of how Brandon's looked when he first woke up in the morning. A thought Paul was very careful to keep to himself. "Paul Dunham," he answered, shaking hands with Eric and Anita and tapping Liam's tiny shoe with one finger. "Brandon's told me all about you, of course." He didn't miss the slight widening of Brandon's eyes—a clear *oh hell I'm going to get crap for this from my brother later aren't I* look. "I've been looking forward to meeting the brother who features so heavily in all Brandon's embarrassing stories."

Eric threw his head back and laughed. "Oh, I definitely like you. You two coming to the house for lunch afterward? I've got tons more embarrassing stories I'm sure Brandon hasn't told you yet. There was this one time—"

"Yes, okay, thank you," Brandon interrupted. "Gosh, we better get moving, shouldn't we? Wouldn't want to miss the prelude."

Anita flashed Paul a silent smile, but it was a sign of welcome. They split, the friendly old lady to go take her place in the back pew "before someone else claims it" and Anita to shuttle Liam to the nursery and Kimberly to the children's service. Eric led Brandon and Paul to the sanctuary and to what Paul assumed was their semi-regular place.

"It's pretty relaxed here," Brandon whispered as they got settled. "The pastor's new—well, she was new last year—but I doubt there will be anything really different than what you're used to."

"Pretty sure even the fact that there's a female pastor would be enough to upset some of my parents' church friends," Paul whispered back. "This is beautiful, though. I don't know what I was expecting, seeing the church from the outside, but this wasn't it."

And honestly, it really was gorgeous. The sanctuary was an irregular shape, wide curves along the back and obtuse angles in the front, but it worked. The stained glass windows were modern and abstract and colorful in the morning sunlight. The friendly pre-service milling about was familiar. Anita slid into the pew between Brandon and Eric just as the prelude started, and Paul lost himself in the music.

It was a lovely service. Nothing political—about homosexuality or otherwise. The pastor was funny and the choir was very good and even though Paul really wasn't used to the whole "slideshow of song lyrics" method of presentation, it wasn't as odd as he thought it would be when he first saw the projector. It helped that Brandon had a gorgeous voice—it was easy to get lost in the experience, listening to Brandon singing on one side of him and the rest of the congregation on the other and everyone so astoundingly *relaxed* about being there together to worship God. It felt like they were all a comfortable family and were happy to welcome him into their midst.

The sunshine was pleasantly warm as they exited the church afterward, a beautiful spring day. Paul and Brandon were stopped a few more times on their way out the door—more people coming to say hi and to subtly or not-so-subtly tell Brandon they were excited to see him "with someone." But then Eric and Anita reappeared with the kids and somehow there were confirmed lunch plans. Brandon extricated the two of them from everyone else wanting to wish him well, and they escaped to the car.

"So what did you think?"

"It was wonderful." Paul wasn't entirely sure how to verbalize how eye-opening the morning had been—wasn't sure *he* was able to parse it all yet. He'd known more liberal churches existed, in theory, but *being* in one, being a part of the worship community … Paul leaned back against his seat and closed his eyes. "I didn't realize how much I've been feeling trapped, honestly. I don't want to have to give up being a Christian, but I've never been terribly good at toeing the line. It always felt like if I failed to keep myself away from this big temptation, I was failing God."

Brandon nodded, but stayed silent while he pulled out of the parking lot and headed back toward the highway. The radio was off, the sun was warm and bright through the windows, and St. Benedict's was a long way away. Paul watched the traffic outside and smiled quietly to himself for the rest of the drive.

Chapter 16

"So how do you know Brandon, then?" Eric poured four glasses of lemonade and started handing them around while Anita sliced some French bread and fiddled with whatever was in the Crock-Pot. "I hope it's not too awkward if I mention that he doesn't often bring guys to church."

"We reconnected recently." Paul smiled politely, hedging a bit. Brandon really hadn't said whether it was okay to allude to their... Well, it was hard to call it anything other than a relationship between them at this point, but Paul was still a bit vague on whether "fuck buddies" or "exceedingly persistent one-night stand" was the most accurate. And with Brandon in the living room with the kids, there wasn't really a frame of reference for how he was supposed to answer.

"You've known each other long?" Anita asked, looking up. She caught Eric's expression and shrugged. "I'm always interested to hear what your brothers were like before I met you; you know that. Especially Brandon, he's changed so much even since we were married."

"He did mention a bit about that," Paul said. "We hadn't seen each other for almost ten years before last week—we were in the same hall at St. Benedict's, freshman year. Brandon transferred out that summer, so we were only friends for a semester or two, but—"

Eric sputtered and choked on his lemonade. "Holy crap, you're *that* Paul? My God, that's...wow."

"You don't have to make it sound so dramatic," Brandon announced from the doorway. He had Liam on one hip and Kimberly twined around his other leg, practically sitting on his shoe. "But yes, he's *that* Paul."

"Holy crap," Eric repeated.

Paul looked back and forth between the two brothers. They really did look very similar—slightly different build, and Eric lacked Brandon's beard, but they both had the same dark-brown-almost-black hair with a hint of curl, although Eric's was longer. Same shaped nose, same eyes, and they were shooting each other identical expressions of sibling affront Paul knew *very* well from seeing it on his own sister's face so many times. "Should I be worried?" he asked.

"Oh, they're both capable of behaving," Anita declared breezily. "Given the proper incentive. And something to do. Eric, could you please get Liam changed out of his nice new polo shirt before he spills something on it? Kimberly, you may help your Uncle Brandon set the table. And Paul, I could use a hand transferring the chicken dip to a serving bowl—could you grab me one? That top cupboard there. I hate how nobody designs kitchens for short people like me. It's not like I'm the only five-foot-two person ever."

"It means I can hide your Christmas presents on the top shelves and you'll never find them," Eric retorted with a grin, before pressing a kiss to the back of her head in passing and taking Liam from Brandon's arms. Kimberly started talking a mile a minute, then, all about some TV show Paul had never heard of that she had conned Brandon into watching at least once before, and fifteen minutes later they were all settling down to some absolutely amazing lunch. The adults spooned the chicken and cheese mixture onto slices of freshly-warmed French bread and ate them as open-faced sandwiches; Kimberly and Liam resentfully dragged both their bread and their fingers through the puddle of chicken dip Anita had insisted on depositing on each of their plates. It was the kind of comfortable, home-cooked meal Paul hadn't had in years, and he was generous in his praise of both the food and the company.

"You don't get this much anymore, do you?" Brandon asked with a grin after Paul gave Anita another, perhaps overly, enthusiastic compliment. "I get the impression you cook more than I do, but it's not the same when it's only for yourself, is it?"

"Yeah, well, just because I *can* cook doesn't mean I do." Paul hadn't realized how much he'd missed this kind of domestic scene. It had been the standard at home growing up, but then he and Danielle had gotten into high school and there were soccer games and youth group meetings and they'd never had time to eat together as a family anymore. Now the big family meal experience was reserved for holidays and whenever Danielle was able to get back home, and it was always awkward in a way it hadn't been before he'd had such a big secret to keep. He took another bite. "I would say I need this recipe, but I know realistically I'd never have an occasion to cook a whole Crock-Pot of chicken dip at once. We don't really even do potlucks much in my department."

"Paul's teaching at St. Ben's now," Brandon said. "And it kind of blows my mind that I'm old enough to have peers in positions of authority."

"You and me both," Eric quipped, and Anita smacked his leg under the table where the children couldn't see.

"I have a teacher too," Kimberly announced. "Her name is Miss Stevenson and she's really pretty and she said I'm the best at counting in the whole class."

"You are?" Paul asked, the distraction welcome. "Are you in kindergarten yet? Or is this preschool?"

Kimberly was happy to monologue for the rest of the meal, with occasional prompts from Paul and Brandon. Conversation only wrapped up when Liam decisively slammed his little palm down in his chicken dip and smeared it through his hair before Eric could stop him, and Kimberly started laughing so hard she lost her train of thought but didn't want to surrender the floor. Anita scooped up Liam and shooed the rest of them outside to enjoy the sunny weather while she cleaned up. Eric led the way to the back porch, which had a patio table and chairs and a fair assortment of toys. Kimberly selected a purple ball that came nearly up to her waist and was off in the grass chasing it before the adults had even had a chance to sit down.

"So, St. Benedict's," Eric said. "What do you teach?"

"Psychology," Paul answered. "It's not a huge department, so I've got a random smattering of courses instead of just in my discipline, but my research focus is on human behavior. Specifically on logic and decision-making."

"No rats in mazes?"

Not any more, thank goodness. "That was undergrad. Worked in the lab for two summers, literally running rats through a radial-arm maze. They smell, they take forever to learn anything, and the breed I had to use was known for biting whenever they got the chance. It was a miserable job."

"So you decided to specialize in something with fewer rodents."

"Oh, definitely. In cognitive psych, all I have to deal with in experiments is freshmen."

"Let me guess," Brandon interjected. "They get extra credit in your class?"

"Nope. One of the school-wide course requirements for Psych 101," Paul answered with a grin. "It's not like I'm the only one needing test subjects. If they don't want to participate, they can write an extra paper instead, but nobody does that."

Eric sat forward, looking honestly interested. "So, what, you're running the college students through the mazes?"

"Almost. Decision-making scenarios." Paul thought back to the research proposal he'd been tweaking for the last month. The one he should have been finishing up this weekend, since the deadline was in five days. "Right now I'm studying how emotion affects the decisions we make: Do you make less rational decisions when you're angry or happy or bored or stressed? If so, why? The concept seems pretty simple, I know, but designing an experiment which gives useful quantitative data is harder than it looks. We make choices every day, and they're rarely the 'right' ones from a pure logic perspective. Human emotion is a weird thing."

"I don't know," Brandon murmured. "I find I'm kind of enjoying it right now." He eyed Paul up and down and flashed a slow, sensual smile.

Eric rolled his eyes with predictable sibling annoyance at his younger brother's expression, but Paul couldn't find it in himself to care. He knew he had the exact same goofy grin on his own face.

* * * *

Paul stuffed his weekend clothes back in his duffel and tossed it in the backseat. Brandon packed with a little more care, but they managed to get on the road with no real complications.

They both sat in silence. Paul tried to find something on the radio, but all the stations on Brandon's presets turned out to be on commercial. "So that was your brother," Paul finally ventured.

"Yep. Creepy how much he looks and sounds like me, right? Everyone always says that."

The lunchtime visit had wrapped up mid-afternoon when Kimberly threw a bit of a tantrum and Liam had needed his nap, but Paul couldn't remember the last time he'd felt so *welcomed.* Eric and Anita had seemed fine with hanging out to chat, which had eventually devolved into Paul and Brandon and Kimberly sitting on the floor playing with toy cars while Liam toddled around them babbling cheerfully in mostly-incomprehensible toddlerese. It was nice to sit there and just *be.* Paul had always had Danielle as a companion when they were kids, but he couldn't remember his parents ever being as engaged with them as Eric and Anita were with their offspring.

"I did notice," he said when the silence was about to get uncomfortable again, "that Liam's hair sticks up exactly like yours does when you first wake up in the morning. I figured I shouldn't say it, though. Might have made things a bit awkward."

"Yeah, thanks for that." Brandon shot him a sidelong grin. "I'm going to get teased enough about you already."

"About that. Um." Paul stared out the window a minute. *How do I word this?* "Not that they weren't lovely, but… It seems like we went from 'nice to see you again, let's get off together' to 'meet the family' awfully quickly. I'm not sure how I feel about it, to be honest."

Brandon sobered, but he didn't dismiss the tentative not-actually-a-question out of hand. "I didn't mean for it to come off like that," he said after a moment. "Although I see what you're saying. You said some stuff last night that got me doing some thinking too. About how you were approaching your sexuality like it was this big forbidden thing. That you felt like you had to 'pray yourself straight.' And I thought it shouldn't be like that. For you or for anyone. And if you were feeling held back by the idea that God couldn't accept you as a gay person, I wanted you to see that not every Christian says that. Getting to play cars with Kimberly and hear Eric tell you all my embarrassing childhood stories—which you totally bluffed about already knowing, by the way, so screw you for that—that was all a bonus. I'm going to get teased, probably for quite a while, but I decided you were worth it."

For one long moment, Paul let himself imagine it: himself and Brandon, living in some suburban house like Eric and Anita's, coming home from work and kissing each other hello and grilling burgers on the back porch and who knows, maybe even a kid or two playing in the yard. The American dream. The thing he always assumed he'd have to marry a woman to get. They could join a church somewhere—an open church, where they'd be welcomed and not have anyone try to "fix" them—and he could finally stop hiding. Could he do that? Was he even *capable* of maintaining a relationship? It's not like he had the best track record, and his parents would—

Hell. His parents would hate him forever. It wouldn't just be some new freedom to "be himself," it would be burning bridges with everything and everyone he ever cared about in his life to date. He'd have to give it all up for even a chance at the dream. He took a long breath and slumped against the back of the seat. *I hate this.*

"I'm sorry," Brandon said abruptly. "I guess it was kinda presumptuous of me. To assume you could just turn it all around like that." He kept his eyes on the road, but his grip tightened visibly on the steering wheel. "Not all churches are the same, so I totally won't blame you if you want to tell me to go jump in a lake or something. I suppose if you grew up with a stricter religious background, it might make the more liberal churches look…well, fake, I guess. It's okay."

Paul stared at him for a long moment. *Screw it—he's here, I'm here, and I'm not going to balk now.* "Come stay with me," he said instead.

"Hmmm?"

"When we get back to St. Ben's." Paul hadn't thought it through before he spoke, but he suddenly realized he very much meant it. "There's no reason for you to be paying for a hotel room every night, and—" *I want you in my bed with me.* "—I don't want to avoid my apartment forever. Staying there alone that one night was horrible, but I don't want to let Christopher—or whoever—keep me from my own home."

Brandon looked dazed. "You sure?"

I'm sure I want to wake up beside you every chance I get—and if those chances are running out, then all the more reason to keep you near me. "I'm sure."

"That would be nice." Brandon cleared his throat. "Let's find somewhere to pull over up here and I'll call the hotel."

They stopped at a gas station at the next exit. Paul filled the tank, since it was only fair that he pay for gas after bumming most of his meals for an entire weekend, while Brandon looked up the hotel and called. He wasn't technically supposed to be able to get a refund for that night, since it was a same-day cancellation, but having a corporate account got you little perks like that. He was wearing a smug smile when Paul got back in the car.

"Done," he announced, and leaned over to place a chaste kiss on Paul's lips. "I'm all yours now. Bodyguard, bed-warmer, and all."

Paul didn't want to admit to himself how nice that sounded.

* * * *

They got back to the apartment right as the sun was setting. There were still adequate groceries in the fridge from the previous week—mostly because they had been eating out so much—so Paul threw some cubed pork and apples together in a skillet with some walnuts and a bit of brown sugar and Brandon deemed it the best home-cooked meal ever. Which was patently not true, but by the time they sat down to eat they were both shirtless and more than a little turned on, and Paul could have been eating shoe leather for all he would have noticed. They left the dishes in the sink and spent the rest of the evening in bed.

It was fantastic.

Chapter 17

Brandon headed off to campus early the next morning. Getting up at seven required two cups of coffee and a lot of aggrieved muttering, but he came back into the bedroom to kiss Paul one more time before he left.

"Meeting," he grumbled. "It's with all the people who need to give me permission so I can dig further into your Christopher's records, so I'd better be charming."

"He's not 'my' Christopher," Paul countered. And then softened under Brandon's renewed kiss. "Thanks, though," he added.

Brandon pressed a last, chaste peck to the top of Paul's head. "May not be him at all, for all we know—although from what you've said, he fits the profile. Introvert, tech-savvy, and with a grudge against the school. I'm kind of hoping it is him, at this point; it would mean my half of the work will be a lot easier."

"Your half?" Paul raised himself up to a sitting position and scrubbed a hand over his face. "Gah, sorry, still mostly asleep. You were in a hurry."

"Not *that* much of a hurry." Brandon nudged Paul over and sank down on the mattress next to him. "It's only fair you should get the whole story, I guess. You know how you're supposed to be my liaison with the psych department?"

Paul nodded.

"The original plan was for me and my team to go through everything on the university servers, file by file, and run each one by someone who should know what's supposed to be there. It's—if I can be blunt—a spectacularly stupid idea."

"Why?"

"It would take forever. And so far, they're only letting me look at *most* of what St. Ben's has sitting around—I'm supposed to let my departmental liaisons look at any 'sensitive' files and report back to me if something looks off."

Paul snorted. "I highly doubt Dr. Kirsner would approve of me snooping through anything like that. No wonder this is so hush-hush."

"Like I said, a fucking stupid plan. I'm hoping to talk my way into getting unlimited administrator access, though, so I don't have to go through intermediaries. Which would also be stupid of them to allow me, but it's the easiest way to get on top of this, and someone up the chain is already not too bright because the president has administrator access anyway."

"That's bad?"

"You've met him, I'm sure. Do you really think a man like that needs to be able to make back-end changes to the official website? Or to go mucking around in the salary database?"

Paul thought back to his last conversation with the current St. Benedict's president—the man was practically a Luddite. Albeit good at glad-handing and securing donations from rich alumni. "I see your point."

"I'm going to go out on a limb and say he didn't trust your IT department, so he demanded an administrative account so he could 'keep an eye on things.' He's the president so, of course, no one will say no to him. I'm going to make another wild guess and say that he's probably not very good at picking passwords."

Paul blinked. "You think Christopher—or someone else—guessed his password? That's all there is to it?"

"That plus the technical know-how and actual physical access to the server room, yes." Brandon leaned in for one last, take-no-prisoners kiss, then forced himself up off the bed. "Right. Off to work. You enjoy your no-classes-until-eleven Monday morning schedule and I'll see you tonight, all right?"

It wasn't quite a "see-you-later-I-love-you," but it felt close. Paul spent the next two hours catching up on housework and wondering whether he liked it that way or not.

* * * *

Brandon sent a text at 5:30 that he was in the car, but he didn't get back to the apartment until closer to six. Paul had supper well on the way when Brandon walked in the door.

"Hi, honey, I'm home." Brandon grinned and set his laptop case down next to the kitchen table. "That smells amazing. Probably sounds pathetic to say this, but I've been thinking about you all day."

"It's mutual." Paul gave the chicken another poke with his spatula. There was something comforting about being *able* to cook, even if he usually didn't bother. Usually on a weekday evening—well, *any* evening—he was already sitting on his sofa and burying himself in a game and pretty much zoned out for the rest of the day. This afternoon, though, he'd zipped off campus as soon as his two o'clock seminar finished and swung by the grocery store on the way home. He wandered the aisles, wondering about what sort of fruit Brandon would like best, whether he drank skim milk more often than 2 percent, and whether he might prefer salmon to tuna. It had been a while since Paul last did a good stock-up-the-pantry grocery run anyway; he told himself it wasn't *entirely* because he wanted to impress Brandon.

Still, though, by the time he got home he had all the makings of chicken Florentine and another hour (or two) until Brandon got back. Enough time to throw in a last load of laundry, finish cleaning the bathroom, and generally become shockingly domestic in a fantastically short amount of time. Paul knew he hadn't done this much cleaning all on the same day since—

Since Christopher. Crap. Some of his all-day happy buzz melted away.

Brandon pressed a kiss on his lips right there in the middle of the kitchen, as if they'd been doing this forever. As if he could make this their daily routine. "Got a voicemail from my mother today," he announced after they finally broke the kiss so Paul could stir the chicken and spinach mixture. "Anita called her and she's decided she wants to meet you."

Paul blinked and turned to look at him over his shoulder. "What happened to 'it's not like that?'"

"I told her we weren't dating. She wants to meet you anyway." Brandon pressed up against Paul's back as they faced the stove, leaning his chin on Paul's shoulder and wrapping his arms around his waist. "Mmmm—I love the way you smell, you know that? Anyway, she asked if I'd be willing to bring you along to the house party she's holding the Saturday after next. I said I'd ask you about it."

"I…" *Saturday after next. He's expecting to be around that long?* Paul pulled away slowly, sliding sideways to get out from between Brandon and the stove. "You mean, like, almost two weeks away?"

Brandon shot him a puzzled look. "If you're already busy, that's no problem—I didn't say yes yet."

"It's not that, it's…" Paul held up his hand to keep Brandon from coming closer. "You just—you presented this like it was some convenient thing while you happened to be in town. And now you're inviting me to meet your mother." A casual post-church invitation to lunch was one thing, but a pre-planned "meet the parents" date was something else entirely. Something Paul felt very sure he wasn't ready for. Something that smacked of a permanence and a commitment he wasn't entirely sure he would *ever* be ready for. "It just, you know? Taking me to meet your parents? You've been really upfront about how you don't 'do' anything more than casual, and this feels like more than that."

Brandon opened his mouth, then closed it again. "You don't want this to continue?" he finally said. "Because it's clearly gone beyond a one-night stand at this point. I don't bring my casual fucks back to my apartment for the weekend. Hell, not even for the whole night. I don't cuddle with them on the couch, or spend time just playing games, or take them to church because I think they're unhappy with the way their own church has always treated them and I care about their well-being. We may not be 'dating' in any formal sense, but I assumed we'd be able to still see each other sometimes even after I go back to Atlanta. Not just a week-long hookup. Turns out I want more than that with you—I thought I'd made that obvious."

Yeah, he had, and Paul had the sinking feeling it was entirely his own fault for not picking up on it earlier. He'd convinced himself he didn't need a commitment when Brandon wasn't offering one. He could scratch that annoying gay itch he'd been ignoring for so long since Brandon would be gone in a matter of weeks. Then he'd compounded it all by going along with Brandon for an entire weekend—staying at his stupid apartment, for goodness' sake—all without ever having a conversation about what "this" was. What it was very clearly turning into. And it wasn't something he could walk away from with no explanation, not now.

Paul turned his back on Brandon, rather than answering, and pointedly focused his attention on the skillet. "You said you wanted this because you were bored and you were going to be in town for a week or two," he said without looking up. "You said you *liked* not having to deal with someone else in the morning. We've had a week and it's been fun and all, but it's… I'm not looking for a boyfriend."

"I see." Brandon's tone was flat, empty, but Paul didn't dare turn around.

"I have enjoyed it." Only fair to make that point perfectly clear.

"I know," Brandon answered. His footsteps retreated to the living room and changed to muffled rustling as he wandered around on the carpet instead of the kitchen's linoleum floors. "You seemed like you were okay with this yesterday. *Very* okay with it, actually."

"I've got no complaints about your technique in bed." *Quite the opposite.*

The pacing stopped. "Then tell me I'm not imagining that you just pulled a fucking June Cleaver on me not five minutes ago," Brandon demanded.

"You were happy to see me, you kissed me back, you're cooking me dinner. You didn't have to do any of that. Do you see how you're sending mixed signals here? Why I might have assumed we both want something more than a while-I'm-in-town-and-convenient fuck? Because I know you do, Paul. Don't lie to me."

"It's…" *Damn it.* "I'm just not in the market for a long-term thing. Not with a man, anyway."

Brandon's sigh was nearly inaudible, but Paul was listening for it and caught it anyway. "You're still chasing that 'perfect family' dream, then?" he asked quietly. "After everything."

Chasing and chasing and being with you means going in the wrong direction. Paul said nothing. The chicken looked done and the spinach was nearly wilted past the point of edibility. "Dinner's ready."

The weight of Brandon's gaze on Paul's back was making his shoulder blades prickle. "Okay," Brandon finally murmured, defeat in his tone. "You want to eat at the table? Or on the couch?"

"Couch is fine."

They sat on opposite ends of the sofa and watched half of some terrible reality show because it was the first thing that came up when Paul turned on the TV and neither of them bothered going to the effort of changing it. The chicken was overcooked after all. Paul found himself wanting to tell Brandon about his day, but there was nothing much to say. Same old same old. They ate mostly in silence.

"I should probably get some more work done," Brandon announced when they were nearly finished and the TV show was over. "Get a head start for tomorrow."

"Use the kitchen table—there's an outlet right there for your laptop if it needs to be charged."

"Thanks." Brandon rinsed his plate and left it in the sink with the other dishes, then pulled out his computer. "I've still got to go through a ton of old spreadsheets to see if anything's been altered—mind if I do the psychology department first? Since you're here?" He focused overly intently on the process of plugging in the laptop and turning it on, not looking up to gauge Paul's reaction to his question. "I mean, if you'd rather I leave you alone, I can do something else and we can talk about it tomorrow. An official meeting, if you want. Sticking with the original plan."

Crap. "Brandon, I—"

"Or I guess—is it all right if I stay and work here? I don't mean to assume. I can call the hotel if you'd rather have me out now. Thanks for dinner, by the way."

"Brandon." Paul slid into the seat across from him and forced Brandon to meet his eye. "I'm not kicking you out; you're welcome to stay. For as long as you're working at St. Ben's. I really do appreciate that you're doing this for me, I'm just..."

"I get it," Brandon said softly. "I'm good enough for a casual fling but I'm not long-term material. You're not the first to feel that way about me—I should be used to it by now. I've had practice getting over it, anyway. So thanks for letting me crash here in the meantime. I'll try to get this job finished as soon as I can so I don't impose too much."

"Wait." Paul reached across the table and grabbed Brandon's hand. Brandon startled a bit, but didn't yank it away. "It's not that, and you know it. You're a wonderful guy and if I were looking for that, you'd be at the top of my list. This has been great. Eye-opening, even. But I can't keep it up forever, and I've been upfront about that since the beginning. I'm sorry."

Brandon grimaced and dropped his eyes back down to his computer screen. "Thanks. I'll deal, I suppose. Sorry for assuming too much."

Paul squeezed his hand and offered a pasted-on smile. Brandon returned it.

* * * *

They spent the next few hours in semi-awkward silence, apart from occasional questions about various spreadsheets and psychology department projects. Brandon only got up from his seat when he needed to get himself a drink or to use the bathroom. Paul played through a handful of missions of a first-person RPG without taking in more than a few words of the story. They both stood up by unspoken mutual accord somewhere around eleven o'clock.

"You want to brush your teeth first?" Brandon asked. "I feel like I need a shower before I go to bed, so it might take me a bit."

"Sure. Thanks." Paul raced through his nighttime routine, threw on some pajama pants, and curled up on what had become "his" side of the bed. Would Brandon want sex tonight? Paul wasn't opposed—this had been a week of personal firsts, and most of the sex-related "firsts" were things he'd enjoy seconds and thirds and fifths of—but maybe Brandon wasn't in the mood. Even just getting to sleep next to him would help ease some of the tension, though. Paul lay in the near-dark and listened to the sound of the water running in the shower. Imagined what Brandon looked like when wet. Thanks to that little interlude in Atlanta, he knew *exactly* what he'd be seeing if he were in there with him. Not that his bathroom was anything to brag about, and not that two people would *fit* in his shower, but still.

He was nearly asleep when Brandon finally came out. There was a click as Brandon turned off the hall light, then a long silence. Paul's last waking thought was the realization that Brandon wasn't coming to bed—a thought which was confirmed by the squeak of sofa springs. He must have still been mad enough to prefer the old, lumpy sofa to Paul's bed as long as Paul was in it.

The bed felt cold all night.

Chapter 18

Paul drifted through his morning lecture on autopilot. Usually he enjoyed this class because this section of students happened to be generally motivated to learn something, behaviorism was inherently interesting, and unlike Grace's 8 AM section of the same course, almost nobody overslept a ten o'clock lecture. They were finally past the basics of Pavlov and Watson and up to the interesting bits like Tolman's latent learning, which was obvious when you thought about it—surprise surprise, you can learn things by doing them regularly even if you never get a specific reward—but ended up being surprisingly revolutionary at the time. Logical, easy-to-understand eureka moments lent themselves well to undergraduates paying attention in class, which was good for everyone. Paul really had no excuse for being even more out of it than his students were.

Well, he did—his thoughts were almost entirely on Brandon. Not a good excuse, but an excuse nonetheless. Brandon, who had smiled politely and thanked Paul when he offered to make their morning coffee and who had generally pretended everything was fine even though he'd slept on the hideously uncomfortable couch. There'd been an invisible wall between the two of them, though, and Paul hadn't been able to break through. It was physically painful to think about, so why couldn't Paul stop poking at it?

It's excuse enough. And maybe he wasn't quite as energetic about his odd historical anecdotes and punny bad jokes as he usually tried to be—it's not like his students were in a position to complain. Everyone did seem relieved when he released them a few minutes early, though. Maybe his teaching really was suffering more than he thought.

"Hey, you!" Grace caught up to him in the hallway and flashed him a cheerful smile. "How go the behaviorists?"

"About as well as expected." She was wearing a mid-length floral sundress and low yellow heels. The outfit was probably a bit more summery than the weather would warrant, but it looked good on her. Not particularly "professional," but good. Her hair was down in loose waves cascading over her shoulders, and all Paul could think was that she'd look right at home on a sunny Sunday morning at his parents' church.

"Have time for lunch?" she asked, falling into step with him. "I was on my way to grab a sandwich, but I'm not feeling picky. And I don't have anything until two."

"Me either." Paul checked the time on his phone, even though class got out at the same time each day and this late in the semester he really shouldn't have had to look. Having someone to talk to would help keep his mind off the whatever-it-was with Brandon from the previous night. "I'm up for whatever—want to take our chances at the cafeteria?"

Paul noticed the day had warmed up quite a bit over the course of the morning as they walked across the quad. Maybe the sundress wasn't such an unseasonal choice after all. It was nice. Pleasant. And chatting with Grace was comfortable. They'd known each other long enough to have lost any awkwardness between them ages ago, but the psych department was spread out enough that they rarely got a chance to simply catch up. It's not like there was a central water cooler to hang out around. Most of the time Paul didn't mind—he had very little in common with most of the other faculty—but right now it was nice to trade mild gripes about schedules and students and school politics.

"I heard you're heading up the big secret project," Grace said, nudging his shoulder with her own. "Did you make up with Dr. Kirsner, then?"

"What pr—oh, the computer one?" *The one I'm supposed to be working with Brandon on.* "Didn't really have much of a choice."

"Is it really some big super-secret thing?" She brushed a lock of hair out of her face and grabbed cafeteria trays for them. "There was a definite air of mystery surrounding the rumor—all I heard was that some consultant needed a 'departmental liaison' and Dr. Kirsner centered on you."

Paul shrugged. "He said I was best for the job because I'm the biggest slacker in the department and therefore I had the time. Not quite in those words, but you know how he is."

"Wish I didn't." She grimaced. "Is it that bad?"

"It hasn't been all that much work so far," he answered. "Met with the consultant, who turned out to be a guy who'd been on my hall freshman year. Of all the weird coincidences. Anyway, he's doing some sort of hocus-pocus with the whole university's databases and needed someone who knew where all the bodies were buried. Or something." He pasted a casual smile on his face. "May not even need me after all, he said. It's probably nothing."

"Someone from our year? Here? Who?"

"Do you remember Brandon Mercer? Little taller than me, dark hair, computer geek?" *Amazing chest, gorgeous brown eyes, and a seriously tempting little smile that promises a multitude of sins?* He very carefully shoved that last part back down into the recesses of his brain where it belonged.

Grace pursed her lips. "His room was on the second floor next to the stairs? I didn't get to y'all's wing of the dorm much—I mostly spent time with the other girls—but I think I do know who you're talking about. Transferred somewhere else early on through, is that right? All I remember about him was that he had a nice smile. And he was pretty outgoing for a comp sci major."

"Pretty outgoing for anybody," Paul said. "He still is."

"I think it's cool that you're getting to reconnect." She handed Paul his tray as they got in line. "I mean, I know you weren't close, but sometimes it's fun to see how people have changed."

You have no idea. All, Brandon had gotten sexier. The beard was a good look for him. And Paul was incapable of going ten seconds without mentally drooling over the man. *Darn it.*

They got a table near the wall at the far end of the room. The dining hall was busy like usual around lunchtime, but most students tended to sit in the same general places each day and the farthest section ended up being unofficially reserved for faculty and grad students. Grace handed Paul a napkin (long-standing habit between them, since he invariably forgot to grab one on his way through the cashier's line) and said a silent prayer before picking up her sandwich.

"How's Danielle doing?" she asked.

"She's good. In the States for a few weeks. My mom and dad are all in a dither because she met some guy who lives in the apartment across the hall from hers. She sounds positively giddy whenever she talks about him."

"Ooh!" Grace's eyes lit up. "Someone French? She's in Paris, right? Is it serious?"

"French-Egyptian, and yes to both. I think my dad is disgusted she couldn't find a literal American in Paris."

Grace snorted, coughed, then daintily covered her mouth until she finished her bite. "I can't—wow, I mean, from all you've said about her I guess I *can* believe her finding a French guy, but that makes visiting the family hard. Good for her, though. Everyone deserves to have someone. Even if he's French."

"You and my mom would get along great. I swear, Dad was about to blow a gasket, but Mom must have talked to him because I haven't gotten any tearful calls from Danielle and it's been a whole week now since she dropped the bomb on them. I went home that weekend and it was awkward the whole time."

"That's how it works at your house?" Grace winced. "I've always wished I had a sister. For that kind of thing. I mean, not that I've made all that many tearful phone calls home, but..."

"Oh, I get you." They'd had a good long talk a few years ago about what it was like to be a twin, and Grace had confessed to being insanely jealous that Paul had always had someone there for him. She'd even met Danielle a few times, over the years, although never anything more than a passing conversation. "I guess this is where I admit I haven't made many either," he added. "Maybe one or two. That I'll admit."

Her eyes widened for a moment, and then she ducked her head and snickered. "Sorry, I just—I don't see you as the whole melodramatic type. You're always so...so ..." She waved vaguely at him across the table. "You're *you*. Unflappable, is that the right word? Dependable, maybe. I feel like I always know where I'm at with you."

I'm glad you do, because even I don't usually know where I'm at, Paul's inner voice snarked. *Dependable? Unflappable?* Those both sounded like good synonyms for *boring.* Paul's sandwich churned unpleasantly in his stomach.

"Boring" had its advantages, he reminded himself. It was safe, for one. And it didn't get him in the middle of complicated relationship messes with people like Brandon Mercer, for another. The whole idea of having a family, settling down, moving gracefully into middle-age—those were "boring" at the core. And yet.

"Speaking of types." Grace set down the last remaining bite of her sandwich and leaned forward, as if she was about to tell him a secret. "The computer consultant you're working with—Brandon—what do you think of him?"

"Um." *Crap, isn't* that *a loaded question.* Paul quickly sorted through a whole variety of inappropriate answers until he finally settled on, "He's nice, I guess?"

"Still at least passably good-looking?" She bit her lip, failing to hide her smile. "You're a guy so you probably wouldn't notice, but I remember him being...yeah. I've got an idea."

"He's better-than-average, I guess?" Paul absolutely couldn't bring himself to say *gorgeous* to Grace. "Short hair, programmer beard, no creepy scars or missing teeth or anything. And now I'm kind of scared to hear what your idea is."

She swatted his arm. "Nothing bad, honestly. It's just—you remember my friend Anne? Adjunct in the English department? She went through an awkward breakup a few months ago. Not that her boyfriend didn't deserve to be dumped, but it was rough on her too. And better-than-average nerdy guys are *definitely* her type."

"Oh." Paul took a too-big gulp of his water.

"Anyway." She took a much daintier sip of her own. "She gets free tickets to the spring play. Sounds like half her students are in it, from the way she's been passing on second-hand stories about the rehearsals. They're doing *The Mousetrap*—it's an Agatha Christie mystery, all 'theater in the round' and up-close and whatnot. And it occurred to me that it would be a nice venue for a date. If you think Brandon would be into that sort of thing."

"I really wouldn't know." Paul could feel his cheeks heating, now, and prayed the lousy lighting would hide his blush before Grace noticed. "We weren't friends all that long, back in undergrad. He was only here for the one year. I'm not sure I'd be comfortable setting him up on a blind date—"

"See, that's the thing." She popped the last bite of sandwich in her mouth and smiled at him, all innocent excitement. "I agree that it would probably be weird and awkward to just shove them together for the evening. But if we call it a double date, it wouldn't be so strange—and if they absolutely hate each other, we can just all watch the play and it won't be a big deal. I know you've suffered through worse, and this play is a pretty good one. We could all go out to dinner afterward or something, depending on how it goes. They're general seating tickets, no specific date, so we can be flexible about what night we go—I think it starts on Thursday."

"I ..."

"Oh, come on." She reached across the table and grabbed his hand, squeezed it. "Worst that could happen is that you get a free night out with me and the 'mystery' turns out to have been the butler the whole time. You'll live."

That was hardly the worst thing that could happen, but Grace's eyes were wide and shining with enthusiasm and Paul found he really didn't want to turn her down. Didn't want to mention that Brandon probably wouldn't be interested in Grace's friend. Didn't want to announce, *"Actually, Brandon Mercer and I are kind of 'fuck buddies' at the moment—I think—but he's also disappointed in me for not wanting to sign up for an exclusive relationship so it might not be that fun of a night after all. We probably wouldn't get to that dinner."*

Instead he squeezed Grace's hand, pinched his lips together, and nodded. "I'll ask him," he heard himself promising, "but I'd say don't tell Anne until I let you know how it goes."

Chapter 19

Paul picked up Thai again that night. Cooking would have been too much of an admission that yes, he did want that "perfect family" dream, and yes, he was even willing to bend over backward to make the house (or apartment) a happy home for his partner and himself. He had done it with Christopher, for all the good it did then. Because at the time, it had felt like getting to take care of someone was the most important thing in the world. *Not going to repeat that mistake.*

"Hey." Brandon offered a tired smile this time, but no middle-of-the-kitchen kiss. "Thanks for doing dinner again—at least let me pay you back? I know I'm a lousy cook, but I want to contribute something."

"It's fine." Paul forced himself to return the smile. "I know we had a lot of takeout last week, but I didn't feel up to cooking today."

"You're already being incredibly generous by letting me stay with you here," Brandon said. "Don't feel guilty if you don't want to do a whole bed-and-breakfast routine." He stepped up to the counter and opened the brown paper sack to peek inside. "Thai tonight? You remembered what my favorites are—it looks good. Where are your forks?"

They worked together, Paul giving occasional directions when Brandon couldn't find something, to get the food dished out onto plates and the table set in at least an approximation of civility. Paul felt oddly formal sitting down at his kitchen table with another human being, especially with honest-to-goodness napkins instead of paper towels and food on real washable plates instead of straight from the to-go containers. Eventually the lack of conversation between them started to get awkward, but Paul didn't know what to say.

"I made some progress today," Brandon eventually commented. "Proof that whoever did this was indeed using the president's administrator account. Given what you told me about Christopher and the details I could get from HR, I started looking at the backups from right around when he was fired last year."

"Fired—not laid off?"

Brandon shrugged. "Employers always cover their asses for that kind of thing, but his record says he's 'not eligible for re-hire' and that sounds an awful lot like 'fired' to me. Anyway, I *did* find some discrepancies. Doesn't prove it was him, but it does prove that this has been going on for at least that long."

"What kind of discrepancies?"

Brandon pinched his lips together, then let out a long breath. "I'm probably not supposed to say. Nothing to do with you, though."

"Oh. Um. Okay." There was no reason to feel bothered about it, so why did it hurt so much to be shut down? It's not like Brandon hadn't said right upfront that this project was supposed to be secret. Well, sort-of secret. In any case, there was no reason for a psychology professor who didn't even have tenure yet to know the intimate details of a complicated electronic forensic operation.

"I promise I'll keep you in the loop on anything I think you need to know," Brandon offered.

"All right, thanks." Paul pushed back his chair and stood up. "You want some more ice water?"

"Yes please."

Paul took their two glasses over to the counter and set them down so he could use both hands to prod at the ancient icemaker in the freezer. It was a crappy machine, probably original to the apartment building, but it did eventually produce ice when given enough time. Which then usually melted into one consolidated lump, often with the wire thingy embedded into it. There was a ding from somewhere behind him.

"Text," Brandon said. "From someone named Grace? She says..." His voice trailed off.

Crap. Paul plunked a misshapen lump of ice in each of their glasses and turned around to go retrieve his phone. Which was currently in Brandon's hand. Being stared at blankly by Brandon.

"Thanks, I'll just..." Paul took the phone with a bit of a stale smile and thumbed the lock off.

We still on for our date? Thursday or Friday work best? Having dinner with Annie tonight, so let me know :-)

"Paul," Brandon asked in a deceptively calm voice, "who is Grace?"

Crap. Crappity crap crap. Paul felt his face begin to heat, which was so *not* helping. "She's a colleague," he offered lamely.

"Is my presence here this week interfering with your social plans?"

"No, of course not." Paul dragged his hand through his hair and took a deep breath. "It's not what you think."

"Ah," Brandon said. "I'm misconstruing the word 'date,' then? There's some other definition I don't know about?"

Shit. Somehow "crap" wasn't working well enough as a mental expletive anymore. "I had lunch with her today," Paul said. "There's not—we're not dating or anything."

Brandon's gaze lowered pointedly to the phone.

"It's just…" *Damn it.* Paul sighed. "Fine, so we ran into each other and had lunch, right? She and I have known each other for even longer than I've known you—she was in our freshman dorm too. Plus we had a few classes together. She's the closest thing to a friend I have in the psych department. Anyway, we had lunch and she asked me about you—"

"About me?" Brandon interrupted.

"About the mysterious computer consultant I was supposed to be the 'departmental liaison' for," he clarified. "She wanted to know if you were attractive."

Brandon blinked. "You told her about us?"

"*No!* Christ!" Paul tossed his phone back down on the table, the text message still blinking accusatorily between the two of them. "She asked about you, I said you'd gone to St. Ben's with us back in the day, she said she vaguely remembered you. And that her friend, Annie, in the English department is recently off a bad breakup—"

"Oh *hell* no," Brandon muttered.

"—and Grace had this brilliant idea of us all going on a double-date. Together. This weekend."

Brandon just stared at him.

"I froze up and didn't know what to say so I told her I'd ask you," Paul finished, "and now I have. There. That's it."

Brandon was still staring.

"I didn't…" Paul had to look anywhere other than that betrayed glare. "I didn't plan to go through with it, if that makes you feel better," he muttered. "Was going to tell her you were busy."

Brandon sucked in a long breath, then nodded. "I get that you don't want a boyfriend. You've made that *perfectly* clear. You want the white picket fence and the lifetime tenure and the girl your parents would approve of. But you'd expect me to, what? Go back in the closet and pretend I'm straight for a night so you can make eyes at someone else? Someone we both know you would never feel anything for?"

God, it sounds terrible when he puts it like that. "It wasn't *my* plan," he countered. "Just something Grace thought up."

"If I did say yes, though." Brandon cocked his head, eyeing Paul. "If I said yes, you'd go through with this."

"I…" Paul had to pause for a long time to get his words together, but Brandon just watched him. "Yeah, I would. She's been hinting around it for a while, but I shouldn't keep putting it off forever. It's kind of inevitable, really."

If Brandon's eyebrows went any higher, they would become part of his hair. "Inevitable how?"

"It just is." Paul spread his hands, at a loss for how to explain it. "It's not like I'm going to meet any other women, not here. The only people I ever see are my colleagues and my students. Grace and I know each other already, we've been friends for ages, and she's *nice*. Sweet. She *is* that good Christian girl my parents would approve of, and if I don't finally acknowledge her interest in me, she's going to get bored and move on to someone else and I'll be out of options. Once you leave, it may be time for me to bite the bullet and ask her out anyway."

"Once I leave," Brandon echoed without inflection. "No qualms about fucking me and then kicking me out, I take it. Thought that was my usual thing, not yours."

"What do you want me to say?" Paul snapped. His flailing arm caught one of the glasses and nearly knocked it to the floor—only his quick reflexes saved it from shattering. He put it back on the counter with a deliberate calmness he didn't feel. "What do you want me to say?" he repeated, more quietly. "That I'm in love with you? That I'll give up my career and my parents and my life for you? We barely know each other, Brandon. I can't announce 'Hey, I'm gay now!' like you did and expect everything to be fine. I thought this was just supposed to be a mutually beneficial thing. We could hang out together, kill some time, and both get off a few times while you were in town. I didn't sign up for a relationship. Even a not-actually-dating friends-with-benefits thing."

"No," Brandon growled. "No, I suppose you didn't. I'm being unreasonable, aren't I? I offered you a no-strings-attached fuck and that's what you wanted." He stood and held his arms out to the sides. "Fine—here I am. Let's do it. Fuck me."

Chapter 20

Paul froze. "That's…that's not—"

"I mean it," Brandon said. He reached up and started unbuttoning his shirt. "You're all worked up right now, and so am I. It's the perfect time for an orgasm or two. To get it out of our systems, since we're oh-so-conveniently both here." He wrenched the shirt off and tossed it to the floor, then grabbed the collar of his undershirt and yanked it off over his head. "You just going to stand there?"

Paul didn't really have a choice—Brandon, angry and shirtless, seemed to have short-circuited whatever higher brain function he had. He could feel himself getting hard, a conditioned response to seeing Brandon's naked chest, and *damn it*, it wasn't supposed to be this way, sex wasn't supposed to be some sort of macho challenge.

"Fine, I'll do it." Brandon stomped over to him and yanked his shirt tails out from his khakis. "Touch me," he ordered, and bent down to suck a wet bruise against the skin under Paul's right ear.

Oh God. "Brandon, I—"

"Less talking, more touching," Brandon snapped. He rapidly worked his way up Paul's shirt, popping the buttons without even looking, until he could yank the two halves apart and skim his palms over Paul's shoulders to nudge the sleeves down off Paul's arms. They caught on his hands, the wrists still buttoned, but Brandon just grabbed the shirt sleeves behind Paul's back and pinned his arms while he slid his other hand underneath the zip of Paul's khakis. With their bodies this close, Paul could smell Brandon's deodorant and shampoo and a hint of sweat. It was all mixed up with the Thai spices on his breath and it was nearly too much, too quickly. He moaned aloud, unable to stop the sound before it escaped.

"Please," he breathed.

"Please stop, or please do *this*?" Brandon slid his hand lower, cupping Paul's balls through the fabric of his boxers, and gave them a firm squeeze.

Paul's breath tangled on a gasp.

"Fuck, yes," Brandon hissed. "You want this, don't you? Want me? You're trying to be all polite, all better than this, but I can tell you want to get off just as much as I do. I. Can. Feel. It." He slid his hand up and down, pumping Paul a few times through the thin cotton, until Paul couldn't stop his hips from nudging forward into that delicious pressure. "How do you want to fuck tonight, then?" he whispered in Paul's ear, low and filthy. "Want me on my knees right here on your linoleum, sucking you off as you lean back against the fridge and gasp? Want me to keep your hands all tangled up like this so you can't move, so the only thing you can do is thrust into my warm, wet mouth? It would feel fantastic—an excellent way to shut me up, just choke me with your big damn cock. Fuck my throat until you get off. That what you want?"

Yes. No. Paul gulped in a deep breath and closed his eyes. This was Brandon feeling hurt, he knew, but the combination of sensations and those filthy words were practically melting his brain. Brandon had such an advantage over him, in this arena—he clearly knew *precisely* what to do, where to touch, what to say. It was too much and not enough all at the same time. But—and it took another two deep, gasping breaths to identify the problem—*everything was all wrong.* He wanted to feel Brandon's mouth on him again, of course, but not like that. Not without the kissing and the touching and the snuggling in bed at two in the morning and the slow slide of wet skin against wet skin in the shower and *damn it*, none of that was his to ask for. None of it. This was supposed to be about biology and one last round of experimentation before setting down with a nice innocent partner like Grace who would never think of offering anything like an after-work against-the-fridge blow job.

"Oh, I get it," Brandon murmured against Paul's earlobe, interrupting his rapidly derailing train of thought. "We've done that already. I'm supposed to be teaching you things you've been missing. Isn't that what I'm here for? Let's try this, then." He let go of Paul's erection and tugged at his khakis instead, managing to work them down to mid-thigh even with just the one hand free. Paul was now pinned up against the door of his refrigerator wearing nothing but his undershirt and boxers, his pants and shirt both half-off and useless. Brandon looked amazing wearing only his work pants, but Paul felt more rumpled than sexy.

"What are you—"

"I'm getting you out of your clothes, obviously," Brandon growled. "Might keep the shirt like this. I like that your hands are tied. It stops you from trying to take control. Lets me show you *exactly* how this is supposed to go." He ground against Paul again, the zipper of his trousers an unpleasant intrusion into what would otherwise have been a seriously hot maneuver. "I've been gentle with you, on account of your lack of experience, but clearly that's not what you want. So merry fucking Christmas, you're getting your wish. I'm going to take you back to your room and lay you out on that bed of yours and bring you *almost* to that peak. Right like you are now, boxers on and all. And then I'm going to stop, and I'm going to make you wait, and I'm going to strip us both the rest of the way. And then I'm going to go dig the lube out of my bag and I'm going to sit across your thighs so you can't buck me off. Positioned just right so your cock is crying out for my mouth or my ass but you can't do anything about it because your hands are still all tangled up in your shirt and I won't let you up. And I'm going to push up to my knees and finger myself for you, right there on your bed kneeling over you, right where you can watch. You liked what we did in my shower back at my apartment, didn't you?"

Yes. No. Paul whimpered something that could have been either assent or rebuke.

Brandon must have interpreted it as agreement, because he delivered another long, delicious glide of his hips against Paul's and this time the zipper wasn't in the way at all; it was just a fantastic hard pressure on the other side of those thin layers of fabric. Brandon groaned too, this time, a truly obscene noise.

"Fuck, yes," he ground out. "Going to lube myself up nice and pretty for you, letting you watch. And then I'm going to sit on your cock and ride you until you can't even remember your own name. My ass is going to be the best thing you've ever had your dick in, I promise you that—going to make you beg for mercy before I let you come. I might even give it to you. Eventually. After I've ridden you long and easy and then fast and brutal and then so slow I'm almost not moving, so you think you're practically ready to die if I don't finally push you over that last little bit. Going to make you come so damn hard—"

"Stop." *Too much, too much, too—*Paul squeezed his eyes closed and fought to regain his equilibrium. "Brandon, I don't—"

"You haven't," Brandon corrected. "That doesn't mean you *can't*. That's what you want me for, isn't it? A convenient hole? Well I'm willing. And I'm an excellent teacher—"

"No." Paul turned his head to the side, sucked in air like he'd never have oxygen again. It felt like he wouldn't. "It's not like that; you know it isn't. Just because—"

"I'm not going to balk just because you've never fucked someone's the ass before," Brandon retorted. "You said it yourself: I'm just good for getting off with. This is a 'mutually beneficial thing,' and I *know* we'd both mutually benefit from me getting to ride your cock. I'm going to show you what you'll be missing when you go marry some quiet little Christian girl who'll never touch you like I'm doing *right the fuck now.*" He punctuated his statement with a little grind and twist, planting both hands on Paul's rear and pulling the two of them tightly together. "This is why you want me—"

"I said stop!"

Brandon froze for a long moment, then stiffly backed away with his hands up in surrender. "Fine. Fuck it—fine. You don't even want me for that anymore—I can take a hint."

Paul struggled with his shirt cuffs, eventually managed to get his hands free. Brandon was just standing there looking stormy. Paul ran his fingers through his hair—a gesture he tried not to do anymore, since it made his hair stick up in stupid little tufts—and attempted to sort through the minefield of his thoughts.

Brandon is angry? Check. Disappointed? Paul took in the line of Brandon's stance, his crossed arms, his posture. *Possibly. Probably. Hurt and embarrassed? Yeah, a bit.* Brandon was glaring, now, but Paul didn't think he was imagining the hint of pain in his eyes. *Okay, a lot.* Ashamed that he pushed too hard and didn't read Paul's (admittedly garbled) body language well enough? Or was it because Paul had turned him down?

"Look," Paul said quietly. "It's not that I don't want you—"

Brandon interrupted with a dismissive snort.

"Hey," Paul snapped. "I told you upfront that I didn't do that stuff. I'm not going to be some item on your damn bucket list. I didn't do it with Christopher and I'm definitely not going to do it with you to indulge your little temper tantrum—"

"You know what? Fuck you." Brandon grabbed his undershirt and pulled it back on, then retrieved his button-down and shoved his arms through the sleeves without bothering to fasten it back up again. "I'll be in touch if I need anything more from you for work—otherwise, you might as well delete my number."

Hell. "Brandon—"

"Shove it," Brandon growled. "I'm headed back to my hotel."

"But you canceled—"

"I'll find another one."

And with that, Brandon grabbed his briefcase and stormed out the door.

Chapter 21

Paul went to bed alone. Woke up alone, showered alone, ate breakfast alone. There was a brief period in which he was not alone, when one of his students finally came to his Wednesday morning office hours and consented to pick a topic for her final paper, but after that he was alone again. Paul reviewed his lesson plans for the next three weeks, checked his e-mail every ten minutes, and gave what was probably the finest intro to developmental psychology lecture in the history of St. Ben's. He polished his funding paperwork until it practically gleamed, wrote his cover e-mail, attached the proposal, and reread it one last time. And then paused when he got to the section outlining the necessity of his study.

Decision-making is frequently necessary in situations that offer inadequate data to accurately predict the statistical probability of desired outcomes. The somatic-marker hypothesis holds that such decisions are affected by emotions, physiological affective states, which then consciously or unconsciously interact with future perception to influence the illusion of statistical certainty. The importance of further study...

Paul grimaced. *In other words, people are terrible at predicting what's going to happen when their emotions are in play.* He pretty much knew the entire experimental justification word-for-word by now—knew all the research standing behind it, knew the ins and outs of every paper in this corner of his field—but never had it hit him before that he was included in that generalization. Never really had a decision worth analyzing before, either. Not since choosing this topic to dedicate his research to, anyway. Breaking up with Christopher had been more of a necessity than a decision, and everything else had essentially been one smooth progression flowing from the initial declaration of "I want to study psychology someday" all the way back in high school.

Staying with Brandon would require giving up everything, though. That's what it really came down to. And the cool, rational part of his brain kept reminding him that he didn't *really* know Brandon that well, not truly, especially after spending a total of less than two weeks together after a full decade apart. It was completely illogical to be missing him so terribly—they'd survived without each other for ten years, and then for eighteen years before that. What if Brandon turned out to have some terrible, hidden secret? An ex-wife and a kid hidden away in Minnesota, maybe. Or a prison record. Or a history of dating naïve guys, coaxing them out of their closets, and then abandoning them as soon as they cut ties with all the homophobic friends and family members in their lives.

Yeah right. He was working himself up into a ridiculous state, all because Brandon Mercer turned out to be the man of his dreams—dreams he'd never wanted to acknowledge he had in the first place. Dreams he couldn't afford.

"Paul?"

Paul shook off his reverie and returned Grace's smile with one of his own. "Hey."

"Hi." She tucked a lock of hair behind her ear and ducked into the room. "Happened to see you were here and I wanted to ask—have you talked to that consultant yet? About the play?"

"I haven't seen him yet today," Paul answered truthfully. "Probably safest to assume it's a 'no,' though—he's been pretty busy."

"Oh." Her face fell. "I was starting to really look forward to it. I guess, um… Let me know if you get the chance? Or if you want to go without him." Her eyes widened and she immediately began to backpedal. "I mean, doesn't have to be a date—"

"Thanks," he said, before she could make the moment even more awkward. "I'll let you know when I have an answer for you."

"Thanks, I'm holding you to that. I appreciate how you're always so reliable." She made an aborted movement, probably an impulsive handshake, but she thought better of it. "I should get going, I guess. Class in ten minutes."

"Me too." Paul threw his notes for his two o'clock seminar into his briefcase and stood up. "I hope at the very least you and your friend will get to see the play." *And I need a long walk, alone, before I can decide anything else.*

* * * *

He headed from his seminar directly to his car, and from there to his usual park. Once again the hiking trails were nearly empty, despite the gorgeous weather. *Sunny and warm just to spite me.* It was a stupid thought, but Paul was grumpy enough to half believe it. He walked until he was exhausted, until he was well and truly sweating through his gray dress trousers, which were in no way appropriate for hiking, but he hadn't wanted to take the time to go home and change. If he went home, he'd end up putting his things on the table (where Brandon had eaten) and sitting down on the sofa (where Brandon had slept) and staring at his game collection (which Brandon had called "impressive") and never getting back up again. How had Brandon managed to so thoroughly infiltrate his life in less than two weeks?

Oh right—because Paul *had* no life. Ninety-five percent of his time was spent either at work or hanging out in his apartment. No friends outside of St. Ben's, no hobbies, no thrilling secret identity going out to fight crime, nothing. His life was in a holding pattern, had been for years, and he'd been too blind to realize it.

Paul slowed to a stop at the trailhead and forced himself to drink about a cup and a half of lukewarm, rusty-pipe-flavored water from the park drinking fountain before collapsing onto one of the picnic benches near the parking lot. He was sweaty enough for his work clothes to be sticking to his skin, which meant he was probably dehydrated—not going home to change meant not bringing his own water bottle, either. The drinking fountain was usually a last resort, but it was a nice amenity to have available for days like today.

"Thought I'd find you out walking."

Paul jumped about a foot in the air and whirled around.

"You look hot—I bought you a bottle of water on the way. Here." Christopher held out a Dasani with a tight smile. When Paul didn't move to take it from him, he set it down on the picnic table between them as if ambushing your ex with bottled drinks was a totally normal and expected part of anyone's day.

"Christopher, what are you doing here?" Paul asked.

"Isn't it obvious?" Christopher sat on the bench next to Paul and leaned back against the table, his body facing away from Paul but invading his personal space nonetheless. "You had a rough day, so you came here to think like you always used to do. Boyfriend troubles will do that—he's not much of a hiker, then, I assume?"

Paul suppressed his immediate instinct to panic. "Sorry, who?"

Christopher laughed. It sounded forced and fake. "Brandon Mercer? The guy you've let stick his dick in you? Really, if I'd known you were that desperate for some action, I would have come to see you sooner. It's been a while."

Paul's gut roiled at the look on Christopher's face. "*What?*" He took a deep breath, let it out slowly. "Christopher. Why are you here? Why are you following me?"

"Because you need me." Christopher crossed his arms and cocked his head to the side, a mannerism Paul had seen him do countless times in the past. "Who's going to take care of you otherwise: you? Your boyfriend?" He nodded toward Paul's sweat-stained work clothes. "You can't even do something as simple as wearing actual exercise clothes when you're going for a walk. You forgot to bring water. You're lucky I remembered, otherwise you'd have to do with that lizard-flavored piss that comes out of the public fountain. And I know how you hate that."

"I..." Paul glanced over Christopher's shoulder at the mostly-empty parking lot. Nobody there to overhear them, although that didn't mean someone couldn't drive up at any minute. As stupid as the idea was, it made Paul feel a bit safer—even if Christopher was completely batshit insane, he surely wouldn't risk doing anything violent in a semi-public place, would he?

"Look, you don't need to pretend with me," Christopher continued when it became apparent Paul wasn't falling all over himself to thank him. "I know you're lonely. I know you miss us living together. And even though you don't deserve it, I forgive you for going out and slutting it up the moment my back was turned. Brandon Mercer has kind of a long history of fucking random men, you know—him condescending to suck you off doesn't make you special."

"Have you been..." Paul opted against spying. "Checking up on me?"

Christopher barked out a canned laugh. Playing the all-around nice guy role, like Paul had just been making a joke that fell flat. "I do still care about you," he said. "Look. I know we all make mistakes. It's part of being human. And you needed some time to realize how miserable you are alone. But I know you, and you deserve more than some traveling faggot who will have completely forgotten about you the next time he's dick-deep in some other faggot's ass. You're better than that. We both are. I was giving you some time to come around, but then I realized you probably didn't know I would be willing to take you back. I'm here to tell you now—I really do forgive you, Paul." He dropped a heavy hand on Paul's knee and squeezed it. The gesture was practically paternal. "My new apartment is bigger than our old one—plenty of space for your videogames and all your nerd crap. It's much better than your current place. Being on the first floor isn't safe, you know—leaving all those games in plain view is pretty much asking to have your window smashed in and your collection stolen."

Crap. Crapity crap crap. Still nobody around in the parking lot. He should have recognized Christopher's car—there it was, an omnipresent white Ford Focus, just like the millions of others out there. Paul had eventually stopped expecting them all to be Christopher's, but maybe he should have been paying better attention. Was Christopher threatening him, or was he seriously delusional? *He's making it sound like our breakup was merely some big misunderstanding, a 'phase' I was going through. No mention of how I finally got up the courage to kick him out and change the locks.*

"Hey." Christopher squeezed Paul's knee again, and Paul couldn't suppress his flinch. "You're still acting like you have to think about it."

No. No thinking required. Paul pulled his knee away and twisted so there was a bit more space between them. "It wasn't a mistake," he said with a good deal more bravado than he felt. "We're not—we're not compatible. God, it was so obvious! How did you not notice?"

"What, because you're trying out playing gay?" Christopher rolled his eyes. "I got over that ages ago."

"Oh, *I'm* playing gay? You're the one trying to talk me into moving in with you."

"Because it's...fuck." Christopher put his hand back in his own lap where it belonged, but he would have rather been shaking some sense into Paul. "It's not like that, and you know it."

"Right—how, exactly?" Paul took the opportunity to scoot backward a few more inches and turn so they were facing each other. "Because from here, it looks like you don't have a lot of room to talk."

"It's different," Christopher insisted. "You and I, we just work. We come home and you play your videogames and I surf the internet and we trade off cooking dinner. We're just roommates who like to get off on occasion. It's not like either of us are going to go get our ear pierced or start listening to chick music or go march in some faggy pride parade—none of that gay stuff. You're trying to pretend for your new fling, but it's not going to work because you're not the kind of flaming fucktoy he usually goes for. Seriously, have you *seen* his friends' Facebook pages? Half of them are drag queens."

He looks so earnest. That was the one thing surfacing above the maelstrom of Paul's thoughts. Christopher seemed to truly believe that Paul was just going through some sort of experimental gay phase and would give up on it sooner or later. And that he'd come crying back for whatever scraps of attention Christopher could be bothered to give him.

And then it hit him: He probably would have, eventually, if it hadn't been for Brandon. If he'd known he'd be facing decades upon decades of being in the closet, of dithering over whether he could pretend to be straight enough to date someone like Grace (who really deserved better) or whether he'd have to constantly deflect attention from his sad lack of a personal life. Eventually he'd have said "screw it" and settled down with Christopher—or someone like him—and maybe he'd have called it a "relationship" and maybe not, but he'd have been *miserable.* Because no "we're roommates, mostly" scenario could possibly be as good as waking up next to Brandon every day. Or of watching Brandon smile that little smile of his and seeing that glow in his eyes that meant he was truly, honestly happy they were in each other's presence right that very second. Of shower sex and sofa sex and bedroom sex with Brandon who in the end didn't *want* Paul for some random one-night stand. Who wanted to hold his hand in public, who wanted them to both enjoy themselves in bed, who could hold his own in a first-person shooter and couldn't cook for crap and was practically a zombie before his first cup of coffee in the morning. And if Paul didn't call and apologize *today*, as soon as possible, Brandon might go back to Atlanta and then the chance would be lost.

Christopher was watching him with his head slightly cocked to one side again, assessing him. Waiting for an answer.

"I'm taken, Christopher," Paul said firmly. "Sorry."

"Oh, that's a damn lie," Christopher said, a hint of a sneer in his tone. "You're not sorry at all, are you? You're thinking about fucking him right now. Even knowing that he's going to leave you."

"Then I'll have to go chase him, won't I?" Paul stood up, mentally willing Christopher to take the hint already. "Look, I know you think you're looking out for me, but please don't. I don't need your protection."

Christopher looked pointedly at the still-untouched bottle of Dasani sitting on the table next to them. "He's never going to understand you like I do. To look after you."

"I'll take my chances."

"You'll throw everything away to go play house with some big-city faggot?"

Right, enough of that. Paul picked up the Dasani and tossed it into Christopher's lap. "Looks like it," he said. "I'm heading out. I don't want to hear from you again."

"Going to go fuck your boyfriend?"

"Guess so," he called over his shoulder as he headed back to his car. "Because unlike you, I actually *am* gay."

* * * *

Paul stopped for gas on the way home, partly to make sure Christopher wasn't following him and partly because he didn't want to wait until he was all the way back at the apartment before he could call Brandon. The phone rang through but went to voicemail.

"Um, hi," Paul said above the noise of the gas pump next to him. "Look, I know I—it was bad, last night. I owe you an apology for all the mixed signals I've been sending. You were right; I was being a dick. I hate that I made you feel unwanted, because nothing could be further from the truth." *God, he's probably feeling so rejected right now.* "I, um. Yeah. I've been thinking about you all day, and—maybe—can you call me back? Or could you come over tonight or something? We can meet somewhere neutral if you'd prefer, I just… We need to talk. I'd like it if we could talk. I'm not good at this, but I want to—I want to try. To have it be more than a temporary thing. I went for a walk after class today and ran into Christopher and… Well, mostly it just made me want to apologize to you as soon as possible. So. Call me. Please?"

God, it was a terrible rambling mess, but he hit "yes, save" anyway when prompted and hung up. Now it was all up to Brandon.

Chapter 22

Paul didn't realize how tired he was until he sat down on the couch to take his shoes off and then couldn't find the energy to get back up again. He watched TV for a while, vaguely aware that he was hungry but not desperate enough to do anything about it. Nothing sounded good anyway.

I want Brandon back. That single statement felt truer than anything else in his life. Brandon Mercer was offering something: a life where being gay was normal and acceptable and not indicative of a major moral failing. Even better, that life would have Brandon in it. For the long-term, presumably. Sleepy mornings together and late-night cuddles on the couch and *don't forget the milk* texts in the middle of the afternoon and always, always, someone to have his back. And to care for in return. Paul had known in the abstract that some people's lives were like that, but even on his more optimistic days he'd never pictured it working out like that for *him*. The best he'd ever hoped for was the outward appearance of the American dream: the smiling wife and two point four kids in a house with a white picket fence, and if he smiled enough in return everyone might assume he was happy.

He fell asleep imagining Brandon mowing their hypothetical lawn, shirtless in the summer sun, smiling and waving at their hypothetical children every time he passed the window.

* * * *

The phone jolted Paul out of a very pleasant dream some time later. He groped for it and brought it to his ear without waking up enough to read the display.

"'lo?"

"Paul." Danielle's voice, with a hint of panic in it. Paul mentally jolted himself awake the rest of the way and sat up.

"Danielle? What's wrong?"

A pause. "You haven't seen it, have you," she declared.

"Seen what?"

"Shit." There were sounds in the background, the clicking of a keyboard. "Look, I just forwarded you the e-mail. Which supposedly came from you about fifteen minutes ago. It's… Well Dad's at work so I can't tell you about his reaction, but Mom was on her laptop when it came in so she saw it at the same time I did. And she's pretty broken up about it. Someone sent this long, rambling coming-out letter from your address, pretending to be you. I know it *wasn't* you, because you're a better writer and don't use anywhere near that kind of profanity and the whole thing just sounded really bitter, but I think a lot of things finally clicked for Mom and now she's doing that thing she does where she refuses to talk about it. I'm not sure what to say to her."

"Shit," Paul echoed, and dove for his laptop. Took forever to turn on, to get the internet open, to get to the staff portal and pull up his inbox.

Danielle waited silently while he read. If anything, it was worse than what she described—an eight-paragraph confession of just how much he loved taking it up the ass, how he'd enjoyed "putting one over on all you uptight nutjobs" but didn't want to bother hiding anymore, with some liberal profanity and graphic details included for good measure. The final paragraph referenced attached photos, but Paul couldn't bring himself to open the folder underneath.

"I, uh, didn't look at the pictures," Danielle volunteered after a long moment of silence. "Figured they were probably something you wouldn't want me to see."

"Yeah, that's…good." It was hard to see any *good* in the current situation, honestly, but Paul was still having trouble coming to grips with the whole concept in the first place. It was Christopher, of course; it had to be. It's not like there was *that* long a list of people who even knew Paul was gay. (Christopher, Brandon, Danielle … Yeah, that was about it.) Paul had a sinking feeling he knew exactly what picture (or series of pictures) Christopher had shared.

Shared with who? Paul flipped over to his sent messages folder, saw the "COMING OUT SURPRISE!!!" e-mail at the top—

And nearly threw up. A *long* list of recipients—it looked like Christopher had gone through Paul's entire address book. Possibly everyone he'd ever exchanged e-mails with. Dr. Kirsner received it, as did Grace and the rest of the psychology department—some of them two or three times, as they were on various mailing lists he shared. His parents. Danielle. Brandon. The handful of people he'd interacted with for events at his parents' church. All his students. *Shit.*

"You okay?" Danielle asked. "I can come over there if you want. Or we can—I don't know. Go somewhere for a while. I would say you could come home, but…"

"But Mom and Dad are eager to disinherit me," he finished for her.

He could hear her wince even over the phone. "I don't think it's *quite* that bad," she said, "but they're going to take some time to come around. Dad especially. It would be easier if you were to deny everything—but you can't, can you? I mean, obviously you didn't write it."

He sighed and finally succumbed to the instinct to lie down before he passed out. The sofa was still warm from his nap. "Fuck."

That startled a bit of a laugh out of her. "If anyone deserves the right to use that kind of language right now, it's you. Any thoughts about what to do now? Damage control? Who would even do this?"

Even thinking was exhausting—he wanted to crawl into a hole and hide for a while. The next decade, perhaps. "I've got a pretty good idea who's responsible, but I can't think yet."

"You want me to come by? I was going to go up and visit Christine and Derek tomorrow—the friends I shared an apartment with that one summer, you remember?—but they'll understand if I have to cancel."

A knock at the door jolted Paul to his feet. He barely had time to formulate the vision of his father showing up to yell at him in person when Brandon's voice cut through the panic. "Paul? You home?"

Thank God. Paul let out a shaky breath. "Look, Danielle, I've got someone here now, so I think I'm okay. But thanks."

"Someone?" The word dripped with curiosity.

"Someone I—someone who can help," Paul admitted. "I'll explain later, but—talk to Mom for me, please? I know I can't *make* her accept me the way I am, but having someone rational around right now would probably be a good thing."

"Will do," Danielle promised. "And Paul? Whoever your *someone* is, I hope he makes you happy."

* * * *

"Hey."

"Hey." Paul breathed a sigh of relief. *Thank God.* Brandon didn't look mad; if anything, he looked worried.

"Um, can I ..."

"Oh. Sure, sorry." Paul opened the door wider and stepped back to allow him inside. Brandon had his laptop with him, which he set down on the kitchen table.

"Look, Brandon, I—"

He was interrupted by a rib-cracking hug. God, how had he not known how much he needed this? It was wonderful of Danielle to call, and even better of her to offer to drop everything and come running to help him escape what were probably soon to be the shambles of his regular life, but Brandon was holding him tight and he smelled amazing and somehow the world seemed a lot more positive than it had been five minutes earlier. They stayed like that for a while, neither needing words to communicate. When they finally drew apart by mutual consent, Brandon dragged in a deep breath and ran his fingers through his hair.

"You meant it, then," he said quietly. "In your message."

I'm such an idiot. "Yeah."

"And you saw the e-mail?"

"Only right before you got here. The voicemail didn't have anything to do with that."

"Oh, I know. It's just—I couldn't stop it, Paul." He rubbed one hand in gentle circles over the nape of Paul's neck, soothing even as his own posture belied his frustration. "I saw it right away and did what I could to get the pictures off the server before too many people could download them, but I couldn't stop it from going out."

"I'm surprised you could do anything at all." He swallowed hard. "I—I didn't look, but I'm assuming the pictures are of you too."

"All three were shots from that first night," Brandon said quietly. "And yes, I'm in them too, but he didn't get my face. The only saving grace was that you were on some lists that didn't allow unauthorized attachments, so those got flagged right away—I yanked the file down from the St. Ben's mail client, but that's only a stopgap measure. Anyone who checked their e-mail before I got to it received the full thing, and there's no way to know who that might be."

"And of course if even a handful of people saw it, they'll forward it to everyone else pretty much as soon as possible." Because that was how the world worked, wasn't it? "Apparently my mother is having a meltdown."

Brandon closed his eyes. "Fuck. I'm so sorry, Paul."

Paul dropped a chaste kiss on his collarbone. "Not your fault. Danielle called me to say that she doesn't know how my dad's reacting, but my mom's freaking out. I'm sure she's on the phone with him right now."

"Not going to be supportive, I assume?"

When hell freezes over. "Danielle is, and that's what matters."

"Did you tell her about me?" The question was casual, but Paul could feel how Brandon was tensed for another rejection.

And he was thrilled to not have to deliver one. "Not yet," he confessed, "but I alluded. And I was hoping you might get to meet her in person before she goes back to France." *That would be an interesting conversation.* "I suspect I'm going to be having a lot of free time soon."

"God, I'm sorry," Brandon said, his voice muffled against Paul's hair. "I couldn't do anything about the text itself, or the addresses not on your mailing lists—they sent pretty much instantaneously." He tightened his grip and started rocking them gently. It felt wonderful. "And I'm sorry about last night. I knew in the abstract why you felt you had to stay in the closet, but I was upset. I hate that you're having to live the doomsday outing scenario now."

"Don't be sorry." As good as burying his face in Brandon's neck felt, Paul forced himself to pull back and settle down a bit. "Obviously this wasn't how I meant to come out, but that's not your fault. And I—I want to. Be out. With you. For good."

Brandon stilled. "You're serious?"

Paul nodded. "I'm not sorry this happened. I'm *furious*." As he said it, he *felt* how true it was. Almost like a new wave of energy washing over him, rinsing away the last of the lethargy and self-pity. "I'm furious that I've spent all this time working toward tenure and now it's wasted. And you deserve to hear this from me when I'm not dealing with a stupid career crisis, but Christopher took that chance away. I wanted to apologize and—heck, I don't know. Do something especially nice for you. And now we're both stuck cleaning up the mess Christopher threw us—*me*—in."

Brandon's breath rushed out in a startled huff. "Damn," he murmured. "I'm really glad I'm not going to have to meet that ex of yours face to face. I've never wanted to punch someone so badly."

"Any chance he can get in trouble for this?"

Brandon choked on what had probably been a laugh. "You could say that, yes. I was on the phone with legal on the way over—that's essentially the other half of what my company does, so really all we can do is wait it out." He pressed a quick kiss to Paul's lips, then drew back far enough they could look each other in the eye. "If I can make a suggestion, though…not here?"

God, yes. Paul glanced over at the closed curtains, but the thought of Christopher potentially watching him again still sent a shiver down his spine. "Where?"

"Throw something in a bag and I'll tell you."

Chapter 23

At Brandon's insistence, Paul just transferred the contents of his dresser to a suitcase.

"It's a lot," he warned.

"My car has a big trunk. And I'm not bringing anything; I'll have one of my guys pick up my suitcase in the morning. I was already mostly packed. I was planning on returning to your place before all hell broke loose."

Paul paused and stared at him, but Brandon just shrugged.

"I was hoping to convince you to come home. To my apartment. I'm not short on clothes back there, after all."

Traffic was light that late in the evening, so they made good time back to Atlanta. Paul was feeling a *tiny* bit paranoid about Christopher having followed them to the city—or to Brandon's hotel or to anywhere else they'd been in the last week—but the lack of cars on the highway helped.

"I turned my phone off," Paul confessed as Brandon reached over him and keyed in the combination at the gate to the complex. "You and Danielle are pretty much the only two people on the planet I'd even consider talking to right now, and she already called me earlier."

Brandon shot him a glance out of the corner of his eye as he pulled up in front of his apartment. "Are you teaching in the morning?"

Hell. "We'll find out, won't we?"

"What, they can't fire you if they can't reach you?"

"Sure, we'll go with that for now."

Brandon frowned, but didn't call him on it. Paul hauled his bulging suitcase into the bedroom, then came back out and joined Brandon on his tiny balcony. It was quiet except for some faint road noise in the distance. A decent-sized stand of trees blocked some of the surrounding light pollution, so there was a clear view of at least the brighter stars. They stood in silence for several minutes.

"Good to be away for a bit?" Brandon eventually said.

"Never want to go back." Paul could practically feel the last of the tension draining away. It was cool enough he wished he'd brought a jacket, but the quiet was beautiful and Paul let himself drink it in.

Brandon leaned on the railing next to him, studying his face. "You mean that? Or is it just the stress talking?"

"I think I do mean it." *Dang, who'd have thought I could walk away from it all without feeling at least a guilty pang of regret?* He already didn't miss it, though, and that perhaps surprised him more than anything else. Although... "I really do owe you an apology," he added.

Brandon immediately shook his head. "I was being an ass. Last night wasn't your fault."

"It kinda was." Paul tore his eyes away from the stars and turned so they could see each other face to face. "I was so convinced I had to hide what I am that I ended up unwilling to consider anything that might threaten what I thought I wanted. Even though what I *really* wanted was you." He smiled weakly at the stunned look in Brandon's eyes. "I know, we've both been careful to say it's 'casual' and all. And it hasn't been long enough for me to be all serious like this. But...yeah. I thought you should know."

"You want me, specifically?" Brandon asked quietly. "Or just what I represent? The freedom to be out and be true to yourself?"

That startled a totally inappropriate laugh out of Paul, which he quickly suppressed. "I'd be lying if I didn't say that was at least partly a factor, but..." *God, this is harder than I ever imagined to admit.* Brandon deserved to hear it, though, so he could decide for himself. "I didn't know it could be like this. So *comfortable.* I assumed I could only get that with a more traditional relationship, because I assumed being gay was... Well, you know what I thought. Heck, you lived the stereotype for a while yourself. And."

Brandon huffed. "I could absolutely see you with sparkly product in your hair, you know."

"Shut up and let me finish." Paul nudged Brandon with his elbow to make it obvious he was teasing back. "It's hard enough to admit this without you interrupting."

"Oh, is this a declaration?" Brandon faked an innocent look. "Sorry, I was mostly looking forward to the part where you say you want me and that the "something nice" you want to do for me involves sex."

Paul was all ready to elbow him again, to take one more run-up at getting this *right*, but something in Brandon's eyes stopped him. It wasn't just the lust, although that was certainly at the forefront. There was a sense of…maybe not disbelief, but insecurity. Brandon needed reassurance that Paul really did want him for real and not only as a convenient source of temporary sex. Perhaps this was one of those times where actions spoke louder than words.

"Brandon," Paul said in a low voice, "it's not just sex. I want to keep you for as long as you'll have me. But I would very much like it if the next several hours of that time were in your bed."

* * * *

They didn't *sprint* to the bedroom, but it wasn't a leisurely stroll either. Brandon kept alternating between tugging Paul forward and halting to kiss him breathless up against whatever vertical surface happened to be the most convenient, which meant they were both grinning when they finally made it to the bed. They landed on the mattress with a thump, the springs squeaking loudly in protest.

"You really want to do this," Brandon confirmed, wonder in his voice. "As in, not just for tonight or for convenient weekends. You want to do the whole real relationship thing. For how long?"

"Let's play it by ear. If that's okay with you." Paul grabbed Brandon's hips and slid himself closer, so they were lying on their sides and pressed together from chest to thigh. "I know neither of us have a lot of experience with actual real relationships, but I find myself wanting to try my best for you. It's probably horrible to say this, but I honestly don't care what happens tomorrow, so long as I've got you here with me. Or I can be with you wherever you are. If I'm going to be unemployed anyway, I might as well be unemployed in Atlanta."

"Jesus." Brandon seized his face with both hands and kissed him thoroughly before pulling away again. "Yes. Hell, yes—move in with me here. Get away from that toxic environment and let me introduce you to the benefits of being in a big city. I know some people at Emory and Georgia Tech—I can even ask around for you, job-wise. Not that you need to—"

Paul silenced him with a quick and dirty slide of his tongue into Brandon's mouth, taking him completely by surprise. "More important things to worry about right now," he murmured against Brandon's lips. "You've got other ways of making me feel better."

And was treated to the delightful sight of Brandon's eyes instantly darkening. "You've picked up on that, I see," he answered once they broke far enough apart to speak. "Tell me, any particular requests? Because I intend to make you feel very, very good. It's become rather an obsession of mine." He nipped at Paul's bottom lip. "One I intend to indulge."

Paul rolled over onto his back, pulling Brandon on top of him. "I've been doing some thinking lately. There's something I've always been afraid to try, but there really isn't any reason to be afraid, is there? Not with you."

Brandon pulled back a bit at that, his forehead furrowing. "I didn't mean we have to right—"

"I want to, though." *So much. Spent most of the drive here daydreaming about it.* "I've been thinking. Pretty much constantly since I saw Christopher again. And I realized something." Paul looked up into Brandon's brown eyes and let himself go. "I realized that I wasn't afraid of anal sex."

"That's—*oh.* Okay." Brandon was making a valiant effort to not react to Paul's body below him, but Paul could feel the tremor in his spine. *Gotcha.* Not so unaffected as he wanted Paul to think.

"More than okay," Paul said. "It hit me—pretty much immediately after I realized I wanted to make this last with you—that I was afraid of sex with someone who treated me like Christopher did. Who saw me as weak for being physically attracted to men. I was afraid to try it because if I did, I might enjoy it. And if I enjoyed it, then clearly I was lying to myself about being able to be happy without being gay."

Brandon sucked in a breath. "And now?"

"Now I've got you," Paul answered simply.

Brandon stared down at him for a long moment, eyes wide. *Hopeful.* And then he seemed to snap back to himself. His kiss was rough, forceful, demanding—everything Paul needed more than air right at that moment. Brandon seemed to understand his desperation, keeping up the ruthless assault until Paul was literally scrabbling at his shoulder blades with the need to do *something*, to pull their bodies even tighter together.

"You have a preference?" Brandon murmured. "Top or bottom? Because I'm perfectly happy to switch, however you think you might like it. I'll walk you through it either way."

Paul sucked in a breath. *God, this is it.* "I think—if you don't mind—you seemed to like it, in the shower …"

"Your finger on my hole?" Brandon slid a hand under the waistband of Paul's pants, palmed his ass, and squeezed gently. "I did. I do. You want to finger me again?"

"Want you to do it to me," Paul admitted. "It looked good."

"Oh." Brandon's eyes darkened even further. "Yes, we can do that. Hell, I can't *wait* to see what you look like with my fingers inside you. But first—strip."

Paul sat up and shed his shirt with a minimum of grace or elegance. Brandon was a bit slower about it, more deliberate, but then he was crouching on all fours over Paul, pinning him to the bed by the weight of his sheer presence, and Paul was already halfway gone.

"Jeans," Paul gasped. "Need to—"

Brandon dipped his hips and ground his pelvis against Paul's. Only for a moment, but Paul couldn't hold back his groan. Brandon grinned wickedly and did it again.

"We'll get there," he promised. "Good things come to those who wait—you've heard that, haven't you?" He repeated the motion, adding an extra little twist at the end that left Paul literally panting. "Are you ready for some good things coming, Paul?"

"God yes," Paul groaned. "Brandon, please—"

Brandon didn't. He did, however, slide himself slowly down Paul's body, licking and sucking at every square inch of skin in his path and deliberately dragging the entirety of his torso against Paul's cock as he did so. Paul was practically whimpering by the time Brandon's mouth got down to the waistband of his jeans. Brandon popped the snap with a twist of his nimble fingers, then lowered his head again and caught the zipper in his teeth.

Paul slammed his eyes shut to keep from coming right on the spot. The loss of visual input did nothing to impede the onslaught of sensations, though: the warmth of Brandon's chest against his thighs, the slight vibrations as the teeth of the zipper unfastened, one by one, the contented hum coming from Brandon's throat. Paul felt a slight tug at his hips, nudging him upward, and he wordlessly lifted them so Brandon could tug his pants and boxers down and off. When he opened his eyes again, Brandon was standing naked next to the bed and watching him with a blatantly predatory expression.

"You look like you're going to eat me."

Brandon quirked an eyebrow. "Tempting, but going to take it slow. At least for tonight. You're sure you want this?"

"I'm sure," Paul said. *Surer of this than I've been about anything in a long time.* "You were worth waiting for."

Brandon stilled. "Are you sad that I didn't?"

"What? No, I…" Paul sat up far enough to grab Brandon's hand and squeeze. "I was kind of hoping you'd show me a proper fucking."

The poleaxed look on Brandon's face was absolutely worth the uncomfortable crudity of the expression. He recovered quickly, the predatory aura back almost immediately. Followed by a very literal growl as he dove back down to pin Paul to the bed for a thorough—*very* thorough—kiss.

"Stay right there," Brandon commanded in that low voice that always seemed to short-circuit any other thoughts Paul might have had. "I want you to touch yourself—*slowly*—and think about how much you want to feel me inside you. Don't stop, but don't let yourself come. Can you do that?"

Paul nodded frantically, then reached down to rub himself as lightly as possible. He was already keyed up, practically vibrating with it, and it didn't help *at all* to see how gorgeous Brandon's body looked nude as he rounded the other side of the bed and dug in the drawer to pull out a small bottle and a condom.

"Move farther up on the bed," Brandon said, and slid onto the mattress from the opposite side. He positioned Paul carefully, pulling the duvet off the bed and slipping a pillow under Paul's hips so he was in the exact center of the soft blue sheets. Paul felt oddly decadent, fondling himself while Brandon tugged him this way and that, but the end result was hard to miss—Brandon had an erection rivaling his own and it hadn't even been touched yet.

"I'm glad you know what you're doing," Paul admitted aloud. "Because this isn't at all what I thought it would be like."

Brandon shifted over to lie next to him and pressed a firm, reassuring kiss to his lips. "What did you think it would be like?"

"More unsettling. Scarier. Out of control."

"And you wanted to do it anyway?"

Paul returned the kiss. "I trust you."

Brandon's hand slipped down to cover Paul's as it languidly slid up and down. "I know," he whispered. "And it's amazing." His fingers wandered even farther south, cupping Paul's balls and kneading them gently. He withdrew them momentarily, taking the time to slick his fingertips well with lube, but a moment later his hand was back between Paul's legs. He traced a gentle trail over Paul's balls and the sensitive skin behind until his pointer finger was running gently up and down Paul's crack and Paul had to let go of his cock entirely for fear of coming too soon.

"Spread your legs a bit," Brandon murmured.

Paul complied immediately. And Brandon rewarded him by pressing a little bit harder, angling his finger a bit, until his fingertip was skittering around the rim of Paul's hole and it felt so, *so* good. "More," Paul breathed.

Brandon smirked at that, but he sat up a bit and refreshed the lube. His other hand went back to making soothing circles on Paul's belly, thumb tracing the bottom edge of Paul's ribcage and barely brushing the very tip of Paul's cock on every third or fourth pass, but Paul's attention was almost entirely focused on how Brandon was touching his hole. He was almost reverent in his gentleness and—despite the arousal—Paul had never felt so cherished in his life. When Brandon finally slipped his fingertip in through that rosebud of muscle and pressed gently, Paul felt nothing but relief.

"Feels good," he mumbled.

Brandon slid his finger in farther, agonizingly slowly, until—

"Oh!"

Paul blushed the moment the noise escaped his lips—*it's not like I don't know the mechanics, after all!*—but Brandon's gaze sharpened and he brushed over Paul's prostate again. And again, over and over until Paul couldn't keep still anymore and his hips twitched upward of their own accord.

"More," Paul breathed. "Want you in me."

"Patience." Brandon bent down to lick at the tip of Paul's cock, which was already moist with precome. "My pace, not yours." He did add a second finger, though, which prompted another wordless groan.

Paul flailed blindly for the condom on the mattress beside him, but Brandon beat him to it. He did allow Paul to tear open the little foil packet—a concession which was possibly related to how he refused to stop the inexorable drag of fingertips in and out of Paul's hole or the teasing brush against Paul's prostate on every third or fourth pass—but he rolled it onto his cock himself.

"Want you," Paul said, and fell back against the mattress.

"Good. Because if I go any slower it might very well kill me." Brandon ducked under Paul's knee and settled himself down between his spread legs. "I'll make it good for you, I promise."

The blunt pressure of Brandon's erection against Paul's hole felt completely different than the teasing glide of his fingers, but it was a good kind of different. Paul took a deep breath and tried to relax. Brandon—despite his words—was going so slowly he was almost not moving at all. Which meant that Paul felt every last millimeter as Brandon slid slowly home. It did hurt, a bit, but the physical burn was insignificant in comparison with the heat in Brandon's eyes.

"Fuck," Brandon breathed. "Paul, you feel—*fuck.* So incredible around me. Please say you're ready for me to move."

"Please. Do it." Paul tightened his internal muscles, drawing a groan from Brandon. "Fuck me."

Brandon dropped his head to hang loose, like he couldn't be bothered to hold it up anymore, but he slowly tilted his hips backward and then pistoned sharply back in. Paul caught his breath on a gasp.

And that was Brandon's cue to move. He dropped all pretense of being slow and gentle and began to show Paul what, exactly, he'd been missing all this time. Paul reached down toward his own cock, but Brandon knocked his hand away.

"Not yet," Brandon growled. "Together. When I say. I'll take care of you, I promise."

Paul would have answered, would have said something about how sexy it was when Brandon got all commanding like that, but then Brandon changed his angle slightly and anything Paul might have had to say was swallowed up by the fireworks exploding behind his suddenly closed eyelids.

"Found it." The smug expression on Brandon's face was obvious even though Paul's eyes were closed. "Like that, do you?"

Paul could only moan and tilt his hips farther up, silently begging. Brandon picked up his pace, hitting that one indescribable spot again and again until Paul was digging his heels into the sheet and practically tossing his head back and forth with desperation. Only then did Brandon finally consent to close his hand around Paul's cock and pump him in counterpoint to the firm thrusts. Paul didn't last long before everything coalesced and he seized up with a sharp cry. He could feel Brandon's body stiffening between his thighs, could hear Brandon's breathing stop entirely for a moment, then they both shuddered and collapsed together in a limp pile of satisfaction.

"That was amazing," Paul managed several minutes later, after they'd mustered the energy to disentangle themselves and spoon up together but not enough to get up and clean off. "I didn't know."

"It's not…" Brandon nuzzled Paul's hair, his beard tickling the back of Paul's neck. "It's not always like that. Hell, it's *never* like that. That was…" He let the thought die away in favor of pulling Paul closer. "Stay," he murmured.

"Right this minute? Or forever?"

The words were out before Paul could properly censor them, and he winced at how needy he sounded. Brandon didn't seem to object, though. He tightened his arms around Paul's chest and murmured something into his hair.

"Sorry, I didn't catch that."

Brandon shifted his body upward. "I said," he whispered distinctly into Paul's ear, lipping the sensitive lobe, "forever is good for me."

Chapter 24

It was pure hell to get up the next morning. Paul awoke to discover himself practically cocooned by Brandon, who was wrapped around him and snoring ever so faintly. Paul lay in Brandon's embrace for several minutes, enjoying the warmth, before his stomach reminded him that they never got around to eating last night and he was therefore absolutely starving. Then his brain kicked in and pointed out there was probably still no food in the apartment—and worse, he was pretty sure he used up the coffee last time. *Darn it.*

Brandon awoke in stages: first murmuring groggily and snuggling closer, then opening his eyes and yawning, then favoring Paul with a heart-melting smile before coming back to himself and remembering their situation.

"Welcome back, sleepyhead," Paul announced, pressing a brief morning-breath-friendly kiss to the corner of Brandon's mouth. "The good news is you're waking up with me. The bad news is there's no breakfast and no coffee until we get ourselves back on the highway and find a Waffle House or something."

"Damn, then this can't all be just a dream—my subconscious couldn't possibly come up something as diabolical as a morning with no coffee." Brandon stretched, pressing his very clear morning erection against Paul's backside as he did so, then struggled up to a sitting position. "Fuck—we have to go back to St. Ben's today, don't we?"

"I suspect I need to get properly fired." Paul couldn't resist another quick kiss, drawing away before Brandon really had time to react. "And you said last night your legal department was taking over, but I'm guessing you still need to sort some things out, right?"

Brandon blew out a long breath. "There's going to be fallout. From that e-mail. It's one thing if someone guesses the president's password and peeks at things they shouldn't see, but—aside from the obvious personal aspects you're facing and the legal repercussions of hacking—Christopher has made the university look bad. Everyone's going to be looking for someone to blame."

"And let me guess, you're the most logical target because you didn't catch him faster? That would be on par with what the administration usually does when cornered."

"Not if we can hand them your ex first." Brandon cupped the nape of Paul's neck and drew him in for a much more extended slide of tongue against tongue, until Paul was somewhat less able to string an entire sentence together anymore. He practically fell out of bed when Brandon's phone chimed out a surprisingly noisy alarm.

"Sorry," Brandon mumbled, and pulled away. "Have to set it loud or I sleep through it."

"Luckily I don't have to pack today." Paul sat back and ran a hand through his hair, trying to get it to at least pick a single direction to stick up in. "I'm starving."

"Mmmm—what for?" Brandon waggled an eyebrow suggestively and glanced pointedly down to his morning erection.

Paul rolled his eyes, but he gave in and allowed Brandon a *bit* more distraction before they finally got out of bed.

* * * *

He didn't even make it all the way through the main doors of the psychology building before being ambushed.

"My office," Dr. Kirsner intoned. *"Now."*

It wasn't a surprise—Paul and Brandon had parted ways in the parking lot and he'd spent the rest of the walk to his building anticipating the reception he was likely to receive—but following Dr. Kirsner back to his office felt an awful lot like the "walk of shame" Paul had promised himself in undergrad never to do.

"Sit."

Paul sat. Neither of them closed the door. Dr. Kirsner rounded the desk and settled opposite him like a pharaoh claiming his throne. He eyed Paul for several seconds, nose wrinkling in disgust, before finally turning his computer monitor and displaying exactly what Paul had initially feared—the same pixelated image of himself and Brandon on his sofa that first night together. Obviously him. Obviously with a man. Obviously sexual. Paul expected to feel embarrassment, but oddly enough he felt…nothing. No, not nothing—*satisfaction.* The knowledge that he *was* going to make it through this, and that Brandon would stay by his side the entire way. That no matter what hurtful things Dr. Kirsner might accuse him of, he'd be able to let them roll off his back because they weren't true. And that, despite the circumstances of the picture, Brandon still looked damn gorgeous.

"I find myself in the rather unique position of not knowing what to say," Dr. Kirsner declared once the silence was nearly unbearable. "Normally when there's been a conduct violation, I meet with the department member in question and at least attempt to get their side of the story—but there's really no denying this, is there?"

There wasn't. Paul shrugged. "I didn't write or distribute the e-mail, if it matters—and I didn't consent to that photo being taken. But yes, that's me."

"Performing an immoral act with another man."

"Being stalked, photographed, and forcibly outed by a vindictive ex-partner."

"Irrelevant."

"If you say so."

Dr. Kirsner frowned. "You don't seem too concerned by this—you realize you're being terminated, don't you?"

Yes, he did. And it did hurt—all that time spent jockeying to get track for tenure, all the ridiculous lengths he'd had to go to in order to get his research funded and his papers published. All down the drain. And yet, on the other side of the scales, was Brandon. For real, for good. Who made everything that happened all worth it.

It must have been apparent that Paul wasn't going to melt down and beg for forgiveness, because Dr. Kirsner finally nodded and broke eye contact to shuffle some papers. "You're being removed from employment at St. Benedict's effective immediately. If you wish to challenge your firing, you'll find the information about how to do so included in the paperwork, which will be mailed to you with your last paycheck. Dr. Carrington will escort you to your office to retrieve your personal effects. The computer has already been removed, since everything on it belongs to the school, but you may pack up whatever items you personally have purchased and brought in for your own use. No office supplies, no paperwork. Everything left behind will be held for ninety days or pending a challenge hearing if you request one, whichever comes first. You will be escorted from campus and—God willing—will never be in a position to corrupt students like this again. Have I made myself clear?"

Crystal. Paul nodded. He had no questions because there was nothing to ask—it didn't matter. Some part of his brain tried to point out that he really ought to be paying attention in case he needed to fight some aspect of this later, but his mind was already filtering everything about his life at St. Benedict's into some sort of mental "before" file folder, never to be worried over again. Or—more likely—to be worried about at length, but sometime far in the future when everything had had a chance to sink in. He didn't even jump when the knock came on the door behind him.

"Dr. Carrington."

Grace nodded at Dr. Kirsner, then offered Paul a tremulous smile. "Paul."

"Security will meet you at Mr. Dunham's office by the time you're finished—and thank you for taking the time to help." Dr. Kirsner stood and held the already-open door for both of them as they exited his office, then rather pointedly shut it behind Paul the moment he was outside.

"Mister" Dunham. I guess that is *me, again.* Paul wasn't sure when he'd gotten so used to being "Professor"—probably related to how he never had much of a social life outside St. Ben's. He did still have his doctorate, so he should technically be "Dr. Dunham," but refusing to show even that much respect was obviously Dr. Kirsner's way of twisting the knife a bit further. Not that it mattered. Grace's wide eyes and forced smile hurt much worse.

"I take it everyone saw the e-mail, then," Paul said softly as they walked down the nearly-empty hallway together and headed for the stairs.

Grace blushed and looked away, but he could read the guilt in her expression even so. "Just the confession at first. One of the grad students forwarded everyone the pictures a few hours later, though. I didn't want to believe it was true."

"I'm sorry." Paul drew to a stop ahead of her on the stairs, forcing her to stop too and look up at him. "For what it's worth, I would have liked to have felt that spark for you. And I didn't write that e-mail—that was crude and small-minded and intended to hurt by outing me in the worst way possible, which it did. But I *am* gay and I'm not going to deny that."

"I know." She smiled at him sadly. "I guess I've known for a long time, but I never wanted to admit it. And Paul... I'm not going to pine. But I will be praying for you."

There wasn't much he could say to that. She obviously didn't mean it in the snarky, judgmental way some people did when they used that phrase, the "you're going to be in so much trouble when Our Father gets home" kind of way, but in some aspects that made it worse. She thought he was so beyond human redemption that his only chance was divine intervention. Nothing Paul could say would change her mind, and certainly nothing she had to say on the subject of homosexuality would change his. They walked the rest of the way to his office in silence.

It took less time than he thought it would—*much* less time—to clear out all signs of himself from his office. There wasn't a lot to pack: the framed picture of Danielle from right before she left for France, the handful of action figures from various old video games he kept scattered around his desk, a box and a half of textbooks and paper copies of research journals he had brought with him when he first was given his own office with actual office hours and the possibility of students stopping by. Grace stood in the doorway and watched. She didn't offer to help, but she didn't breathe down his neck and challenge him over every item he threw in the box, either. The desk already looked naked without the monitor and keyboard on it; removing the scattering of nerdy knickknacks only made it look more bare and impersonal. He ignored everything in his drawers and the papers stacked in neat piles near the window—he had electronic copies of everything related to his research on his personal laptop anyway, and nothing else was worth keeping.

"I guess I'm done."

Grace looked at the two file boxes full of his things, looked at him, and nodded. "Need a hand getting those to your car? No point waiting here for security to come and escort you out when I'm headed that way anyway."

* * * *

It was just as well Brandon had left him the keys, or the whole situation would have been even more awkward than it was. Paul loaded the two boxes in Brandon's trunk, daring Grace to comment on the obvious fact that it wasn't his car, but she said nothing. The campus security guard caught up with them as he finished. Grace stammered her way through an awkward good-bye, hesitated long enough over shaking his hand for Paul to consider going in for a hug just to give her gay cooties, then escaped back to the psychology building. The security guard eyed him with significantly more sympathy.

"So you're the gay one," she said matter-of-factly. "You're not going to do anything stupid now, are you?"

He snorted. "Define 'stupid'?"

"Usually it involves coming back here and trying to start a fight with your former boss or co-workers." She tilted her head to one side and studied him. "I wouldn't blame you for being mad, you know—it's total crap that they can fire you for stupid stuff like this—but that's what happens when you work for a religious college. For what it's worth, I think you're going to find something better. You were faculty, right?"

"Psychology. Yeah."

"So go do something else for a while and come back to the field when the shitstorm dies down. I mean, what do I know? Students all seem to think I'm barely a step up from mall cop. I never went here or anything. But you don't look like the usual kind of idiot I have to trespass off school grounds, and I'm hoping that means this is a step up for you and not a step back. Good luck."

"Thanks." Paul sucked in a deep breath. *Get fired, get pitied by the woman I once thought I might marry, get kicked off campus*—all of that he could take with his chin up. And yet one random stranger, a blunt-spoken woman in a security guard uniform, managed to slip through the cracks in his armor and get to him.

He accepted her nod of dismissal with a nod of his own and pulled into a gas station a few blocks away before calling Brandon.

"Let me guess," Brandon said by way of greeting. "You've been asked to leave?"

"'Trespassed off school grounds' is the term the security guard used."

"Can you give me another twenty minutes or so? I requested to be removed from this contract, since I'm not a neutral party anymore, so I'm passing off as much as I can to my team and then I'm free to head out with you. I suspected we might need the manpower so I pulled in a few favors. We've got three more guys on-site as of this morning, but they're still settling in." He covered the phone and answered someone's muffled question in the background. "Sorry about that," he said when he came back. "Right, so as much as I'd like to stick this out and personally slog through every piece of data St. Ben's has, I pretty much got to cherry-pick the fun parts and then pass the boring stuff on to the guys with less seniority." A laugh from somewhere else in the room. "Yeah, that's you, Jacob—learn to love it." There was the sound of a door closing, then the background noise dropped off and Paul's tone sobered considerably. "All right, I'm leaving those clowns by themselves for a minute. Honest question now that nobody's listening in: How are you holding up? I mean, truly?"

Paul was mildly surprised to discover that yes, he honestly was. "Probably still in shock a bit, but I'm fine. I think."

"I really do want to get that bastard for what he did to you," Brandon said slowly, "but this was a logical time to admit to my personal stake in the result of this investigation. Everyone on my team has been really understanding and supportive, despite being called out here on no notice. I've been told to take a day or two off and let them all mop up the details before I come back to the office. Hope that doesn't disappoint you too much. I'm still leaving them strict orders to keep me in the loop as much as they can, though, even if I'm not technically on this contract anymore."

"It's okay." More than okay. "I ... kind of don't want to be alone right now. And I don't want to go back to my place. I know it's silly, but I keep thinking about Christopher lurking around outside with a camera, and I just—"

"Totally understandable," Brandon interrupted. "I'm in the admin building on the north side of campus right now—tell me where you want me to meet you and I'll be out as soon as I can."

Chapter 25

"Christopher has been picked up by the police for questioning," Brandon announced as soon as they both were in the car. Paul hadn't adjusted the seat or the mirror, but Brandon fiddled with them anyway the moment Paul surrendered the wheel. "They're still figuring out what exactly to charge him with, but there's a pretty long list to choose from—and a good chunk of what he did to get into the more secure databases in the first place falls into federal anti-terrorist territory."

Paul slumped back against his seat in relief. "God, I didn't realize how much happier hearing you say that would make me feel."

"Me too, to be honest." Brandon smiled suddenly, then lunged forward for a quick close-mouthed kiss before sitting back and putting on his seatbelt. "Sorry." He didn't look sorry at all. "Was thinking I wanted to kiss you and realized I could. In public and everything."

They weren't exactly "in public"—Brandon had walked to the McDonalds across the street from campus so Paul didn't have to risk getting arrested for trespassing by driving on school grounds to come pick him up, which meant they were literally just sitting in a parking lot—but the McDonalds was far from empty and they were getting at least one double-take from another driver. Paul didn't care. "So what now?"

"Now we detour by my hotel room to let me get my stuff and officially check out. Maybe a quick grocery store run because I am *not* going another morning without coffee if I can help it. And after that…" He grinned. "Then maybe we can go back to my apartment and find somewhere to walk around holding hands and looking soppy. But mostly I'd be in favor of us staying in bed so I don't have to take my hands off you for at least twenty-four hours."

It sounded like a fantastic plan.

* * * *

They did end up grabbing lunch together on the way back to Atlanta. Brandon held Paul's hand under the table and didn't look at his phone until they got back in the car, even though it kept buzzing. The relief of *finally* putting St. Ben's in the rearview mirror was enough to have Paul grinning stupidly the entire time.

"I shouldn't be so happy."

"Yes you should." Brandon looked up from where he was either texting or e-mailing something, his thumbs flying across the tiny keyboard. "There'll be time to freak out about everything later—enjoy the giddiness while it lasts."

That drew a startled laugh out of Paul. "You think I'm giddy?"

"I may be projecting a bit." He flashed a grin. "Although you are getting to keep me around, so…"

"Twit." But Paul couldn't help but grin back.

* * * *

Paul didn't even think about his own phone until they got back to Brandon's place. He'd turned it off when they left his apartment the previous day and he really, really hadn't wanted to turn it back on again. He needed to face the music eventually, though, so while Brandon unloaded his suitcase and their meager selection of groceries (i.e. "whatever had looked good at the Publix they'd passed on their way out of town"), he powered it back up and ran through his missed calls.

Grace. His parents. Danielle. His parents again. Christopher—Paul was suddenly very glad he didn't see *that* name flash on the screen yesterday. His parents. Brandon. And about twelve calls from Danielle over the course of the last two hours.

"Anything important?" Brandon asked, coming around beside him to peer over his shoulder.

Only the real world, waiting for me to let my guard down. "I should call my sister."

"Can I say hi? I'd love to meet her in person, but at this point I'd settle for just finding out how much she sounds like you."

Paul snorted and leaned into Brandon's shoulder—his warmth and solidity felt fantastic. Grounding. "I guess so." He dialed, put it on speaker, and followed Brandon over to the sofa so they could put the phone down between them to talk.

It only rang once before being picked up. "Good morning, honey."

Paul froze. "Mom? Why are you answering Danielle's phone?"

"She left it here when she went out, and you wouldn't answer for me. And your father wants to talk to you. *Bill! It's him!*"

Damn it. He wasn't ready for this conversation, wasn't ready for the cross-examination his father would undoubtedly want to throw at him.

Paul's mental castigation was cut off by the nudge of Brandon's knee against his own. He looked up to see Brandon studying him with a worried expression.

You okay? Brandon mouthed.

And somehow the sight of Brandon being right there—open and attentive and ready to have his back—made Paul's panic recede a bit. He still didn't want this, didn't want to have to hear what his parents were going to tell him, but it was going to happen, and it was better with Brandon at his side rather than some surprise ambush later on. Paul took a deep breath and nodded.

There was a soft clunk on the line, most likely his mother picking up Danielle's cell and putting her end on speakerphone as well, and then Paul's father's voice came on. "Do you... You're not working at St. Benedict's anymore, are you?"

Not something I want to go into details about. "No."

"We saw your e-mail."

"I didn't send it."

"Your sister mentioned that. But it was you. In that picture."

Paul swallowed against the sudden tightness in his throat. "Yes."

"So you're a..." His father faltered for a moment. "You're a gay."

Brandon squeezed Paul's hand, tight, but he stayed silent. Just as well. "This wasn't how I wanted you guys to find out," Paul admitted.

His mother's voice, hesitant but clear. "Are you sure? I mean, you never really dated much..."

That drew a little strangled laugh from Paul's throat. "I'm sure, Mom. I've known for—well, for a long time. And I was planning to pretend I wasn't, as long as I could, but I couldn't hide anymore."

"The other man?" his father asked. "The one in the—was he a prosti—? Are you being safe?"

"Boyfriend, Dad." Paul squeezed Brandon's hand back and flashed him a tiny, private smile. "The word you're looking for is boyfriend, and yes, he and I are dating now. His name is Brandon and he's from Atlanta and I'm moving in with him as soon as I can get the rest of my stuff packed up from my apartment. I would love it if you could both be happy for me—this isn't how I wanted to come out, not at all, but he's the most wonderful person I've ever met and I love him very much."

Brandon's eyes widened beside him, and Paul suddenly realized what he'd done. *Damn, did I really admit that for the first time in front of my PARENTS?* Brandon's expression brightened so much, though, that Paul could barely keep from tugging him down into a giddy kiss right there with the phone between them.

There was silence from the other end of the phone. And more silence. "Mom? Dad?"

"I don't know what to say," Paul's father finally admitted. "I just—I wish you could have been happy with a woman."

It was no more than he'd expected, but it still felt like a lead weight dragging him back down to earth from whatever clouds he'd been inhabiting while avoiding the whole mess his life was turning into. "I wouldn't have been," Paul said.

"You never tried."

"I spent ten years trying."

"You never dated—"

"Mom?" Paul asked before his dad could start pontificating on his disappointment.

"What do you want me to say?" she asked quietly.

"Say you're glad that I'm happy?"

There was another long pause, and then a sigh. "I still love you," she said, almost too soft to hear. Then, louder: "Is he a Christian?"

* * * *

"That was depressing," Paul announced for Brandon's benefit after he'd said his awkward good-byes a minute later and hung up. "I mean, I knew they'd disapprove, but I'm sorry you had to hear that."

"They're not the first I've gotten the sentiment from," Brandon answered, and reached out to pull Paul closer to him in a wonderfully warm embrace. "And they won't be the last. The other side makes up for it, though."

Paul exhaled sharply into his shirt collar. "What, the sex?"

Brandon's chest shook under him in a soft chuckle. "Well, sure, that too. But I want to show you something." He pulled back from the hug and thumbed through something on his phone. "Here."

"What am I looking at?"

"Just read them."

Paul scrolled down the list—twenty or thirty e-mails, all from today.

He skimmed a few at random.

...Dr. Dunham was the best professor I've ever had...
...It's ridiculous that he be fired for such a trivial...
...and any college would be lucky to have him on the...
...I don't know how much weight student opinions carry, but...

Paul blinked back up at Brandon, not quite able to absorb what was going on.

"Recommendations," Brandon murmured. "Your mailbox is full of them—I've had my guys forwarding a sampling of them to me as they come in. Word gets around fast, but your students seem to be much more understanding than your department head was. I'm assuming someone started a campaign on your behalf. They all seem eager to provide you with as many references as possible, presumably because St. Ben's is probably going to be less than helpful. One student testimonial about how awesome you are might not carry much weight, but an inbox full of them..."

"Oh my God." Paul was startled to realize he was blinking back tears. "They would... They care?"

"They'll miss you." Brandon pulled him back in and pressed a soft kiss to his forehead. "Is it really that amazing that you've made a difference?"

"I—you just, you try your best and hope something soaks in, but—"

Brandon cut him off with a kiss. A long, achingly sweet kiss, one that was wonderful all for itself and didn't feel like a temporary stop on a frantic pathway to somewhere else. Paul felt himself relax into it, simply absorbing the feel of Brandon *being there*. When it drew to a natural conclusion, Brandon broke it off and pressed their foreheads together.

"I love you too," he murmured, cupping Paul's face with his palms. "Just so you know. I love you too."

Epilogue

"She's gorgeous," Brandon breathed.

Paul nodded in agreement, but Brandon didn't look up. He seemed unable to take his eyes off the tiny baby in his arms. Danielle was sweaty and a bit pale, but beaming.

"Not me," she told the approaching nurse, waving her away. "They're the dads. I'm just the DNA."

Paul grabbed his sister's hand and squeezed hard. She returned it. Brandon merely looked awestruck as the nurse carefully repositioned their daughter against his chest and showed him how to support her tiny head.

Paul couldn't remember ever having been so happy. Two years—that's all it took. Christopher and the whole St. Ben's debacle were a distant memory, he and Brandon were still disgustingly head-over-heels for each other, and now they had a *baby.* Chalk up one more advantage to having the most wonderful twin sister in the world. They hadn't even had to ask; she had *offered.* And now their daughter was the closest thing to being genetically "his" and Brandon's as she could be.

"I think she's got your nose," Brandon murmured, still mesmerized by the tiny wrinkled body in his arms.

"Your hair, though."

"Yeah."

They traded her around among the three of them while the labor and delivery nurse bustled in the background, entering something in the computer and taking occasional measurements from both Danielle and the baby.

"So do I finally get to learn her real name?" Danielle asked, cradling her niece gently. "Calling her '2.0' works fine in utero, but I figure you guys came up with something better."

Paul caught Brandon's eye and nodded.

"Emily," Brandon said quietly. "Emily Louise Mercer."

Danielle looked up, surprise on her face. "You two are giving her Brandon's last name?"

"It's…" Paul and Brandon exchanged another glance, and then Brandon squeezed his hand and grinned. "Brandon proposed to me last night," Paul admitted. "We're getting married this fall, hopefully. And I'm taking his name too."

Danielle's ear-splitting squeal—hastily muffled—startled the nurse and possibly most of the rest of the maternity ward. "My *God*, you guys! Why didn't you mention it earlier?"

"We were going to, but Emily was kind of in a hurry," Brandon said. "You were a bit busy, going into labor early and all."

"But *married!*" She looked from Emily, up to Paul and Brandon, then back down again. "God, you two are ridiculous, you know that? I swear, ever since Paul was little he's always wanted to settle down somewhere quiet and have kids. And now he has that wonderfully flexible teaching-from-home job and y'all have the charming little house and everything is creepily *perfect.* When do I get my happily ever after? Because it wasn't in Paris, so I'm still waiting. Any time now would be good." She wrinkled her nose at them, but the look of adoration she gave to Emily took any possible sting out of her words.

"You're welcome to visit as much as you like," Paul offered. "Teach Emily how to be all girly; heaven knows she won't get that from us."

"Oh, I definitely will." Danielle heaved a sigh, but handed Emily back to Paul. "Dad will come around, you know. Eventually. Mom won't let him be responsible for losing her even a minute of potential time with her first granddaughter."

"My family is probably in the waiting room right now," Brandon said. "I texted Anita on our way here and I expect she probably spread the word."

"Have them meet us upstairs in the recovery ward, then." Paul ducked his head to nuzzle at Emily's wild tuft of dark hair. "We can introduce them to Emily and let them all know at once that Brandon's going to make an honest man out of me."

When they got moved to the recovery room forty-five minutes later—Danielle in a hospital-mandated wheelchair with Emily sleeping peacefully on her lap and grinning at Paul every time he looked her way—they were met by Brandon's family. His *entire* family.

"We left the kids with Anita's mom," Eric said, offering Paul and Brandon a brotherly hug, "but Jordan and Marshall made arrangements to come down months ago."

"Caught the first plane I could, little bro," Marshall said. He was a taller, thinner version of Brandon, with lighter hair but the same eyes. "Didn't want to miss meeting my new niece."

"And I was going to visit Mom and Dad this weekend anyway," Jordan interjected. "Didn't take much to convince them to meet me here instead, once we got Anita's text."

"This is convenient," Brandon murmured privately to Paul, then pointedly cleared his throat. Everyone quieted down immediately. "It works out well that you're all here," he said more loudly. "Because while we're on the subject of expanding the family, Paul and I have another announcement to make...."

Worth Waiting For

If you enjoyed *Worth Waiting For*, don't miss Wendy Qualls's

Worth Searching For

A Lyrical Shine e-book on sale February 2018!

CPSIA information can be obtained
at www.ICGtesting.com
Printed in the USA
LVHW030308310821
696470LV00004B/770